We Should Write A Book Someday

A Story of Illegitimate Shame and How it Hurts

Howard Glass

Disclaimer

Dedication

To the victims of illegitimate shame.
Some were driven by it; most were overwhelmed by it.

Acknowledgment

Cover illustration by Bethany Haizlett Narajka

About the Author

Howard Glass has been a writer at heart since he was young. In 2001, he impulsively submitted a piece to his local newspaper. He got serious about writing when it made the front page without editing. Dropping any hope of making it a livelihood after a harsh critique at a writer's conference, Howard opted to trust his muse and measure success by the number of tear sheets and feedback from readers. He reminds himself often that the art pros of Van Gogh's day thought Vincent was no painter. Howard has published and won awards in several magazines, a newspaper column, and two previous books.

Howard Glass Previous Work:

To Catch a Cradle

The Sieve of Angkar, with Savonnara KY

Get in touch with Howard at: heglass1954@gmail.com

All of us had our moment, the time when we packed our meager wardrobe into some bag—the impulse to run away. Impossible, we knew. One would say, "We should write a book someday."

Preface

These summer evenings, I long for. Many times, such nights have slipped by me because of more important things, mostly the demands of rising early for work. But now I am old, with time and perspective. I sit here in the cool, dark air, listening to the singing of crickets and peepers. The train will go by tonight. The blare of the horn and the mellow sound of the engine, softened by distance, are poetry, setting the tone for my mood so pensive.

I savor the life I struggled through. Now I know there is so much that doesn't matter. No storied monarch had a better throne. They say old people treasure memories because they are all we have. Nonsense. The ancients knew it. A person lived long and was 'full of days.' And when you are full, activity can add nothing. They say memories change with time. That, too, is nonsense. Hazy details do not cloud understanding.

Understanding is rare in this world, but I have gained it. Death, in its time, is the right thing. That much is clear. The sands of sin are miry. No one is free. So it was with me. So it was with my family. The people have passed. The story can now be told.

Chapter One

June 1951

Roger was shaking as he entered the out-kitchen. Shaking in a way that Bonnie had never seen. It alarmed her. His face was sweaty, even worse than hers. He held the rifle in the crook of one arm like a baby.

"Where you been, Roger? You didn't go out lookin' for Luther again, didya?"

Her brother's voice trembled, "I knew you'd be comin' up the hill. I was waitin' for him, Bonnie. The sumbitch won't ever bother you again."

"Where? When?" asked Bonnie.

"Only a minute or so after you ran by me. You must have heard the shot."

"I guess I did. I didn't think nothin of it. Figured it was Timko pestering the groundhogs."

She put the stack of plates she'd been drying on the low shelf, took the dishrag out of the soapy water, and wrung it, preparing to wipe the table. She had heard the shot all right. She knew where the path ended at the road and that it would be the best place for Roger to wait and shoot from. She hadn't looked back because she wanted to pretend it had not happened. Roger was angry, and he meant business the first two times he took the gun out looking for Luther. He didn't find him either time.

"That was you?" Bonnie asked.

"Damn right. I saw how scared he had you. He's dead, Bonnie. I drug him off the road into that ditch." He leaned the rifle in the corner the way Dad always did when he meant to use it again that day. "We gotta do something, Bonnie."

Roger was sixteen years old and full of tricks. Tormenting his younger sisters with foolish pranks was a hobby of sorts. She tried to think of a snappy retort, but the gravity in his voice disabled the idea.

"We gotta get rid of his body. We gotta hide it or something. It was all I could do to get him off the road. It might be that car that came by saw me. I'm pretty sure he's outta sight, but I can't know for sure.

"You're not trying to trick me, are you?" asked Bonnie, hopefully. "Who drove by?"

"I didn't even try to see. They didn't slow down more than usual. Everybody rides the brakes going down the hill. I had to get him out of sight. It's mostly downhill, you know, once you're away from the road."

"Are you sure he's dead?"

"He bled a lot. You could smell it."

Bonnie went back to putting the supper dishes away. A sick sensation struck deep down in her belly, like the fear of falling from high on the barn rafters. The idea that her brother had killed the man who had been tormenting her was impossible to take in. He had talked about shooting him several times; he'd taken the gun out in search of the man twice before. She had assumed the worst that could happen would be some kind of warning shot. Or maybe having a gun pointed at him would be enough. Now Roger claimed that it had happened, and he needed her to tell him what to do next. Nothing like this had ever happened before. She didn't know how to react.

"What can we do? He's out of sight now, right? We gotta act like we don't know a thing about it. Nobody except us knows you were out with the gun," Bonnie said.

"They'll miss him. He walked off the job, didn't he? Like the other times?" Roger asked.

"I don't know. I guess so. He always seemed to come out from that alley by the smokestack. I never knew how he could get away with doing that. But that was his problem."

Bonnie had initially felt relieved upon arriving home. She felt safe there. Safe from the awful man who seemed determined to get his hands on her. Now, the secure feeling was replaced by a frantic heartbeat that she could almost hear.

She gathered her courage like she always had when things went chaotic and her brothers and sisters were threatened. "Let's get the flashlight and go see once it gets dark. I'll get Beth. She'll be done feeding by now," Bonnie said.

Roger felt better now; he could count on the support of his two sisters.

The Metts farm was a mile and a half from Parker and uphill the whole way, even across the bridge. The incline on that four-span steel structure was the steepest roadway across a river in the whole United States. Nobody knew how to prove that, so, of course, it could not be disproven either. It was all the bragging rights the little town had. A two-lane, blacktop road ran straight down to the bridge, ending at a T intersection. To the left and downstream stretched the business and industrial part of town. Mostly a glass bottle factory, the largest employer for miles around. Luther Banks worked in the hot end of the plant. The highest paying and most miserable working conditions. Also, the spot where the operator's skills made the most difference in the quality of the product.

The men who worked the hot end were higher on the factory's pecking order, such as it was. There were openings in the walls at the hot end, with catwalks that overlooked the street. The men could stay cooler and be only a few steps from the controls and gauges. They watched people walking by, saw the boats on the river, and kept track of the trains that ran up and down the river. In the winter, they monitored the ice flowing by.

Luther had noticed Bonnie walking by with a sack of groceries. He had left the plant several times, whistling and calling after her, following her across the bridge and partway up the hill. He couldn't catch her; he liked the sport of it. He always gave up where the hill got steeper. Once Bonnie let Roger know that Luther had been hounding her, Roger had to do something. Luther's crude behavior was rumored. Roger thought about telling their father, but everyone knew that Ward Metts overdid everything. Ward spent eight months in the state hospital two years before—after shooting up a beer joint—and the kids were terrified of how he might handle someone threatening them.

"Don't say nothing to anybody else," Bonnie insisted. If the three of us can't figure out what to do, we should keep our mouths shut and hope for the best. Time we get there, it'll be almost dark." Bonnie knew that tomorrow being Saturday; she would go talk to Maggie. She'd know what to do.

The three siblings knew the path through the pasture and the woods well enough to walk it in moonlight. It was a shortcut for foot-traffic only. Since the Mettses had no car, it was their primary route to Parker. In mid-summer, on most nights, the walk would be magical, the country air cooler as the sun went down. The shadows stretched long across the gently rolling hills. The Metts kids always played outdoors on evenings like this, embraced by peace and security. A treasure they never realized had vanished, replaced by the dread of the unknown. Roger had only fired the rifle a few times before. Had only killed one deer. Dad had taught him how to sight and squeeze the trigger, but nothing more. Ammunition was an expense that crimped Ward and Dorothy's beer budget.

The Metts kids had all helped butcher cows, pigs, chickens, and even deer when they killed one, hanging the carcass for skinning. The body of Luther Banks was something else. His right leg had been nearly torn from his body. The bullet struck the man's femur in mid-thigh. Jagged, white bone stuck out from a bloody pant leg, surprisingly visible in the darkness.

"Where'd Beth go?" asked Roger.

"She must have fainted," Bonnie answered.

"Gosh, what now?" Roger seemed ready to panic.

"Rog, Rog, settle down." Bonnie watched her brother do his best to stiffen himself. "You know guys have lied about their age to get into the Army. They must have. Shooting someone has to be done sometimes. You were protecting me. You were protecting Beth too. It's going to be okay. I can't let you get into trouble, maybe go to jail for doing the right thing. You said we'd have to do something. I've thought about it, and you're right. We get this mess into the woods a little way, and maybe nobody will know what happened. We've gone this far."

"Watch out, Bon," Roger stepped aside a little and vomited. Bonnie had to fight to keep from following suit.

A shrill voice cut into the quiet night air, "What do you think you're doing?" It shocked Bonnie and Roger. Bonnie shivered and felt a hot sensation in her crotch as she lost control of her bladder. She had instantly feared the worst and then was relieved and angry upon realizing that it was her twin brother Carter's voice. In the darkness, maybe none of her siblings would see how she had peed herself. She didn't care if they did.

He had come walking up the lane just in time to see the silhouettes of three of his siblings trailing each other down the path toward town. He could not imagine where they were going at that time of day, so he quietly followed them. Seeing an opportunity to make them jump out of their skins once they stopped and were focusing their attention on the ground was too much to pass up.

"Carter, you bastard," said Roger, recovering from the shock, relieved that the intruder was their brother. "Were you following us?"

"Obviously. What is so important that you're sneaking down here this late?" Though he looked where the others were focusing, he did not initially recognize it. Slowly, his eyes began deciphering the dull image, and he understood that a human being lay stock-still on the ground.

"What happened, Rog?"

"It's that pervert Luther Banks. He's been chasing Bonnie every day when she comes home from the store. She's been scared to death that he'd catch her. He won't chase her anymore. I shot him, Carter."

"You what?"

Roger's proud tone melted in the shock of Carter's voice. He stopped denying the awful truth. What he had foreseen as a gallant defense of his sister was worse than the reckless act that got his father locked up. Would anyone care that a man bent on rape, a man three times Bonnie's age, had been terrifying her? Luther Banks had become a more hideous brute, a larger problem, lying there motionless than he could possibly have been alive. Fear, stacked on anger, made the whole thing get-away-from-me ugly. They all knew that life had changed.

Bonnie knelt beside Beth and patted her face a little. She didn't know what to do; none of them had ever swooned before. They had only heard about it. "Let's rest here a little while," Bonnie said.

Roger's upchuck restored his courage some. "Let's make sure Beth's okay."

It didn't take long before Beth drew a deep breath and sat up. "What happened?"

"I think you passed out, little sis," said Roger gently. "It's okay. I threw up. I better now."

It was a playful thing to say, and the humor of it usually served well. They would pretend to be hurt or heartbroken by some event. They would feign deep anguish, crying intensely, then stop abruptly and announce, "I better now."

"I better now too," Beth said, begging for levity that would never come. Bonnie looked out at the road and saw a little of the man's blood on the pavement. Most of it had soaked into his jeans or the black dirt on the shoulder where people walked. There was a pool of it, thick like jelly, but with plenty of loose dirt and rocks to kick loose and scatter down across it. Other messes were crudely tidied like that. What was visible in the dimming light seemed acceptable, as well as she could tell with the flashlight. Fortunately, only their family walked this road regularly.

"I guess this is the best we can do. There's no way to dig a hole here," Bonnie said. The toughest of the four, she always took charge whether they were working, playing, or scheming. "Let's drag him as far in as we can. We can wash ourselves off in the creek. Good thing it isn't shift change time. There'd be a string of cars; someone might see."

Roger and Bonnie each took an arm. Bonnie was so averse to the corpse that her muscles defied her intentions. The initial tug took all the strength they could muster, as if the man's body had begun to grow roots and had to be broken free. Roger's stomach heaved again. Nothing came up.

Carter stood still and silent as a tree stump. Roger pleaded with him. "Aren't you gonna help us?" Carter moved and took the arm from Bonnie. She freely gave it to him, relieved that he would not run home to tell their parents.

A tangle of rocks and tree roots and small brush scraped their legs and faces as they tugged and pulled the body. They meant to go away from the road, but for every foot they went, the body slipped downhill some. They had to pull together, one on each arm, gripping Luther's wrists. The jagged leg bone stuck out and caught on the ground, and they had to shake it by the foot to free it. Soon, they were in the stream, their shoes filling with water up past their ankles.

"I wonder if we can get him downstream the whole way to the culvert below Indian Rock?" Roger said. It was an inspiration, as if they had been granted a solution. None of the others responded. They kept moving mechanically, their thoughts frozen. The man's jeans caught on a tree root, and they nearly pulled them off before they realized what had snagged.

Carter resigned himself to being part of what the others had started. "If we can get him down there, we can push him into the culvert. Nobody will see him there." They had played in and explored this creek a time or two on days they were bored, blundering through the rugged terrain looking for snakes and salamanders or playing cowboys and Indians.

The stream gushed from the springhouse on the Metts farm. It meandered around through the pasture and under a dirt road, the southern border of their property, and flowed faster and wider as another unnamed run added to its flow. The grade grew steeper, flowing toward the river. At the bottom were a railroad track and a gravel road beside it that ran for miles up and down the river. The creek passed under the roadway and the tracks through a big pipe to where the water cascaded onto a pile of rocks and into the river like all the other little runs and brooks that drained the hillside.

Down the wet, rugged, rocky hill they went. Beth held the flashlight, already starting to dim, just enough ahead so Roger and Carter could see to step. "My god, he's heavy," said Carter.

"Beth, turn that off. We can see good enough," Roger said. A full moon helped a lot. "Save it. Those batteries are about shot."

In a few hundred feet, the streambed leveled into a wide pool, almost deep enough to float the body. The passage under the road, partly obstructed by a deadfall, forced them to wrangle the corpse to one side. They managed to get the body past it, with Roger gripping the jagged bone, desperately shoving. Luther was not a large man, and the three were glad of it. Clear of the obstruction, aided by the flowing water, the corpse went easily into its grave. The water flowed by on both sides, invisible without crouching the way they did.

"Will a heavy rain wash it out?" Beth asked. No one answered.

They clambered back up the stream, reversing their course. The flashlight dim, their progress clumsy; they barely kept their footing, moving slowly upgrade, every step putting them farther away from the hideous body. As far as they could tell in the darkness, only the scuffed shoulder where Bonnie had worked to hide the spilled blood indicated any disturbance. Upon reaching the familiar path, they broke into a run. It was past ten o'clock when they got back to the house.

The younger ones had gone to bed shortly after sundown without so much as wondering where the older ones had gone. On Friday and Saturday nights, the older ones always went to the homes of their friends and classmates in Perryville, the village that had sprung up behind the electric co-op. There were long-standing instructions to be home before dark, but none of them had ever been punished for failing to be. Mom and Dad never went upstairs to check. The kids were always home when needed to weed the garden, chase the cows, or do other chores.

The four gathered in the out-kitchen. They always conspired together after doing anything that might get them in trouble. They all had to tell the same lie.

"Does Dad know you got it out?" Carter asked, pointing to the rifle.

"He didn't see me get it. You know how he does. Sits in the bedroom, reads, or listens to the radio. On a payday weekend, they'd be downtown."

"If it were payday, I wouldn't have gone to Carson's, and this wouldn't have happened," said Bonnie.

Ward Metts had been losing his hearing for years and interacted with his family less and less. He had to keep his good ear close to the radio to hear it. What relationship the kids had with him channeled increasingly through their mother. Many things that went on in the household were now beyond his ken.

Carter picked up the rifle and worked the bolt; the spent cartridge clattered to the floor. He dropped the magazine out and slid the other three rounds out into his hand.

The kids knew how things worked. When mom and dad were away, the oldest kid at home was in charge. But they could all see that Roger had no mind to boss anyone now.

"Put these back in the box, Rog," said Carter." He picked up the empty cartridge, carried it out onto the porch, and threw it violently into the pasture. He went back into the out-kitchen, scratched a match, lit a burner, and set the big tea kettle on so they could wash up.

"Change your clothes. We'll hang the wet things up on the rack upstairs. Soon as the suns up, look them all over. If they need washing, we'll do it ourselves. Don't let Mom see if you can help it. You guys get up to bed like nothing happened. Listen to me. We can't say anything about this where Mom or Dad or any of the kids can hear." There were promises made all around to keep this secret. They had kept secrets before.

Roger and Carter shared a twin bed, Jack and Richard shared another, as did Bonnie, Beth, and Mary. There were three bedrooms upstairs in the farmhouse. The kids didn't have many clothes, except when some friend from school would share castoffs with them. There were no chests or closets to keep extra clothes in if they had obtained any. A few nails and a bushel basket did the trick.

Their older sister, Carol, had left home to live with their Aunt Polly in Grove City, thirty miles to the west, a place where she got work as a housekeeper.

A memorable line from Georgia Baker, one of Dorothy's friends from the beer garden, was often repeated when the whole brood was together. "Ward, you and Dorothy need to quit making babies; you're out of places to keep them."

Bonnie and Beth rarely touched each other in bed. Now, they wrapped their arms around each other and spoke in a whisper. The grim sense that life had changed was upon them. Neither of them knew how to talk about it or even if they should. "What will happen if they find the body?" asked Beth.

"If nobody knows what happened, why would they look for his body? That's our only hope that people will wonder where he went. It wouldn't take much for them to hear about Luther chasing me."

"What happens when someone disappears?"

"His family will look for him, surely?"

"Do we know anything about his family?"

"I don't. Mom and Dad probably do. I'm going to see Maggie tomorrow. She'll know what we should do. For now, we need to make sure not to talk about it where anyone else can hear. The less we say the better. Remember what Uncle Curt told us about the war, 'Loose lips sink ships.'"

As Roger lay in bed, he could tell that Carter wasn't asleep either. They often lay there talking quietly. But they had agreed to pretend as if the shooting and what followed had not happened. He remembered Edgar Allan Poe's story, *The Telltale Heart*, from English class and wondered if he or one of the others would feel the need to confess. He knew he had committed a crime. It didn't bother him; Luther Banks had threatened Bonnie and asked for something terrible. Only the fear of getting caught tormented him now.

Sometime in the middle of the night, Bonnie sat straight up in bed. She realized that the next person to walk on the shoulder of the road, where Luther's blood was, might be her mother. Dorothy walked to Parker nearly every Saturday. Buying groceries was her standby reason. Mostly, a friend would drive her home, sometimes with a bag of groceries, always with several quarts of beer. What would her mother think if she saw a mess of blood on the shoulder of the road? What if her cover-up job hadn't been adequate? Would the blood be dried? Half-dried? Would Dorothy's foot slip on it? The rule was to walk facing traffic, but on that part of the hill, the shoulder facing uphill traffic was too narrow. Everyone who walked up or down that hill used the same side. Bonnie wondered if it might be better to tell her mom about Luther after all. Bonnie didn't need another thing to worry about, but there it was.

Chapter Two

It was past 10 a.m. when Bonnie left the house. Any earlier and Mom would have cautioned her not to bother Maggie that early. Bonnie had nearly worn a path leading past the barn, across the hayfield, and into the woods.

A little creek, fed by another spring higher up the hill, drained into the stream they had spent hours in the night before. Maggie's house had a wide porch where they could sit and watch the wild critters.

People often remarked that a photo of the home would make a nice postcard. Maggie's husband Abner shot all the venison they cared to eat, right from the porch and had no worries about the Game Warden. With no sight or sound of the nearest neighbor, the house was a retreat and Bonnie felt safe there.

Maggie Porter had become a second mother to Bonnie. Her influence grew stronger than Dorothy's as Bonnie matured. Not long before, Bonnie had sensed her own ignorance.

Her mother was overworked, distracted, inadequate, and drunk at least two days a week. Maggie never meant to take Bonnie under her wing; the girl wiggled her way there and intended to stay.

Maggie hoped that the important things she taught Bonnie, like keeping herself clean, would be passed down to the younger Metts kids. Maggie thought they might be better off as orphans. The county had a home where such children were cared for.

Maggie was hanging sheets on the clothesline when she heard Bonnie's greeting. Immediately sensing crisis, she finished putting another couple of pins into the sheet and turned around to face the girl.

Bonnie looked more and more like a grown woman each time Maggie saw her. Early development in any girl troubled Maggie. She had been anticipating Bonnie's confusion and had pondered how to talk to Bonnie about it.

Dorothy had told Bonnie about her coming monthly cycle and showed her where the 'little blue box' was kept. Bonnie knew nothing about why the bleeding occurred. Maggie had explained as best she could.

"You sound a little glum, Honey," Maggie said, trying to sound cheery. "Did you start?"

"Yeah, Sunday afternoon. It's done now though."

"Has your mom said anything about getting you a bra?"

"No, you think I need one?"

"It won't be long now you've got your monthly. It's hard to get used to. Keep in mind, it happens to all of us. I feel like congratulations are in order. It means you've become a woman." Maggie expected a smile, instead, Bonnie's face contorted, and tears sprang to her eyes. Maggie sensed that it wasn't Bonnie's first monthly that weighed on her.

"Something awful happened last night," Bonnie said.

"Let's sit down here on my garden bench. You can tell me about it."

"Remember me telling you how that man always whistled at me and hollered as I walked by the factory?"

"Sure. That's gotta be Luther Banks. He's awful. His favorite pastime is annoying anything with a skirt. One of these days he'll bother the wrong man's wife and get himself thrown in the river. I told you how your Daddy did."

"You told me." There was a legend about how a young man had gotten away with raping a woman in town. Ward Metts had cornered the fellow in Rottman's bar, knocked him down with a few punches, and carried him like a sack of wheat across the street, down the riverbank, and launched him into the Allegheny. Those who knew the story approved of what Ward had done, then.

"Maybe I should have told Dad. After what happened before, Mom won't let us say anything that might set him off. He could have gone to prison, Mom said."

Maggie kept her thoughts about Ward to herself. They were too mixed up to articulate. The man was a wild card. Ward had shot up Rottman's with a .38 revolver—two rounds passed Cliff Rottman's head—in a fit of drunken rage when they shut him off.

The result had been the county judge offering him prison or committal to the State Hospital. Folks called it an 'insane asylum' at North Warren.

Whether it was the shock treatments or the constant threat of a straitjacket for eight months, the place had had a calming effect on Ward. He had become a mostly peaceful drunk.

Remembering the past, no one drew an easy breath once Ward Metts went beyond two or three beers, which lately, he did every weekend.

"Anyway, Luther Banks won't be pestering anyone from now on," said Bonnie.

"Why not?"

"Last night," Bonnie hesitated, looking around as if checking for anyone who might overhear, "Roger shot him. He had chased me across the bridge and up the hill three times in the last week or so. Roger waited for him last night, where the path meets the road, and let him have it with the 30-30. He's dead."

Maggie's face got pale. Bonnie thought maybe Maggie would faint the way Beth had. "You're not foolin', are you?" Maggie asked.

The idea that Bonnie would make something like that up was unthinkable. The idea that Roger had shot someone was also unthinkable.

"No Maggie, I helped hide his body."

Maggie was flabbergasted. Abner had worked the midnight shift at the factory. He came home as usual and went to bed, saying nothing to her about Luther. She resisted the impulse to go immediately and wake him up to ask about it. Maybe word hadn't gotten around yet.

"You hid his body?" Maggie asked incredulously. She stared at Bonnie, hoping there would be some explanation that would make the square peg of disbelief fit into the round hole of reason. Bonnie nodded gravely.

"You mean you buried it? You four skinny kids dug a hole and buried him?" That couldn't be. Roger was maybe sixteen, strong enough for a grown man's work. Still, it took a long time to dig even a shallow grave.

"No, we hid it."

"Where? Wait, maybe I don't want to know. How well could you hide something like that without burying it?"

"We're gonna pretend like we don't know anything. Roger says he got him off the road before anybody driving by would see him. Carter was there too; nobody else knows. Except you, now."

"So, did you see him do it?"

"No, Roger hid in the brush. He said I ran right past him. He didn't want to shoot, but when he saw me so scared, he got mad, and the gun went off. Luther never made it onto the path."

"So did he shoot him in the head?"

"In the leg. I didn't think you could kill a person with a bullet in the leg, but he's dead all right."

Maggie thought a little. "There's a big vein in your leg. If something like a bullet cuts through, you'll bleed to death quick. Too quick for even a doctor to help. Did Roger mean to kill him?"

"We've heard a hundred times; don't point a gun at anyone unless you mean to kill them."

"I guess it doesn't matter. Can the four of you keep your mouths shut?"

"I know I can. It won't be hard for me. Anybody else knows, besides us, they'd call the cops or tell. I figure it will be deer season before anybody goes around where he's lying. Maybe not even then." She looked Maggie straight in the eye and asked, "You won't tell on us, will you?"

Maggie looked into Bonnie's eyes pensively and long enough to unsettle her young friend. "Bonnie, you'll look long and hard and not find anyone who cares less about Luther Banks than I do. He had a wife once; she couldn't stand him and left. She was from Oklahoma or someplace, not around here. That's what I heard. No one around here would have him."

"Listen, we don't know what's gonna happen, how this thing will play out. I don't know how much family he has or who might ask questions. A person can get in big trouble if they lie to the police. Maybe for now, we should do like you say. We can't talk about it to anyone. Abner will pick up whatever talk there is at work. If his body turns up, there'll be hell to pay."

They sat for a long time in uncomfortable silence, Maggie pondering. "How many people knew about him chasing you?"

Bonnie thought for a minute. "Only the ones who know what happened last night. School's out, so I don't see Kathy or Trish much."

"Don't tell anyone you see. Folks are gonna be asking questions. You don't want people to know you had anything to do with that man. Did anybody see him running after you?"

"There might have been a car or two saw me hustling up the hill with him coming after me. Nobody said anything. Not to me anyhow."

"While he was on the sidewalk, people could drive by and not see him. It isn't far from the end of the bridge to where the path meets." Maggie nodded her head up and down, bobbed it from side to side, measuring the possibilities, pondering the whole situation in her mind.

"Listen, Bonnie, whenever something happens that we want to keep secret, we tend to fish around and ask questions trying to see what other people know. That makes them suspicious. Understand what I mean?"

"I guess so."

"Don't do that. You gotta pretend there's nothing you need to hear. I know how you kids like to run around, but for a while, you'll need to stay home and mind your own business."

"Mom sends me to Carson's three or four times a week. She'll expect me to keep it up."

"Who do you see when you're there?"

"You mean besides Joe? He's always there. It's not like I see the same people all the time. Some I know, some I don't."

"Is there anyone who might be aware that Luther was after you?"

"No! I wouldn't tell anybody," Bonnie said.

"Why not?"

"I don't want anyone to know."

"Not even me?"

"No. I'm telling you now cause of what happened."

"Why do you want to keep it to yourself?"

"I don't know."

"Did he scare you?"

Bonnie nodded slowly.

"Do you have any idea what he had in mind, child? What he'd have done if he caught you?"

Bonnie lowered her head and wept softly.

"So, you know what he might have done?"

"Some."

"Darlin, there's a lot I need to talk to you about. I should have done it already. The thing is, I feel like it's none of my business, not my place. Has your mom ever told you about the 'birds and the bees?'"

"No."

"You do understand sex, don't you?"

"Isn't it how you make babies?"

"Yeah. But it isn't that simple. I wish it was."

"I think Luther wanted to touch and kiss me. He called me a 'pretty little thing.'"

"Lord, girl," she said, shaking her head and gnashing her teeth, "What that man would have done if he had caught you."

"Isn't that how sex starts? With touching and kissing?"

"That's pretty much the way it starts. But only when a girl is married and wants to do it."

"Uncle Curt did it to me."

"Did what?" Maggie's voice was sharp and angry.

"He stuck his fingers down my unders. I could feel him breathing hard into my ear. He kissed me a little on the cheek. It about made me sick."

"Let me guess, he had you sitting on his lap?"

"Yeah."

"When was that?"

"A while back. I think I was eight."

Maggie shook her head in disgust. "So, when did Luther say you were pretty?"

"The first time he followed me. I'm not sure if he meant me to hear, but I heard. That's what Uncle Curt said too."

"Bonnie, like I said, there's a lot I want to tell you. With what's going on now it seems a waste. If this all blows over, I'll get to it."

"Okay, Maggie."

"Bonnie, you trust me, don't you?"

"I trust you, Maggie. I wouldn't come back here talking if I didn't trust you."

"You go on home now. I got to do some thinking." She stood up and faced Bonnie. The girl she beheld was too innocent for this kind of thing. "You're fourteen, right?"

"Almost. Next month."

Maggie looked away, not wanting her expression to betray what she felt. She had not wanted to admit, even to herself, that she felt good about Luther Banks' death. But she was glad, and no mistake. She couldn't let Bonnie see that. Maybe the disappearance of Luther Banks would be a mystery that nobody cared to solve.

Bonnie's pace was faster now, the burden lighter. Maggie always knew the right way of things. Bonnie's mouth would stay shut. There was a lot to do around home.

She would get Carter, Beth, Jack, Richard, and little Mary and go up the hill to pick strawberries. Roger would probably go too. Unless Mom needed some chores done, she would be glad to let them all go.

Maggie watched Bonnie until her slender form disappeared among the greenery. She sent her along because she knew Abner would be getting out of bed soon and might ask if something was wrong at the Metts house. He didn't sleep as late on Saturdays since his midnight shift ended when he got off Saturday morning. It was back to daylight for him on Monday.

Maggie couldn't tell Bonnie how she had herself been raped by Luther Banks while Abner was away fighting the Japanese. She was not the only one.

The war years had been a dreary routine, raising kids on her own, working at the factory, rotating shifts as Abner did now. Like a long string of cloudy days, loneliness leeched the joy out of life.

Luther had been slick. He could sweet-talk a lonely wife. Abner's platoon had sung, "Jody's got your gal and gone" to quick-time cadence, but it wasn't Jody who got some of the ladies left behind. Luther got them.

Luther was cursed with flat feet and a heart murmur, a cruel fate in 1942. The men who were too old or too young to get into the service didn't hold back their disdain for anyone who appeared healthy; Pearl Harbor had to be avenged and no able man should stay safely at home.

In their eyes, Luther Banks was as healthy as anyone. The fact that Army doctors didn't want him fell on deaf ears. Ward Metts had come close to suicide because the government would not let him leave his farm and go to war. Milk, eggs, and meat were essential. People understood that. Luther's limitations were humiliating.

Luther took more than his share of abuse on the home front. No one would defend him except some of the women. He got good at singing the blues about being left out of the noble cause to young women longing for their man and after a while, longing for any man.

"Girls need some romance and excitement," Luther told himself. In some situations, you have fun any way you can. After slipping easily into the bed of the first one, it happened as if the women were talking to one another, sharing the knowledge of where to find excitement.

He discovered that once a married woman allowed herself to be alone with him, conquest was certain. Didn't matter if her conscience pushed back when things got heated because being alone with him was already too far.

Saying "no" or "stop" when you didn't mean it, made it more exciting for both. She could not complain that he had forced her without the question of how she let him get close being sufficient condemnation.

Luther knew that the war wouldn't last forever and the females who favored him so easily when there was a shortage of men would look right past him when the soldiers came home.

And Al Stone, the old druggist, smiled at him when he began buying condoms regularly. Luther made hay while he had sunshine.

Maggie had every intention of telling Abner about Luther's abuse when he came marching home. But the man who came home was so much less than the one who left.

Chapter Three

The strawberries up the hill were wild. The cultivated kind for sale at Carson's, when they were in season, were a lot bigger but much less flavorful than the ones the Mettses picked.

The kids ate one for every one they put in the bucket. The amount needed for Dorothy to make a couple of pies for the family usually consumed an entire afternoon.

Once on the hill, out of sight from the house and surrounded by goldenrod, Queen Anne's lace, thistles and a dozen other varieties of weeds and brush, groundhogs, robins, rabbits, and crows, the kids were in a world of their own and free to play or talk about whatever they would.

The burden of filling the bucket was secondary. The usual carefree chore was not so carefree now. The four older ones paid little attention to their younger siblings, even three-year-old Mary; there had never been any danger on the hill.

Bonnie looked around to be sure that neither Jack, Richard, nor Mary could hear. "Maggie told me we need to say absolutely nothing, even among ourselves about what happened last night."

"I'm beat," said Beth. She had picked up the saying from her mother.

"Isn't that because none of you slept last night?" asked Carter.

"Did you?" said Beth.

"Not much, I guess."

"What's with you guys? You're pickin' berries faster than usual," said Carter.

"I can't get my mind off of what I did," said Roger quietly. "Still, let's do what Maggie said. The more we stir this up in our heads, the harder it will be to keep it secret. Let's talk about something else."

'Something else' among the Metts kids always had to do with their family situation, the low quality of their home compared to the rest of the community, their default narrative, and the sad account of a heritage lost.

The Metts farm had once been a showplace. It had the largest barn in the area, built with laminated planks, not squared timber; a slate shingle roof; two silos along with many other things that made a farm great.

A smokehouse and pigpen with stone foundations; a corncrib and chicken coop; an apple, pear, cherry, plum and peach orchard; walnut trees; raspberry and blackberry patches; three separate vegetable gardens and grapevines.

It had a springhouse with a deeply cut stone trough that kept cans of milk cool; plenty of wood for timber and firewood, along with an oil well from which natural gas had been tapped.

The Mettses had free gas piped to their house in exchange for whatever the gas company took. That made wood burning obsolete and freed up a lot of time for tending the dairy herd. Add to that an elaborate outhouse with three holes, one just the right height for children.

Grandpa John Metts had grown up during the years when the farm had been established. No one knew exactly when because John didn't keep any record.

A date, 1895, was chiseled into the barn's cornerstone. His father had passed him copious knowledge he brought from Europe. John inherited it all in due course. His first wife Minnie had given him four children and died in agony delivering the last one.

He quickly found a second wife and four more farmhands came along. Grandpa John thrived on hard work, finding satisfaction in the plenty that surrounded him. He kept his family busy with labor, all he'd ever known.

Regretting his father's lack of foresight, Ward had begun keeping a diary for posterity's sake. There were so many details about the place that were lost over time.

Ward planned to remedy that, but since he caused a lot of regrettable incidents that impacted his family, he left a lot out of his diary.

After a while, he secretly regretted coming back to the farm and taking over. His older brothers had moved on to factory work or the railroad. One got a job with the Post Office.

It wasn't an unwelcome event for Ward when, in 1945, as the war ended, he lost most of the dairy herd in one day. The door to the granary was left open.

Neither boy would admit responsibility and they were too young to be held accountable. While Ward was away and the boys were at school, the cows went into the granary and ate their fill of wheat and oats.

Dorothy had noticed the cattle going in and out of the barn. It was unusual and harmless as far as she knew. If she had been raised around cattle, she might have known that they cannot eat much whole grain.

By milking time, they were all down and bellowing. By the next morning, fourteen were dead. A pet food company hauled the carcasses away.

Ward soon got work in Grove City, where his sister lived. She knew someone in the big mill there and put in a good word for him. His reputation didn't range that far from Parker.

When things slowed down post-war, he was laid off and then got on the painting crew for the Parker Bridge. It lasted four months and was within walking distance of home. Work was sporadic for him after that. He still had produce from the farm for his family to live on and he didn't need much cash.

The R.E.A. had begun stringing lines to farms before the war. Post-war, it played catch up. An electric co-operative was established across the main road from the Metts farm. It was another place Ward could walk to, and he got hired despite what people thought about him. He joined the clearing crew, keeping trees and wild growth from fouling power lines.

Since he no longer worked his land, he rented his acreage to Pat and Betty Hughes, the farm beside his. The Mettses kept one or two milk cows, a team of horses, and a few pigs. Chickens ran around the place and fended for themselves. There was always a cat or two and a dog named 'Jim.' Ward named every dog he had 'Jim.'

Talking about their family was gloomy. Once prosperous, they had fallen so far. Ward and Dorothy married when the end of prohibition was in sight. Like wild birds breaking free from a hated cage, the young people became enthralled with demon rum.

Ward saw the work his forebears had thrived on as drudgery. He escaped as often as he could to the newly opened beer gardens in town, with their flashy décor and risqué culture, so different from most of the neighbors, who clung obstinately to the Methodist Church and its stodgy support for temperance.

The religious folk had been proven wrong and whatever sway they once had over society went underground like a woodchuck in winter.

Slowly but surely, the land lost supremacy in Ward's life. As his appetite for alcohol grew, the health of the farm drained into a urinal at the American House Tavern in Parker.

The kids knew and were proud of the fact that, in 1926, Ward was offered a contract as a professional boxer. He never spoke of it unless he was drunk, and even the kids sensed that he exaggerated. Why it didn't work out, no one seemed to know. Those who knew Ward assumed that his inflated ego had something to do with it.

Richard came into the circle of older siblings and asked a question that turned their talk into something else. "Where do Mom and Dad go on Saturdays?" Each of them in turn had raised that question as they grew up.

Nine-year-old Jack had come within earshot, holding Mary's hand in his. "They go to the beer gardens."

"What's a beer garden?" asked Richard, his seven-year-old mind trying to imagine how something held in a bottle or glass came from a plant.

"Beer joint," said Carter. "I don't know why they say 'garden' unless it makes it sound nicer." He shrugged. "And they don't go every Saturday. Only on the weeks when Dad gets paid."

"Did he get paid yesterday?"

"No, it only comes every other week, on Friday."

"They do so go every Saturday, Carter," said Beth. "Mom usually walks. You know that. They even go on Friday nights."

"So where are they going now?" Richard pointed through a gap in the foliage and the others stood up to see. A familiar green sedan headed down the lane.

"That's Georgia and Nick's car. Can you see if they're in it?" asked Roger, although he knew they probably were.

"I'll run down and find out," said Carter.

"Like it will make any difference," said Bonnie. She figured Carter needed to do something different to settle his nerves.

"Why don't we have a car?" asked Richard. "Mom said we used to."

"Dad lost his license because of the last wreck he had," said Roger. He preferred that lie to the truth. A neighbor boy had explained why his father quit driving. Something about the whole thing, Roger didn't understand.

When something big happened in the area, everybody talked about it. But when something big happened within his family, none of their friends would mention it.

Omer Tallman was no friend. He lived out the road past the Metts farm with his poor and frail grandparents. People called him shiftless, and not to be trusted. He had dropped out of school and run off with a carnival company.

He returned in the winter months and stayed in the rickety old house. Word was that a few years back, Lorraine Martin, the school nurse, drove Omer's younger sister to Doc Masters on a school day because of a strange and powerful odor.

When Doc examined her, he found the nipple from a baby bottle had been inserted into her vagina, a sort of homemade diaphragm. In tears, the girl told the school nurse that, "Omer put that up there."

How the story escaped from a circle of people sworn to keep such things secret was unknown. Some events defy boundaries. Lorraine lamented that in a dull-witted family, the sharpest of them, Omer, had the worst character.

When Roger encountered Omer at Carson's store back in March, they had spared each other no indignity. "Metts, so your old man knocked down a porch in Monterey, I hear."

"Why would my dad go there?"

"Drunk as usual. I heard Barney McCall filed a lawsuit against him. Then the lawyer found out your old man didn't have anything they could take. So, he made your dad agree to never get behind the wheel of a car again, or else he would press charges. They'd put your old man back in the booby-hatch. Hell, he'd probably never get out."

"Right. Like my dad doesn't own a hundred-acre farm."

"Ward Metts don't own that farm," Omer spouted gleefully.

"So what? Barney McCall does?" Roger wanted to pound Omer, but the Carsons could see them through their front store window. He wasn't sure he could best Omer in a fight anyway, especially since he had been away from Parker, and nobody could say if he carried a switchblade. Roger had heard that all carnies carried a knife or brass knuckles. He'd seen both and didn't want to feel either.

"No, dummy, I told you. Your old man don't own it. Your grandma left it to you guys, the pups. She skipped right over his sorry ass. Smart woman, all the folks around here say."

"Blow it out your ass Omer," said Roger dismissively. He turned on his heel and walked away, smarting because what Omer told him had the ring of truth.

Chapter Four

Carter returned, slowly climbing the steep hill while the others continued picking berries. "Mom left a note," he said. "That wasn't Georgia and Nick's car after all. They left with Judson Johnson."

"That's nice," said Beth. "I like Jud."

Bonnie smiled with relief. Going to Parker in Jud's car, the parents wouldn't encounter the blood that might still be visible. They would breeze right by the spot and never give it a thought.

The kids all liked Judson; partly because he was the only black man they had ever seen up close. His lively personality was quick with a joke. He sensed the awkwardness they felt about his color and knew how to make them comfortable.

Judson had been hired to work on the bridge painting project at the same time their father had. Ward quickly made friends with the man because he knew most of the other men would not.

Since nobody gave Ward a hard time, nobody dared give his friend a hard time. After a while, the whole crew came to respect Judson. When he visited the Mettses, he often remarked about the good times he had and the good money he made on that painting project.

"Remember what mom said last time he was here?" asked Roger. "'Don't you boys dare use the word you hear all the time. It ain't Jud you'll need to worry about either. If the subject comes up, Mr. Johnson is a negro. Your dad hears that other word, he'll box your ears.'"

"Last time he came," Carter said, "Dad had me take him down to the springhouse so he could fill up some jugs with our water. He told me, 'You'll never make a pimple on your daddy's ass.' He hurt my feelings, so he said, 'Shucks kid, if you turn out to be half the man he is, you'll be okay.'"

"They won't be out real late either," said Roger. "Jud lives someplace on the other side of Eau Claire. He'll bring them home early. He likes to be home before dark for some reason."

Judson Johnson had not planned to visit the Mettses. On his way to his brother's home in Kennerdell to return some tools he had borrowed, he stopped at Turner's gas station just past the Parker bridge. There was a small garage at the place where they fixed and sold tires.

While the attendant was filling Jud's tank, he conversed with a man inside the garage. Jud cocked his ears when he heard his friend's name. "That dumb bastard should know better than to bother one of Ward's daughters," the man pumping gas said. He was half-turned so his words would carry to the fellow inside.

Judson had daughters of his own and read between the lines. "Pardon me, sir, it sounds like you're talking about my old friend, Ward Metts. Is someone bothering one of his kids?"

"Looks like it. We saw Ward's girl running up across the bridge with a sack of groceries. She does that a lot. We got this mean bastard from town; thinks he should pop every cherry in the county. That girl ain't much more than out of grade school. I guess he thinks if he chases her, she'll stop up there in the woods and wait for him. Thinks he's God's gift to virgins or something."

A voice from inside the garage responded, "I bet he thinks that since Ward's been in trouble, he can get away with anything. He's got another think coming, I say. That kid can't be old enough for what he has in mind. What horse's ass runs after a child? Ward breaks his neck? The bastard had it coming, I say."

"Pardon me, sir. Like I said, Ward's a friend of mine. Can I ask what sort of trouble he had?"

"Ward likes his booze too much. He got a snoot full last year and when they tried to shut him off, he went home and got a .38 revolver." The attendant pointed his hand dramatically, miming Ward's firing the revolver, enjoying telling the tale.

"You might say he 'persuaded' the bartender to serve him another round. He gave him another beer and somebody called the cops. Both of Ward's shots went through the wall into the dining room of the place. Lucky he didn't kill somebody."

"Did he go to jail for that?" asked Judson.

"He went to the state hospital in North Warren. Not much different than jail."

The attendant hung up the hose and put the gas cap back on Judson's car. He took the cash from Judson, went inside, and brought some change out.

Judson pulled out onto the road and instead of going upriver, went back the other way and turned up over the bridge. His friendship with Ward meant a lot to him and he had to do what he could to help.

When he got to the farm, he expected one of Ward's children to come down to meet his car. When none showed up, he got out and walked up toward the house. A dirty, white-haired mutt of a dog came off the porch and barked at him.

The dog stayed close to the porch though, so Judson moved cautiously onward. He was almost to the porch when Ward stepped out and saw him. Ward smiled immediately. "Well, look who's here Dorothy." He stepped up and shook Judson's hand vigorously. "Long time no see, Jud."

Judson burst out with a hearty chuckle and bent over as laughter shook his body. "I didn't bring no beer, Ward, sorry."

"You don't need to bring me beer. We can go get some though, if you're thirsty. Or we can drink my spring water. I know how much you like it."

"I got to be honest with you Ward. This isn't only a friendly visit. I heard you had some trouble and had to go away for a while."

Ward hung his head a little and lost some energy. He felt trapped. Not a soul in the neighborhood spoke a word to him about his time in Warren. If Judson, who didn't live close by, knew about it, it had to be all over the county.

Something he told his kids came back to haunt him, "You hear people say you shouldn't talk about someone behind their back, right? Well, pay attention. Everybody gets talked about behind their back. What matters is what people say about you." He struggled to hide the shame that engulfed him.

It took a while before the two men sat down and faced each other. "I'd rather take a kick in the belly than have you know what I did," said Ward.

"You hush now partner," said Judson, imitating the comforting tone that his mama had always used when a sad child did something naughty. I don't think any less of you.

You've had a hard time of it, what with losing your herd and trying to keep all these kids fed. Anybody would go off the deep end."

"Well Jud, I have no excuse for it. I had lots of time to think about it and regret it. I don't think jail would have been much worse."

"Well, I heard something a little bit ago that you ought to know about. That's why I stopped by."

"What did you hear?"

"First, let me give you a little advice. Remember how we always used to listen to each other, give each other advice, especially when we were drinkin?"

Ward smiled. "Sure, I do. Drinkin' and thinkin', that's you and me."

"Well, I gotta give you the advice first before I tell you what I heard. It's gonna make you mad."

Ward nodded.

"You know how I told you how us coloreds have always had to take a lot of shit from folks 'cause if we didn't, we'd end up lynched or beat up, 'specially down south?"

"Yep. And it ain't right, decent, hard-working people getting tramped on and pushed around." Ward's voice got shaky from a mixture of sadness and anger. "How many of you went off to France and Germany and fought for the rest of us?"

"Oh man, Ward, I don't mean to get you started. Ain't nobody understands being pushed around like we do. Thing is, when you're the underdog you gotta think about whether you can get even. It's like you gotta pick what battle you're gonna fight.

Sometimes you can't win, no way. But sometimes, if you're smart, you can. The trick is not to make more trouble for yourself. Remember how you said your daddy told you to think about what you were doing on the farm, so's not to make more work for yourself?"

"I know, Jud. I made that trouble for myself. Too proud mostly. Now, what did you hear?"

Seeing Ward's patience getting thin—not that he'd ever had much to start with—Judson cautiously told him, word-for-word, what he'd picked up that morning at Turner's gas station.

"Well, I'll be damned," said Ward. "Luther Banks, after Bonnie. Must be Bonnie; she's the one who goes to the store."

"They didn't say the fella's name."

"They don't have to. I think everybody knows what he's like."

"You want to go find this fella and break his arms now, don't you? And no father in his right mind would blame you. But you see Ward, you're an underdog now, like me."

"It's not the first time I was an underdog, Jud. Believe it or not, I didn't win as many fights as I lost. You usually know when you're not favored to win a fight. It should make you more careful."

"I'm glad you see my point, Ward."

"So, how do I put this fella in his place? I ain't letting him chase my Bonnie girl. I will kill him if he catches her or any of my kids. I don't care what place they put me into. Any man who hurts my family better have a fast gait and a long stride, I guarantee ya."

Jud gave Ward a long pause to settle himself, nodding slowly all the while. "I'm thinking here a minute. Maybe we can go down to the American House. Somebody there's likely to have heard about what those boys at Turner's gas station saw. About all it will take is for someone there to see your angry face. Word will get to this Luther fella, I'd say. If you still think you need to, you can go to town with your girl, except you wait on the bridge. Get behind the big steel or sit down low. That Luther comes after your girl, whoever comes after your girl, you step out in his way and chuck him in the river. Or hell, threaten to chuck him in the river." Both men laughed at the idea of Ward casting the offender over the side.

"Sometime later on, after people forget about what he done, you can catch him by himself when ain't nobody to see and give him what he's got comin'. A few good ones in the stomach ain't gonna show much bruise, right?"

Dorothy heard all Jud said, and a few things dropped into place for her now. She remembered Bonnie coming home out of breath one evening earlier in the week.

Bonnie hadn't mentioned being chased and insisted there was nothing wrong. It seemed like her kids kept more and more from her. She had given Bonnie a warm plate of corned beef hash. That settled her down. She'd concluded that Bonnie's first period made her anxious.

The three of them decided to go to town. Ward went to change his shirt and Dorothy spoke quietly to Jud. "Thank you for coming today. And for giving him that wise talk. He's a good man; he doesn't always think things out the way he should. He's always wanted to show off with his fists. His brother Melvin said he took too many punches to the head when he was young. I don't know about that. It was before I knew him. I know we can't stand him going to jail or back to the asylum. Now that you've given him a plan, he won't need to go off half-cocked. He'll keep his pride this way. Thank you, Jud. Thank you." She smiled and patted his arm affectionately.

Dorothy wrote a quick note to the kids so when they came down with the berries they would know where she and Ward had gone. They sat until 3:30 p.m. at the bar in the American House and never heard a word about Luther or Bonnie or anybody being chased.

Between them, they put away a lot of Valley Forge draft beer though. Georgia and Nick Baker came in about that time and soon there were five of them around a table in the dining room. Jud still had to go and see his brother, so he took off, leaving the Bakers to see Ward and Dorothy home.

Ward thought a lot about what Jud had told him. He would be sure to be waiting for Luther next time Bonnie made a run to Carson's. He relished the thought of confronting a lout like Luther. He remembered Jimmy Brewster, whom he had thrown in the river long ago. That small act of chivalry got him a lot of praise and slaps on the back. A repeat of that would feel good.

Besides Nick and Georgia, the Mettses had a number of friends who would drive them home after a day of drinking. How much of that was due to Dorothy's willingness to spend all of Ward's pay buying drinks for them? No one would ask. Getting to town wasn't hard, except in winter.

Even that didn't stop Dorothy anymore. Ward didn't want as much beer as his wife, nor could he hold it as well as she could. Four or five drafts were plenty for him. Beer got people talking, and when exaggerations or outright lies began to dominate, Ward might blame his ears, avoiding a conversation if he found it disagreeable. Sometimes the beer kept coming without him asking for it. Sometimes the booze had a voice.

When friends drove them home on Friday and Saturday nights, they all would sit in the out-kitchen and guzzle quarts of beer, sometimes harder stuff. It fell to the eldest daughter to cook for the visitors late at night.

That had been Carol until she left home and went to live with Aunt Polly, announcing to her siblings, "I'm finally getting out of this hellhole." The remaining children would parrot the line whenever they became frustrated about the lack of bed sheets, pillows, towels, and almost everything right down to the scarcity of toilet paper in the privy.

Mail-order retailers like Sears & Roebuck mailed catalogs out a couple of times a year. The Mettses made do with those thin glossy sheets and the Sunday newspaper.

Dorothy prepared three meals a day Monday through Friday, and on Sunday she made a big dinner. Sometimes on a Saturday afternoon, she would make some treat for them all, fudge or gingerbread.

On Sundays, when she expected Aunt Polly and Uncle Curt to visit, there might be cookies or a pie for a late afternoon treat, as if Dorothy felt the need to match or outdo what Polly brought.

Strangely, Polly and Curt never had an appetite, even for a sweet treat. They claimed they gorged on Sunday dinner and were prone to heartburn.

The kids learned early on to fix food for themselves. If they asked for anything to eat on the Saturdays Mom was home, she would chuckle and say, "There's bread in there, jumbo and cheese. You kids know how to fry eggs. Anybody can pour a bowl of cornflakes."

When Nick and Georgia Baker's green Dodge came rolling up the lane, it was nearly ten o'clock. All the kids were in bed, mostly because the older ones were exhausted from the nervous ordeal that had begun the night before. Dorothy walked to the bottom of the steps and called out for Bonnie to report to the out-kitchen and fry up some ham and eggs.

"Not tonight, Mom. I'm tired." There was a hint of disgust in her voice that Dorothy didn't like. Bonnie rolled over and tried to go back to sleep. Soon she heard the heavy tread of her father's boots coming up the steps and braced herself, fearing there was a tongue lashing coming her way.

Instead, she felt strong fingers intertwining her hair. Her father hauled her out of bed despite her being nearly naked and threw her bodily toward the staircase. She found herself scrambling to get away from him, clawing her way down the rough steps.

She didn't stop until she was in the out-kitchen, pulling the ham out of the refrigerator and reaching for the heavy iron skillet that hung on a nail beside the stove. Short-order cooking she could do almost without thinking.

Nothing was said to her, and no apologies were offered to their houseguests for such a rough display of discipline. Barefoot and teary-eyed, she mechanically slid the greasy food onto their empty plates while the adults acted as if she were nothing more than a domestic servant. Neither Georgia nor Nick so much as whispered a thank you to her.

Once they were all fed, her father looked soberly in her direction, nodding dismissal. Bonnie padded slowly back to her bed with Carol's erstwhile aspirations echoing in her ears. "Can't wait to get out of this hellhole."

Chapter Five

When Abner Porter got to work Monday morning, his foreman Benny Gardener smiled at him. "You get a promotion Ab, temporary though. Somebody in the hot end didn't show up. Jacobs is qualified so he's gonna fill in. You okay with drivin' towmotor today?"

"Is the pope Catholic? That beats packing boxes any day." So many of the jobs in the factory were repetitive drudgery. After a while, the workers' hands seemed to move independently of their minds, which left their minds free to wish they had a better way to make a living.

A lot of the workers were young men. When Abner heard them complain about the heat or tedium, he would comment wryly, "They tell me the Army has job openings in Korea." The war was unpopular.

Most people didn't think the country had much business fighting on the other side of the world, so shortly after the big war ended. Most people knew of someone who went away ten years earlier and had not returned.

Abner had been to war and was grateful to have returned. So many people didn't appreciate the peaceful lives and good jobs they had. As much as he hated packing boxes, he knew there were people in Asia, probably other places too, who would gladly trade places with him. Being hot and tired in this factory and being hot and tired on Guadalcanal was not the same hot and tired.

Lunchtime came and Abner opened his lunch box without leaving the seat of the towmotor. He pulled it alongside a picnic table where Joe McGinnis and some other men were sitting.

"Ab, you ever know Luther Banks to miss a day's work?" asked Joe.

"Is that who didn't show up? Can't say I pay much attention to that sort of thing. Why are you asking me?"

"Oh, no big deal. I don't recall him ever missing, much less missing and not calling in. Benny's pissed off about it."

As if conjured up by the mention of his name, Benny stepped into view. "Abner, that's your Ford out there next to Luther's, isn't it?"

"That's Luther's? Okay, I guess it is. I didn't think nothing of it."

"Well, that's strange. The man's car is here; the man is not."

"Did you try calling him?" asked Abner.

"I called him around eight-thirty; he didn't answer. I figured he was sick and went to the doctor. Now I'm wondering about him."

Joe McGinnis shrugged his shoulders, "Well Benny, I wasn't gonna say anything, but it looks like you're gonna find out anyway. Luther left early Friday night. Did he clock out?"

"How early?" demanded Benny.

"Not sure, maybe 7:30."

"So, you ran the hot end by yourself?"

"Yep, and you'll see we were never under ninety-six percent the rest of the shift," Joe said.

"Dammit Joe, two men on the hot end ain't only for production; it's for safety. Who would have been there for you if a pressure line blew?" He was visibly upset.

"All my time here, I've been hearing about how those lines can blow. I've never seen one blow," said Joe, defensively. "And it's not the first time one of us was alone. Who watches out for me when Luther goes to the toilet? Or who watches out for him when I go?"

"So, your partner leaves for the better part of the shift and you say nothing to nobody?"

"There's a foreman on that shift too. I don't do his job, he doesn't do my job," Joe said.

Benny turned away. He knew the men would not rat when one of them pulled some stunt or pilfered something from the plant. The foreman on the other shift was Paul Reichart. He'd lost a leg on D-Day and gimped around on a wooden one.

He wasn't a good foreman because he couldn't make rounds as well as needed. The superintendent made allowances for him because of his wound.

"Benny's probably going to check Luther's timecard," said Abner.

"Good thing he didn't ask me how often Luther takes off," said Joe.

"So, who clocks out for him when he leaves like that?"

"He always came back before," said Joe. "And I ain't clockin' out for nobody, least of all Luther. They'll fire your ass for that."

By the time the day shift ended, it had been determined that Luther Banks left his workstation unscheduled on Friday evening and did not return, even to get his car and drive home.

Benny Gardener had gone to Luther's home and finding the front door unlocked, had entered and taken a good look around. There was no sign of Luther.

Oscar Wyant never had much to do in Parker. As the lone policeman in such a quiet factory town, he wrote a few traffic tickets, mostly when people went speeding along Front Street, where workers parked to enter the factory. He made himself visible when teenage boys acted up with petty vandalism and he had stopped a few drunken husbands from hurting their wives, usually for the second or third time. A missing person was something new. He had a serious investigation for a change.

Bad as gossip was, Oscar knew that often it exposed the truth. You couldn't depend on it or get someone convicted of a crime with it, but idle conversation and clues were a lot like the river; you couldn't see the fish, but they were in there. The barber, the hairdresser, the bartender, and his brother the plumber, had all become sources for him over the years.

He had a theory about what may have happened to Luther. Several people in town would be happy to see the man go away. He had taken advantage of women while their husbands were away during the war.

Oscar could have done that himself. Being the town cop, females saw him as a protector, and they trusted him. It also gave him a license to poke around and ask nosy questions.

There were only two other men in town who—Oscar assumed—knew more secrets than he did. They were both ministers and didn't share what they knew.

It had been nearly five years since the soldiers had trickled home from different parts of the world. Some adjustments had to be made. A lot of wives served as a kind of placeholder for their husbands, and it was a simple matter for the man to resume his position at the glass factory. Other women developed alternate relationships in their husband's absence. No simple matter.

Oscar knew, if no one else did, that Charlotte Timko still made herself available to Luther Banks. He had seen them together in Luther's car while patrolling the tank field. A dozen huge petroleum tanks stood in a field across the river, downstream a little.

There was fear of sabotage, oil being essential for defense production. Though the war was long over, and he never saw any oil company people there, he still kept his eye on the place. He thought he was the only person who bothered with the tank field, but he had to hand it to those two.

With so many places to conceal a car, the tank field was a perfect spot for sneaky romance. He kept the knowledge secret. He didn't think adultery was illegal anymore and didn't bother people who weren't breaking laws he was required to enforce.

There may have been no danger of sabotage, but anyone slipping around with Charlotte Timko should know that Ken Timko had sniper training and experience during the war. If the man chose to, he could put a bullet into you from a long way off. He kept his skills sharp by shooting groundhogs. If you heard rifle fire during the summer east of the river, you could bet on Kenny Timko.

Chapter Six

"Aren't you the early bird?" quipped Dorothy when Roger came into the out-kitchen on Tuesday morning. Past nine o'clock and the 'early bird' remark was intended to shame the boy.

His last full night's sleep had been Thursday. He felt raw and wondered if his mother could tell he was anxious. He poured out a bowl of cornflakes and while he was waiting, counted the days in his mind since he had pulled the trigger.

He had slept, or tried to, three nights now, and not one person in the Metts house had said anything about Luther Banks. How long could it last?

He looked closely at the edge of the bowl and sure enough, a lone cockroach came out from under the pile of golden-brown flakes. He had learned long ago to give the bugs some time to evacuate the cereal before pouring the milk.

He wondered how many of the disgusting bugs he had swallowed before he became aware of how vile they were. The kids at the lunch table in school would cringe when a roach would come out of his lunch bag. He had learned back in grade school to watch out for them, but sometime later, it became clear to him that none of his schoolmates had the pests in their homes.

Some didn't know what they were. He let the creature get halfway to the edge of the table before setting his forefinger under his first thumb joint and flicking the insect away. He heard the shell-like body impact the washtubs.

He knew the nasty creature would not be slowed down. It took a lot more than a finger snap to affect the health of their cockroaches. None of the older kids bothered stepping on them anymore. It was tidier to allow them to range free around the kitchen.

The smaller kids would go on stomping sprees from time to time. Mom would insist they sweep the uncountable mess into a pile and dustpan them into a trash box.

One good thing about having an out-kitchen: There were rarely any roaches in the main house where they all slept. They never left so much as a popcorn shell in the main house. Roaches gather where the food is.

Every year in the coldest part of winter, they would turn off the gas in the out-kitchen overnight. When morning came the floor would be covered with dead roaches.

Curiously, the roaches preferred to die in the open spaces, despite the obvious fact that while living, the majority hid under and behind the refrigerator, range, and cabinets.

Roger thought it noble of the roaches to make cleaning up their frozen remains so easy. For a week or so, the Mettses would be roach-free.

He read once, in the World Book Encyclopedia at school, that cockroaches were incredibly hard to eradicate. It disappointed him to learn the knowledge contained in the revered book was incomplete. While it declared that roaches had wings, he had never seen one fly. And the part about them being hard to get rid of, he could have written himself.

Roger wondered if the roaches had anything to do with the lack of mice in the house. Mice were common everywhere and there were rats and mice in the barn. He speculated the roaches were entirely too fierce, if not individually, then in a horde, for mice to compete with.

Carol had once come home from school crying because the other kids teased her mercilessly about eating in the 'outhouse.' The big farm kitchens in the area had once been known by the term and she, in her innocence, still used that nomenclature.

Sometime in the intervening years, farm kitchens disappeared. The word 'outhouse' was used exclusively for toilets now and more of their neighbors were getting inside plumbing.

Ward quickly agreed to change the name of the place to 'kitchen.' But old habits being hard to break, the 'out' was still hanging on, a vestige of the glory days when the farm had been something he was proud of.

Dorothy knew that her oldest son would dawdle if given half a chance. She often had to shame the boy mildly. "Ain't you supposed to help Pat haul hay today, Roger?" she asked.

"You mean 'make hay' don't you?" It wasn't his nature to be sassy with his mother, but in trying to act natural he was confused about what his attitude should be. He'd never taken note of what 'normal' was for him and so he didn't have a reference point.

"Hay's already made when it's laying in the field. It won't get in the barns unless somebody hauls it. But it's a silly thing to argue about," Dorothy said.

"Hear that, Mom?" said Roger. "Clarence is out there raking. It's our hay we make today," nodding toward the dull hum of a tractor engine, audible along with a tinny clatter of a hay rake. Many farm machines had their own distinct sounds.

Rural people could often tell what was being done by what they heard. Of course, it helped that folks knew what to expect in the different seasons.

A plow didn't make any sound, but plowing took all the power the tractor could produce, and you could hear the strain of the engine itself, a giveaway. A hay baler was unmistakable as was a mowing machine.

Clarence Hughes had been driving a tractor almost since he could walk. Starting out learning on daddy Pat's lap, by age thirteen, he'd mastered the hay rake.

The Metts boys were a little jealous of him. They had no tractor to drive, so they felt left out and behind. On the other hand, Clarence had no free time whatsoever. From dawn until dusk, if he wasn't at school, he did farm work.

Carter had already made his way to the hay field. He hung on the side of the tractor and chatted with Clarence as he prepared the field for the hay baler. The rake gathered a swath about ten feet wide and rolled it into a narrow pile for the baler to pick up.

"Guess who's back at her aunt's house for the summer?" asked Clarence.

"Janet, of course. I saw her at the ball field Sunday afternoon. Her boobs are getting bigger, and she knows it."

"Think she'll let you feel them?"

"That depends a lot on whether Nancy shows up this summer. That girl is hot to trot."

"You haven't even tried to kiss her yet and you think Janet is gonna undress for you," mocked Clarence with a chuckle. "T'ain't likely."

"I bet she'll go a long way if Nancy's around. She'll want to keep up and Nancy sure likes to tease."

"Have you kissed anybody yet?"

"I have. Or rather, she kissed me. A long, wet lip-lock."

"Who was that?"

"Kate Bowser, Marvin's big sister. She was on the steps at Marv's house. Marv had to go help his mom with something in the kitchen. Kate put her arms around me like I was her boyfriend and laid one on me. I didn't know what to think. But I didn't try to stop her."

"Ain't she going with some guy from Dutch Hill?"

"Dave Barger, yep. She didn't say anything about him, and she didn't say anything to me when she finished. I think she likes to kiss, and I got lucky. Right place at the right time, like they say."

"You're making that up," Clarence said.

"I'd swear it on a stack of Bibles."

Clarence and Carter shared all they could about girls, the most exciting subject in their lives. Obsessed with them, Clarence believed he would lose his virginity before he got his driver's license.

Pat pulled the hay baler onto the field and began following the rows, the mouth of the bailer lifting the hay and consuming it like a hungry animal.

From the back of the machine, every twenty feet or so, a tightly formed bail would fall onto the ground. Clarence and Carter unhooked the rake and pinned the tongue of a wagon to the drawbar of the tractor. They were finishing the hookup when Roger showed up.

"Want to throw or build?" Carter asked.

"I'll build if it's okay with you." When Carter agreed, Roger took his spot standing on the floor of the wagon. Clarence put the tractor in gear with a long, gear-grinding sound and let out the clutch.

The combination of tractor and wagon began following the path of the baler. Carter walked along and picked up the freshly packed bales by the double twine strands and swung each one up onto the wagon.

Roger placed each one in the pattern Pat insisted on, each layer alternating so that the friction and weight made them stable. If not done well, the load might fall off when the wagon bounced over the dead furrows, which could not be avoided.

Roger worked with a deadpan expression on his face.

"What's with your brother?" shouted Clarence to Carter as they turned the wagon around at the end of the row, where the long radius gave them extra time.

Carter shrugged. He knew that once the wagon was full, they would drive it to the barn and work together in a quieter place. Conversation would be harder for Roger to avoid there.

The wagon was fully loaded with sixty-five bales, so they steered toward the barn. Pat kept driving the tractor and baler. The Metts boys stood on the drawbar of Clarence's tractor, riding so they could all talk. Clarence broached the dreaded subject.

"Did you guys hear that Luther Banks went missing from the glass plant?"

Neither Roger nor Carter wanted to speak at all, but Carter thought hesitation might be suspicious. "Nope. What happened to him?"

"I don't think anybody knows for sure. Dad heard he was missing for a couple of days before anybody knew it." Carter and Roger made eye contact. Roger wanted to jump off the tractor and run.

"I think I know who that is. I never talked to him though. No reason to," Carter said.

"He used to keep a horse at Clint's place," said Clarence. "He'd come on weekends and ride it." Clint was Clarence's uncle, but he never called him 'Uncle Clint.' The Metts kids couldn't get away with such casualness to relatives.

"How's come nobody missed the guy?" Carter asked.

"Must not be married," Clarence said.

As they approached the barn, Roger leaped from the tractor and ran ahead. He made a beeline through the sliding doors of the barn, clearly heading for the water jug. It seemed he thought he should always have the first drink.

The guys were always parched when they came from the field, where the sun beat down on good hay-making days. The others had begun to resent Roger for treating the water jug like his own personal fountain.

"He might be sorry," said Clarence. "The old man's tired of him hoggin' the jug like he does. He talked about teachin' him a lesson."

"How's he gonna do that?" asked Carter. He had no sooner said that when it dawned on him what Clarence might mean. Clarence didn't answer, instead waiting until they could see into the barn.

"Who pissed in this water jug?" shouted Roger, spitting hard to eject the liquid. He had taken no thought for the clarity or color of the water, and with all his taste buds standing on tiptoe, eager for clean water, the rancid, salty taste hit him like the insult it was intended to be; it nearly turned his stomach.

"I guess that answers my question," Carter said.

"Did you do that, Clarence?" Roger asked, though he never thought Clarence would treat him so crudely.

"I did not," Clarence said. "But I have an idea who did."

Roger felt so disgusted and mad; he was determined not to give Pat the satisfaction. "I'll go wash this out and get fresh water. Your dad's gonna be sorry he done that. You just wait."

Clarence was not sorry for what his father had done to Roger, but he dared not say it. His dad could be crude and surly. He rarely forgave anyone who slighted him. "You gotta admit you asked for it. That might have been a dirty trick, but he'll laugh like it's nothin'. Piss ain't poison, ya know."

Clarence, like anyone who worked closely around dairy cows, had been caught frequently beneath one, washing or stripping teats, when the animal cut loose. Cows did not pee gently, and anyone caught there when the flow began would feel small drops of the hot liquid pattering against their face and their hands too dirty to do any face cleaning.

"How about we don't say anything about the water," Roger said as he returned after washing out and refilling the jug. "He'll want to know how it turned out. Let's let him wonder. I don't want to give him the satisfaction of knowing his trick worked."

Clarence backed the wagon in through the doors. The boys liked watching because Clarence could back hay wagons better than his father. The ability to back wagons quickly was a valuable farming skill.

A poor backer wasted a lot of time and got frustrated while doing the job. The Metts boys stood behind the wagon and shouted directions to Clarence. Most of the time, he didn't need any guidance other than a loud 'whoa' when he reached the proper spot.

Clarence spun around on the seat of the tractor and hopped to the ground like some kind of monkey. "Remember when your mom went missing?"

The Metts boys had been sure that Clarence would bring it up. Dorothy and Ward had gotten drunk and had a bitter argument. She had walked away into the darkness and Ward had passed out or gone to sleep. Sunday morning came and Ward could not find her. He sent the kids out to search.

The girls went to the neighbors' houses and the boys took to the fields and woods. Ward went to the home of his foreman, Red Hilliard, who lived close by and asked him for help. They drove to Parker, scanning the shoulder of the road and the yards of neighbors, the few there were between the farm and the bridge.

They asked about her at the only open place, Turner's gas station. They asked a few people in town. Ward knew she wouldn't walk to Parker since none of the beer joints were open.

When the search dragged on fruitlessly till noon, Red went to the Methodist Church as the services ended and enlisted another dozen people for the search.

They grumbled about missing their Sunday dinners and the minister dialed up the volunteer fire company to add to the hunt. The searchers expected that Dorothy had been drunk and found someplace to sleep it off.

That thought led one of the men to search the hay loft, though Ward had already done so. Covered so thickly with loose hay, Ward had missed her.

Apparently, she came to her senses in the interim and shook off some hay. The kids all loathed that event. Every person in the area, including all their schoolmates, heard about the search for their crazy, drunken mother.

"Did this Luther fellow drink?" Carter asked.

"Don't know. Probably some, I guess. Why?"

"Just thinkin.' Maybe he tied one on like my mom did. Does he have a barn to sleep in? Maybe he went to Clint's to bunk with his horse."

"Pretty sure he sold that horse," Clarence said.

"Oh well, I guess he'll turn up soon enough."

The Metts boys went up the hay elevator, a steel-framed thing that looked like an oversized ladder set at a shallow angle that got increasingly steeper as the loft filled. Clarence plugged the motor into the electrical socket and began placing bales of hay onto the chain.

The bales moved slowly up the incline to where Roger and Carter waited to receive them. Roger grabbed each bale by the twine as it topped the elevator and swung it around his body, pitching it toward his brother. Carter would place the bales as tightly as he could and turn around to be ready for the next one.

Clarence had plenty of bales within reach and could load them quickly, while the Metts boys could not move them across the loft and get them placed fast enough to keep pace with him. In no time at all, Roger found himself being pushed by the next bale coming up the ladder.

After he got behind and overwhelmed, he crawled out from under an itchy bale and hollered down to Clarence on the wagon, "A little faster if you can stand it." The three of them cackled as hard at the joke as when one of their fathers had first cracked it years before. It was a summer ritual.

When it got close to milking time, the hay-making had to stop. Pat and Clarence took one tractor and left for their farm in the late afternoon.

The Metts boys went to the out-kitchen for their supper. Bonnie and Dorothy were setting food on the table, knowing Ward would soon be home. They always sat down to eat as soon as he arrived; he got off work at four-thirty.

"You know what that dirty bastard did to me today?" Roger asked.

"Anything like he did to me?" Bonnie asked.

"He peed in our water jug."

"Isn't it his water jug too?" Dorothy interjected.

"He knew us boys would be drinking from it first."

"How many times a day do you refill that jug? Dorothy asked. "Maybe you should go get fresh water every time you get back to the barn. That way, you'll know it's clean. How many steps is it to the springhouse anyway?"

Dorothy knew Bonnie had been another victim of Pat's stupid tricks. Not long ago, he had offered her a sandwich filled with cow manure.

Fortunately, she had not bitten into it. The idea had been repulsive, and her stomach had reacted accordingly. Pat had laughed, of course, enjoying her disgust.

"I know you kids think Pat's a nasty man. That's not all he is. Have you forgotten stepping on that nail two years ago, Roger? Who picked you up, put you in his car, and run you down to Doc Masters? Who comes and plows us out when there's a snowstorm? Who sewed up your dog when he got cut so bad? Your father would have shot the dog, and you'd a been crying. He plows our garden every spring.

"You boys bitch about him paying so cheap when you work for him and ignore the fact that he's a good neighbor. Did any of you notice who helped us out when your dad went away? It was Pat. I know he's not a saint; just give him his due.

All he's ever done is work on that farm. He never had a time when he could get away from those cows. He doesn't have time to go to town the way we do.

Do you think he ever sits on his porch and reads a book or listens to the radio like we get to do? He's even taken you boys to the rodeo a time or two. That's the only fun he has in his life and that's one evening a year."

Carter and Roger both believed that things in their home would be better if their parents, like Pat, never had time to go to town. They didn't voice those thoughts to their mother.

"You kids give me a while. I'll think of a way to get him back that you won't need to be ashamed of. We don't want to turn him against us. That's enough about Pat. There's your father."

Ward stepped onto the porch, with Richard carrying his lunch bucket. One of the smaller children usually went to meet him when he got part-way up the lane on his way home from work in case there was a leftover cookie in his bucket.

Ward made sure to leave one, a day or two each week. "One more thing," Dorothy said quietly. "You kids take notice how your dad goes to work at the same time every morning and always gets home on time for supper. You think Pat has it that good?"

His mother's lecture made the heavy thoughts about the death of Luther Banks fade out of Roger's mind for a few minutes. Although his father usually spoke little about what went on during his workday, Ward would have heard the news of a missing man.

The family got seated around their table, big enough for all nine of them. The platter of meat or whatever the meal consisted of was not touched before Ward took his share. "Where did you work today?" Dorothy asked.

"A substation at German Hill."

Ward's clearing-crew truck left the garage at seven-thirty in the morning and often drove for an hour or more to their work site. It dawned on Roger that the crew also had that much time riding back to the garage.

If you subtracted the half-hour lunchtime, it meant that his father only did actual labor for maybe five hours a day. His crew got paid to ride back and forth.

His attitude toward Pat softened some when he compared his life to his father's. Ward's day had been a lot easier than Roger's and Carter's had been.

Once Ward had taken in a few bites of his supper, he paused. His voice was unusually pensive, and the older kids perked up their ears. "Looks like a man from the glass factory has run off or something," Ward said. His voice had a tone and cadence that suggested a higher power to his family.

"That sounds more like a question," Dorothy said.

"They say he's missing. People are guessing where he might have gone or what happened to him." Ward's eyes focused on Bonnie, who sat to his right beside her mom.

It was quiet. Bonnie, aware of her father's gaze, chewed her food slowly, unable to act aloof.

"Do any of you kids know who that is?"

"He works at the glass plant," Bonnie said.

"Yes, didn't I say that?"

"You did," Dorothy responded.

"Don't men and women run away together sometimes?" Carter asked. "Our shop teacher, Mr. Kinsey ran off, so they say, with the piano player from his church." He looked quizzically at his mom and dad.

"Could be Banks ran off with somebody. As far as I've heard, it's just him they can't find," Ward intoned.

"Something exciting happened in Parker. How about that?" Jack piped up. He did not often speak at the table and Carter thought it might be the opening he needed to change the subject.

"I bet there's an exciting story about why Pat never speaks to his sister," Carter said.

"That story goes a long way back," Dorothy said. "The way I heard it, the land was left to both of them. Pat naturally took over the farm.

Beverly married Jesse Hooker. They were supposed to move to Petrolia to be close to where Jesse worked. Bev wouldn't walk away from a small fortune in land and cattle. They couldn't agree on her fair share.

Long story short, Hookers began building up a house. They fenced in a couple of acres there; like it is now. Over the years, they put up a little barn, a chicken coop, pig pen, planted a big ol' truck patch of a garden, and started havin' babies. Who actually owns all the land and farm stuff is hard to say. Pat don't talk about it, and as you all know, he doesn't talk to his sister either."

"I think I was twelve or so when I learned they were related. I've known they didn't like each other all my life," Roger said. "Clarence tells me that when he waits for the school bus, right there by that garage at the corner of the Hughes property, he stands on one side of the lane and the six Hooker kids stand on the other side. He has never been allowed to speak to them and they have never said a word to him."

"I guess you've all figured out that since we are friends with Pat, it won't do for us to be friendly with the Hookers," Dorothy said.

"I always knew we didn't like them, but no one ever told me why," Bonnie said. "I watched her walk past his place once. She kept her eyes straight ahead as if her brother's house and barn were not there."

"Sad thing. Those Hooker kids could have been the farmhands Pat has been short of practically his whole life. They would both be better off if they would bury the hatchet and treat each other like family."

"Nobody holds a grudge like Pat Hughes," Ward said. "Anytime I tried to talk to him about it, I got nowhere. What bothers him most is Beverly's ground has a better spring and she don't have any cows to water."

"I've spoken to the Hooker kids a little bit at school," Bonnie said. "But never with Clarence around. I've always felt like I shouldn't."

"You go right ahead and talk to them if you want to. Make friends with them if you want to. Pat's fight ain't our fight," Ward said.

After the meal, Ward and Dorothy went out on the porch and lit cigarettes. They burned through a couple of cartons of Camels every week. Bonnie usually had Camels in her shopping bag from Carson's.

Cigarettes were nearly as important as beer to Ward and Dorothy. In Bonnie's mind, the money spent on them should go for better things. It didn't make sense to resent their smoking because most adults smoked. There were ashtrays in every home.

The men who didn't smoke chewed Red Man or Mail Pouch tobacco. Some smoked and chewed. Pat was the exception. He chewed something called Cutty Pipe. It was cheaper tobacco and Dorothy told her kids that he chewed that because 'nobody else liked it and would never bum a chew from him.'

Bonnie walked out the path to the toilet after she finished the dishes. When she exited the outhouse, her father stood in the path, waiting for her. She knew from the look on his face that he wanted something.

"I need to know something, Bonnie." Right away Ward saw her eyes begin to shift around, avoiding his gaze. "I heard that Mr. Banks has been pestering you when you go to the store. Is that right?"

Bonnie's eyes teared up and she began to sob. She tried to hold it back, but the voice of her father overwhelmed her. He had made his daughters cry a lot over the years, being demanding and insensitive. "Tell me this. Did he ever stand in your way or grab you or touch you?"

"No Dad, he just ran after me. I don't think he could catch me. I run fast."

"Why didn't you tell me someone was bothering you?"

She stopped holding back her tears, knowing how quickly they softened her father. She had heard her mom say a hundred times, 'Your daddy can't stand to see a woman cry.'

Ward put his arm around her shoulder gently and led her back toward the house. The question about Luther Banks could wait. The man was missing anyway.

Maybe someone else had thrown him in the river. Maybe they would find him washed up on the riverbank at East Brady. It was a common place to find drowning victims because the river took a sharp turn there and floating bodies would get caught in the tangled flotsam crowding the bank.

As dusk was settling in, the Mettses heard Pat's tractor approaching. Ward could see a good load of hay bales remaining in the field and the radio said there would be rain before the sun came up. Pat and Clarence would work past dark to get the hay under roof.

"Roger, Carter, you boys go give Pat and Clarence a hand. It will be dark soon."

Beth and Bonnie tagged along. They liked riding on the hay wagon when they didn't have to be in the sun. A pleasant summer evening was at hand, the scent of fresh hay like rare perfume. A good rain to wash down the shoulder of the road, on the hill toward Parker, was something the Metts kids were hoping for.

"I hope it's a gully washer," Bonnie said.

"Yep. A real toad strangler," Carter intoned cheerfully.

Chapter Seven

It had been a week since anyone had seen Luther Banks. Oscar saw Charlotte Timko going into the hardware store. He parked nearby and watched for her. He caught her before she reached her car to leave. With no one close enough to hear them; he got straight to the point. "What do you know about Luther?"

"Why are you asking me about Luther?" Charlotte replied, clearly uncomfortable with the question.

Oscar looked her straight in the eyes and waited. The tactic usually worked on guilty people.

There was no point in lying. Obviously, Oscar knew. "I haven't heard from him since a week ago Thursday."

"I know this is tough for you. What can you tell me about him?"

She dropped her eyes along with her voice. "He started dropping in to see me a long time ago. We don't get together that often."

"When did Kenny find out?"

"What makes you think Kenny knows?"

"I assume you've been getting together with Luther since the war. Am I right?"

"How do you know so much?" Charlotte asked defiantly.

"Unlike most people, it's my job to nose around. You can relax. I only use what I learn when I need to solve crimes." He felt sheepish, saying that since there were so few crimes he had ever solved. He got an inspiration and decided to use her angry state.

"You think you're the only lady he visits?"

Charlotte did not respond, but the wheels in her head were turning. He thought he might give them a faster spin.

"A lot of people got mixed up during the war. Last year, I got a good look at it. Someone you probably know came down with Syphilis. You know what that is?"

"I know."

"Well, when that happens, to keep it from getting out of hand, Doc has to find out who's been seeing who. He doesn't have time to go chasing people down and working out times to talk with them discreetly, that is, apart from their spouse. That's where I come in. You'd be surprised how some people get around. I sure was. And no, Luther wasn't in that mix. You would have heard from me last year if he had been."

Charlotte let out a long sigh that signaled her relief. "I would be able to tell if my husband knew."

"You sure about that?" Oscar asked, skeptically.

"What difference would it make if he did know?" Her mouth popped open, and she sucked in a gulp of air as the implication hit her. Her reaction was anger. "You think my husband had something to do with Luther's disappearance? I assure you, Sheriff, he did not." Charlotte got into her car in a huff, twisted the keys, and gave Oscar a nasty look as she pulled away.

Oscar mused as he walked back to his cruiser. His exaggeration about the people who had Syphilis worked well; it was a plausible scenario. And though he wasn't sure it made sense logically, Charlotte had convinced him that Kenny had no reason to hurt Luther Banks. He liked being called 'sheriff.' It was not his title, but since people began watching Western television shows, some thought all policemen should be called that.

Feeling defeated, Oscar reluctantly asked the PA State Police for help. They dispatched Trooper George Peters to assist Oscar. They spent a whole day interviewing any person who normally crossed paths with the missing man. Not a single person bothered to say that they considered Luther a friend. The next day, they searched Luther's home and his car for any evidence that might give them a clue about the private life of the man. They questioned the same barbers, beauticians, and bartenders that Oscar already had, plus a few random people they encountered as they moved from place to place.

Oscar made a list of every person who met with customers at every business in town and spoke to each one, working from the south end of town and finishing at Turner's gas station on the flat just past the bridge.

Wyant and Peters finally asked Doc Masters if he had any information that might be helpful. Doc had a record of Luther's parents showing they lived in a place called Frogtown. There were two burgs in the surrounding counties with the name Frogtown. Neither of these was large enough to have a road sign or be on the map. The police found Luther's folks by asking at the closest post offices. His parents were in their seventies and not helpful. They had not seen or spoken to Luther since around Christmas.

The parents gave them two letters from Luther's married sister, who lived in a small town in Oregon. They did their best to obtain a phone number for her, but in the end, had to settle for telephoning the local police in Oregon and asking them to inquire about Luther with his sister.

"Well, Oscar," said the Trooper, "the only thing we know so far is that other than the glass factory, nobody is going to miss Luther Banks much."

They had nothing to go on besides waiting for the report from Oregon, so they put out a bulletin to all the police barracks in the surrounding counties and waited for something to turn up.

Chapter Eight

The desired rainfall was no gully-washer, but it was sufficient. Bonnie went to Carson's on Wednesday and saw no trace of the evidence she feared might be visible where the path met the road. There were only five people in all the world who knew what had become of Luther Banks, and none of them had any reason to tell the police about it. Even better, none of those were suspected of having anything to do with his disappearance. Not as far as Bonnie could tell.

When she left Carson's and walked home past the noisy glass plant, she dared to glance up at the balcony-like place where the workmen looked out from the hot end. She thought showing interest in those watchers might be dangerous since she had never bothered before. A man leaned over the rail, smoking a cigarette. A week before it might have been Luther watching her go by.

She was eager to get back and talk to Maggie Porter. Abner would tell her what the folks at the glass plant said about Luther's absence. As Bonnie ascended the bridge, she could not keep her eyes off the spot just upriver where the culvert pipe went under the road. Despite being curious about what might be in the culvert pipe, she could not look without someone seeing her and becoming suspicious. The more she thought about it, the better the hiding place seemed to be. She remembered playing in that thickly shaded creek bottom. It was cool and damp, much like the springhouse on the farm, even on hot days. The running water created a refreshing flow of air. Any putrid scent of rotting flesh might be contained in that naturally chilled spot long enough for it to fade completely. She could not imagine a better place to hide a body. In irony, she shook her head. They had been desperate to find any place.

Her three siblings had managed to say almost nothing to each other about their secret. She remembered when she had been smaller and had the fear of monsters under her bed. Carol challenged her to ignore the creatures, saying that monsters enjoy scaring kids, and if the kids don't talk about it, they get bored and move on. Carol's presence made her feel secure, and Carol had always praised her silence. Carol also played the "first to talk" game. They would sit at the table or lie in bed and agree that the first person to speak lost the game and could fairly be ridiculed as a "motor mouth." It was like Roger, Carter, and Beth were playing the game with her.

With plenty of time left in the day to visit Maggie, Bonnie put the groceries away and headed back the path. Maggie was working in her vegetable garden and was glad for an excuse to get away from it. She fixed them glasses of lemonade, and they sat on the porch.

"What news has Abner brought home from work?" Bonnie asked.

"A lot of bullshit. There are guesses about where he went. Nobody thinks he went over the river. In the river, but not over it. Oscar Wyant has been asking a lot of questions to folks. Who knows if he's learnin' anything."

"Roger says he's gonna quit school and join the Army or something. I think he wants to get away from here."

"How old is he?"

"He'll be seventeen in August."

"That's old enough, I think. He should finish school, but all things considered, it might be a good idea. Has he told Ward and Dot?"

"He's told me."

"Well, Bonnie, I think you need to start thinking about your future the way Roger is. I have tried to mind my own business when it comes to you and your brothers and sisters. Lately, I'm rethinking that. What do you think about getting a job?"

"You mean like workin' at the plant?"

"You're too young for that. I have a better idea. You're gonna need things as you become a young woman. You're gonna want clothes and shoes, makeup, soap, dozens of things I can see you ain't gonna have.

Things Carol never had. Your folks aren't gonna buy much for you; you already know that."

Bonnie sat silently, her eyes cast down and on the verge of tears. Maggie took her by the hand. "Bonnie, you Metts kids don't see the way things are. It's not your fault. You haven't lived long enough or been anywhere or met any other kind of people. You come from a house that's poor, just not rightly poor. Do you know what I mean?"

"I'm not sure I do."

"Well, look at that Trish Myers girl. She's your friend, right?"

"Maybe my best friend, outside of you, Maggie."

"That's nice, Bonnie. You call me your friend, and I am, even if I'm old enough to be your mother. You can't compare yourself to me like you can compare yourself to Trish. How many pairs of shoes do you have?

"One. Mom will get me new ones before school starts."

"How many pairs of shoes does Trish have?"

"At least three."

"You answered quick. You've noticed she has more than you. How many different dresses, scarves, skirts, blouses and all that does she have."

"A lot, Maggie. Trish has a lot. She's got a watch and some jewelry too."

"What else don't you have compared to other kids in school?"

"But Maggie, there's so many of us."

"Okay, I'll give you that. There are more kids in your house than in most families. But where does Trish's dad work?"

"Glass factory."

"Does he make better wages than your dad?"

"I don't know."

"He doesn't, Bonnie. Your dad has a good job with the R.E.A., better than factory jobs. Trish's dad has a car. They have an inside bathroom. I hear they have a television. Those aren't cheap. And don't the Myers have four kids? Bonnie, you can look at all the other kids in this area. They all have more and nicer things than you and your family. You must have seen that?"

"I've seen it. What difference does it make?

"Let me ask you some more. Maybe you don't know. Most of the families around here have a mortgage. Do you know what that is?"

"I've heard the word. People pay the bank every month."

"That's right, and it's a big expense. Abner and I bought this place with a mortgage. We raised our kids here, and we're still making mortgage payments. Your dad inherited the farm from his daddy. There's no mortgage to pay. Don't you guys have free gas? That means no bills for heat. We buy coal every year to keep us warm. Most folks around here do that. Your folks pay the electric bill and buy groceries. Your dad doesn't drive a car anymore. Do you know how much it costs to run a car?

"A lot of the clothes you wear were handed down from Carol, right? You'll hand them down to Beth, and maybe she'll hand them down to little Mary. Same with your brothers. Do you want me to shut up?"

"What are you tellin' me all this for?"

"Am I sayin' things that aren't true?"

"I guess not."

"Don't get me wrong. Everybody hands down clothes. Nothin' wrong with that. I just want you to understand somethin'," Maggie said.

"What, Maggie? What do you want me to understand?"

"Bonnie, you ever have something you knew, but couldn't find the words for?"

"I don't know. Maybe."

"Do I have to tell you where your parents spend all their money?"

"No. They spend most of it in the beer gardens."

"That's true. You don't like it, right?"

"That's right; none of us kids like it."

I don't think you understand how seriously it affects you. I'm gonna do my best to explain it. You've heard that story about the ugly duckling, haven't you?"

"Sure, in first or second grade."

"It's kinda like that. You're kinda like that." Maggie breathed deeply and screwed up her determination. "The ugly duckling wasn't ugly. She thought she was. She was actually something different than what she thought she was. She didn't fit in. She got picked on, and she was made fun of. Do you ever feel like that?"

Bonnie took a long time trying to figure Maggie out. "What do you want me to say, Maggie?"

"It ain't about what I want you to say. Bonnie, it's what I want you to see. The ugly duckling wasn't ugly at all. She was in a place where she didn't belong, and she thought she was ugly. She was a misfit. Have you ever felt like a misfit?"

"They call me a misfit sometimes in school. Beth too. They're friendly sometimes and nasty other times."

"It's a sad fact, Bonnie. Girls can be brutal to each other. Kids can be cruel because they don't understand the damage they do. But that's not what matters now, so forget about them. You're not a misfit at all. You are a pretty, smart, energetic young woman. A lot of good things can happen for you as your life unfolds. But as long as you think you're a misfit, you won't see half of them. The way things are, you are gonna feel like a misfit. You're not so much a misfit as you are neglected. Kids should have parents that make sure they know how to take care of themselves and have the stuff they need to do it. It's like you Metts kids are left to raise yourselves."

"I read that book, *Uncle Tom's Cabin*. There was a girl in there named Topsy. Topsy said, 'I wasn't raised, I just grew.' I think that's me too."

"Yes, darlin', you're right about that. Here's what I want you to see. You aren't a misfit. But you are always gonna feel like one. And when you feel like you're something, you're liable to act like that thing. I'll try to think of a better way to explain it. That'll have to do for now."

"Thanks, Maggie. I know you're tryin' to help me."

"So, what do you think about the job?"

"Do you think Mom would let me do it?"

"You already go to Carson's to get groceries two or three times a week. What about working for them at the store?"

"You think they would let me work there and make money?"

"If you work well, they will pay you. You can earn money."

"How much would they let me work?"

"Hang on, Bonnie. I may have said too much. Let me talk to Mrs. Carson. If they are interested in taking someone on, it might be just the thing."

"All right. That's exciting. I never thought about getting a real job."

"A lot of times kids like you don't think about what's possible. It's sad, Bonnie. Do you realize that you're on your own? I mean, that you're the only person that's gonna care about how Bonnie makes out in life."

"Looks to me like you care."

"I do, Bonnie, I do. I know that if someone tried to interfere when I was raisin' my kids, I'd a' been mad. If I'm gonna help you, you need to keep my advice to yourself. Do you understand why I say that?"

"Mom won't like it."

"I think she'll feel put down. She's a proud sort. It's early in life for you to be working away from home, but you can do a lot of what they need to keep a store going. The Carsons are getting older. They will probably start you out sweeping the floor, stocking the shelves, maybe dusting things. In almost any place there are busy-work jobs, jobs that anyone can do. When Joe and Martha are busy sweeping the floors, they can't be cutting meat or putting out produce. If you have to convince anyone to hire you anytime, point that out to them. Some people think they have to do everything themselves. They don't realize that a helper doing the busy-work lets them concentrate on doing the important stuff."

"So, you think you can help me get a job?"

"I know I can show you how to go about it. They may not want help. When is your next trip to Carson's?"

"Probably Friday. Maybe tomorrow," Bonnie said.

"Okay, I'll take Ab to work in the morning. That way, I'll have the car. You come here first if your mom sends you to Carson's. I'll run you down, and that'll give me a chance to talk to Martha. I know her well enough to ask a favor. We'll see what happens."

"What if Mom doesn't send me tomorrow?" Bonnie asked.

"Can you come anyway?"

Chapter Nine

"She needs to dress better," Martha Carson said, matter-of-factly. Maggie, Bonnie, and Martha were standing in the store's office, a place Bonnie had never seen. Being allowed in that lofty room excited her.

"I can help her with that until she gets a few pays," Maggie said.

"Well, I won't promise anything. You say she's a good kid; we'll give her a chance. Won't be the first one we've hired." Martha and Maggie stopped talking about Bonnie like she wasn't there. "Can you be here at eight o'clock Saturday morning, Bonnie?"

"Yes, ma'am," Bonnie said enthusiastically.

"Maybe you could wait out there in Mrs. Porter's car for a few minutes, honey," Martha said.

Bonnie didn't want to say anything to spoil her good fortune. Getting a job where she could have some money was too good to be true. "Yes, Ma'am," Bonnie said. She turned away and stepped dutifully to the door.

With Bonnie out of earshot, Martha reached into a drawer and pulled out a ledger book. "The Mettses are behind in their grocery bill. We only require payment once a month. It isn't right for me to tell you how much. I just want you to know."

"Do they usually pay on time?"

"No. They have always paid, hardly ever on time. As time goes on, they get worse. They've never been this far behind," said Martha.

"Are you gonna take something out of Bonnie's pay to catch up her mom and dad?" Maggie asked.

"Joe's gonna want to. I'll have to see. That family don't amount to much, but that girl seems nice. I'd hate to take it out of her pay, hate to do that to her. She's not gonna make much if she has to pay her family's bill."

"This isn't the only store they get groceries from," said Maggie. "Usually, on payday, Dorothy gives their neighbor money to take her to the store in Callensburg. Dorothy's own private taxi service. Sometimes they run down to Parker and get beer too. That's been since Ward quit driving. The things they need more often, they send Bonnie for. That's why I thought this would be a good place for her to work, since she comes here so much anyway."

"Half the town does that, you know. That store's bigger and moves more stock. They can sell a little cheaper, so they get a lot of the business we used to get. Truth is, they have a better selection of meat too. We go there ourselves once in a while."

"Well, Martha, I think it's fair to say that they need to be able to buy from you. Can't you tell them to pay up or else it's cash only? I'm afraid her folks might be happy to let her pay for the groceries," Maggie mused. "Pardon me, Martha, I shouldn't try to tell you how to run your business."

"How well do you know Ward and Dorothy?" Martha asked.

"Good question. In some ways, they're good people."

Martha rolled her eyes. "Well, let's see how it goes. Maybe if they want Bonnie to work here, they'll settle up."

"Thank you, Martha, for being so good about this."

"I can see you're trying to help this girl get a better start in life. I admire you for that. It isn't her fault the way her folks are."

While walking to her car, Maggie chuckled to herself. If Carsons sold beer in their store, the Mettses wouldn't let their bill get far behind.

"I need to prepare you, Bonnie." Maggie started her car, and they pulled away from the curb, circled the block and headed toward the bridge. "I'm not sure your mom will take kindly to me helpin' you get this job."

"Why not?"

"You remember me saying, 'it isn't my place to teach you stuff?'"

"I remember. You've told me some important stuff. What you said about keeping quiet was a big deal. I'm glad you're involved."

"Maybe you don't remember. While your dad was away, the ladies at the church took a few boxes of groceries and household stuff, laundry soap, and such things to your house and tried to give them to your mom. Mind, I heard this story second-hand, so it might not be exactly what happened. Anyway, one of those ladies made a comment about how often you kids took a bath, or how well you're all taken care of, something like that. It didn't need to be said."

They reached the Porter house and Maggie stopped the car. She turned to Bonnie so she could look her straight in the eyes.

"Your mom got real upset. She told those ladies she didn't need their charity. Said she wouldn't put up with people who thought they were better than her. Called them a bunch of hypocrites. She even said that Ward's momma had warned her about them when she first came here after marrying your dad. Since hearin' that, I've been afraid to reach out to you kids much."

"I know what Mom says about the people at the church. Pretty much what you heard she said, 'They think they're better than us.'"

"How do you see that, Bonnie?"

"I guess she's right. I know some of the kids at school go to church, and they look down their noses at us."

"I need to explain something to you. You're gonna hear that business about how some folks think they're better than others your whole life. You need to see it for what it is. If the truth were known, your mom probably thinks she isn't as good as those church women are. She'll never admit that, not to herself or anyone else.

"Deep down, she knows that spending so much money on beer is wrong. Deep down, she knows her kids deserve better. Now, I don't know how she grew up. Maybe she was neglected and ragged. Someone said she was an orphan."

"She told us that. She lived in an orphanage for part of her life and with an aunt or uncle after a while. I'll have to ask her more about that."

"Here's what I want you to see. And I gotta be careful here because I want you to understand. Some people are," Maggie paused for effect, "better than others."

"Okay," Bonnie said, her eyes wide.

"Think about it. When your mom says those people think they are better than her, what does that even mean?"

Bonnie shrugged, feeling again like Maggie expected her to give an answer she did not have to give.

"Some folks have better habits, better manners, higher standards for themselves, higher ideals. Some work harder than others. Remember how I told you to keep yourself clean so people would like you and want to be around you? Did your mother ever tell you that?" Maggie's voice rose, and the pace of her speech quickened. "If a person doesn't have a house to live in and no soap and water, that's one thing. If you have soap and water and don't use it, people gonna look down on you, and they ain't gonna feel bad when they do it."

"Maggie, do you know you talk different when you get all stirred up?"

"When I get my back up, I get downright hissy, like an ol' cat. I'll try to purr like a kitty when we talk from now on. I went to 'dainty school' when I was a girl, you know, and they taught me to speak perfect English." Maggie held her hand up with her little finger extended as if she were holding a teacup. They both laughed.

"Seriously though, some kids in school study harder than others. If they are in a band, some get better at playing because they practice longer than others. Some people won't tell a lie, or they have a hard time doing it, even when it might be okay to do it. Some people see to it that their bills are paid before they buy things they don't need." She broke her eye contact with Bonnie for that one. "That's the kind of thing they teach people in church. Your mom knows that.

"The reason she finds so much fault with the church people is that they make her feel guilty about the things she does. Do you understand that, Bonnie?"

"I never thought much about it. You're probably right."

"Some people save their money and spend it wisely. Some people spend their money as fast as they get it. Only rich people can throw money around, and we don't happen to know any rich people."

"You seem rich to me."

"Well, Bonnie, once you grow up and can take control of things in your life, you'll be surprised what you can have if you spend your money wisely. That's one reason I want to see you get this job. You'll be able to see the difference for yourself while you're still young enough to form some good habits.

"Abner always says he'd rather be a half-hour early than five minutes late. Isn't he better than the person who's never on time? Some men have dirty minds and chase after young girls. Men like Abner and your dad treat women kindly, and they protect girls. Which man is better?

"Bonnie, you don't ever want to look down on another person. You know how it feels. If you care about how others see you, you must care about the way you live and behave."

"Dad says everybody gets talked about behind their back. What matters is what people say."

"He's right, Bonnie. We have some control over what people think about us, and that determines what they say about us. Some are gonna lie about us. We can't stop that. If people know you're decent, they'll have a harder time believing it."

"Well, I guess I should go home. I need to make sure my best skirt and blouse are clean for Saturday," Bonnie said.

When the Mettses sat down for supper, Bonnie waited for the others to get a mouthful of food. She looked straight at her father and spoke up so he would hear. "Daddy, Mrs. Carson offered me a job working in her store. Is it okay with you? She wants me to start Saturday."

"She just up and offered you a job?"

"I asked for it, sort of."

"I'm thinkin' about a job too," Roger said. "I think it's time I joined the Navy."

"You want to join the Navy, Roger? You've never said anything about that before," Dorothy said.

"Don't you have to be a little older for that?" Ward said.

"I'll be seventeen next month. I hear that one of you has to sign the papers saying it's okay for me to enlist."

"Don't you want to finish school?" Dorothy asked.

"What for? The Navy don't need a high school diploma. Besides that, if I wait until I'm eighteen, they might draft me into the army," Roger said gravely, "and send me to Korea."

"Don't the Navy go to Korea?" Jack asked.

"Sure, they do. But that war is mostly on the ground," Roger answered. "I think the worst that might happen in the Navy would be if they put me on an aircraft carrier. That isn't all that dangerous unless you're a pilot."

"You're too dumb to be a pilot," Carter said. "You ain't even got a driver's license yet."

"The Navy will give me a driver's license."

Roger's plans outweighed Bonnie's job. She resented that until she realized it served her well. There were no objections to her going to work at Carson's.

Maggie made more trips to Carson's than usual in the next few weeks. She enjoyed seeing Bonnie take so easily to store work. She was pleasant and polite to customers. It wasn't long before they let her keep the accounts of regular customers, those who settled their bills on payday. She had crisp penmanship, and totaling accounts came easily to her. Martha began to trust her, and as a bonus, Dorothy paid up their bill as if the Mettses had never been late and never intended to be.

Bonnie worked every day until the school year started after Labor Day, a Tuesday that was marked by Roger's leaving home for the Navy. Like a page had turned, the dreadful event of summer boarded a bus with her older brother and rolled surely toward a distant place called Illinois. The disappearance of Luther Banks was still mysterious; Bonnie only heard about it at the store, and people spoke of it less and less. Concern for the man seemed fixed on the factory side of the river alone, and that was mysterious to Bonnie until she realized that his absence weighed on so few people.

Bonnie was not surprised when her mother announced, in no uncertain terms, that having a job meant she could begin buying her own school clothes. Maggie took Bonnie shopping on a Friday. Among other things, she got her first brassiere. They both giggled, saying she had little more than rosebuds. For the first time in her life, Bonnie had more than one pair of shoes. Soon she was buying clothes for Beth and the younger kids as well.

"You realize how unfair it is that you have to spend your money on things your parents should be buying?" Maggie asked. They were shopping at the five-and-dime store in Parker. It had a smaller selection than the big store in Clarion. Enough socks and underwear to keep Beth, Jack, and Richard from feeling completely ashamed of the way they dressed. The Presbyterian Church in Parker sponsored rummage sales from time to time, and Dorothy made sure Bonnie knew when they would be held. The upstairs of the Metts house became Bonnie's domain. Dorothy rarely climbed the steps.

Roger and Carter had always worked on the Hughes' farm, mostly for no pay. They had always felt obligated to Pat, even though no one ever said they were. Without Roger's lead to follow, Carter stayed at home. Finally, Pat agreed to give him wages. No amount was ever specified, and once a week, Pat would open his billfold and arbitrarily select a few bills for the boy. After a hard week, Pat might give him three dollars. Carter fed cattle, carried buckets of milk, and shoveled manure alongside Clarence every day of the school week, all day Saturday and Sunday. Beth and Jack took care of Richard and Mary.

Chapter Ten

On New Year's Day, the family was sitting at the traditional meal of sauerkraut and pork. "Jack, I guess you're old enough to change diapers," Dorothy said.

Jack was bewildered. Beth instantly knew. "Mom, you're gonna have another baby."

"That's right. Late summer sometime. One grew up and moved out. Need another one to take his place."

"I thought you were gonna quit havin' babies, Mommy," little Mary said.

"That's what I thought too," Jack said.

"Your grandpa had nine kids. Your dad wants to do him one better," Dorothy said, with a wry smile. "I saw Mrs. Dillon at the rummage sale the other day. She offered to bring me a big pile of clothes her kids couldn't wear anymore. She said to take anything we didn't need to the next rummage sale. That'll save us some money."

"You mean it'll save me some money? You never get anything for us," Bonnie said. It was the first time she dared to defy her mother where her father could hear. She cringed inside, remembering his drunken pull on her scalp.

Ward did not appear to hear the comments. The kids wondered if he chose to ignore some things while blaming it on his poor hearing.

When the meal was over, and Bonnie and Beth were washing and drying the dishes, Dorothy came into the kitchen with a disgusted tone. The tirade never varied much; the kids could almost recite it.

"So, I never get you kids anything? Nothin' but work and sweat and cookin' three meals a day for threshing crews. Up all night carin' for you sick kids, plantin', and weedin' garden, cannin', and shreddin' kraut, grindin' sausage, and cannin' beef, and all for what? To be pregnant again with another snot-nosed, shitty-diapered, feverish kid to find clothes for? I'll show you. I'll go downtown and get hellish good and drunk."

"Go ahead, Mom. We're used to it."

The girls always felt guilty after Dorothy cut loose that way. They understood how difficult her earlier life on the farm had been. In calmer times, they had heard the accounts of long, hard days; they knew the misery was real. Didn't all farm women have the same circumstances? Their grandmother had died three years earlier and had endured the same kind of laborious existence. She had taught Dorothy everything she needed to know and do in the kitchen and garden. Grandma didn't get drunk and make everyone in the house feel her pain.

Bonnie regretted chastising her mother the next morning when Dorothy went back to their bedroom after Ward left for work. When some time went by, Bonnie grew uneasy and went into the bedroom to check on her mom.

"Mom, are you awake? What's wrong? Are you sick?"

Bonnie shook Dorothy gently by the shoulder, and she roused enough to mumble, "I took a bunch of pills."

Bonnie ran to the out-kitchen and found Beth. "She did it again. She says she took a bunch of pills. Where's Carter?"

"He went up to Pat's. He took Jack with him." Richard said.

The girls went quickly to the bedroom and pulled the covers off their mother. Pulling on her arms, they could sense that, while not alert, she wasn't completely unconscious. They each took an arm and helped Dorothy to her feet. Bonnie was taller than her mother, and Beth was almost the same height. Richard and Mary were standing in the doorway. Richard looked stunned, and there were tears on his cheeks. Mary didn't know what was going on. The fear in the room was palpable, and she stayed quiet.

"Richard, you remember I showed you how to make coffee?"

The boy nodded and turned around. Taking Mary's hand, he headed to the kitchen. He threw the old grounds out from the coffeepot basket, filled it with fresh ones, and dipped water from the bucket to fill the pot just as the trio of females came from the main part of the house onto the porch that connected it to the out-kitchen.

"I filled the basket up. Is that right?"

"No, it'll have grounds in it. Dump about half of it out," Bonnie said.

"Does it matter? She's gonna need it to be strong," Beth said.

Assuming haste was required, Richard turned the gas up to the point where flames were dancing up the side of the pot.

"Turn that down. You'll have the pot too hot to pick up, even with a rag," Bonnie said.

"Will water help?" Beth asked.

"She said coffee before. Black coffee. Wasn't there some left in the pot, Rich?"

The boy began sobbing. "I emptied it. Mom likes her coffee fresh."

"Let's keep her moving, Beth," Bonnie said.

"Should I run and get Carter and Jack?" Richard asked.

"No. Pat will want to know what's going on. She'll be okay once we get some coffee into her," Beth said, although she didn't feel confident about that.

Bonnie recalled another time when Mom had swallowed pills in a supposed suicide attempt. Carol had been there and was convinced that her mother would not take enough pills to cause her death; no one knew how many that might be. Bonnie wished, not for the first time, that Maggie was her mother.

It didn't take much coffee to remedy Dorothy's drowsiness. She had never been as asleep as she let on. She never asked herself why she did things to scare her kids. The time when she had caused a search party to be gathered was a dear memory. The people it had disturbed, the anxious look in the eyes of her children, the comforting voices of her neighbors, she craved pity. It would keep her going.

By noon, Dorothy was back to normal. Normal for the Mettses was to quietly move on from threatening events, and they did. No one told Ward about it when he got home. As soon as the dishes were finished, Bonnie donned her winter coat and left to see Maggie. The sun was setting, and there was just enough snow to cover her shoes and settle in on her socks. Her feet were wet by the time she reached Maggie's. She knocked on the door. She could see Abner sitting at their kitchen table through the small window in the front door. He got up, strode to the door, and smiled big when he saw her. "Hey there, Bon-Bon. What brings you out on a dark, dreary winter night?"

"I hope you don't mind me barging in here like this."

"Not at all, dear. These winter evenings are too long. A little company will do us good." He could see the disappointment on her face. "I know you came to see Maggie, so I'll just keep myself busy in the basement. It's warmer down there anyway."

Maggie shook her head and pursed her lips as her husband slipped away. "You need to sit here by the stove and get your feet warm, honey. Why don't you give me those socks, and we'll get 'em dried out." She hung each sock up on a wire hanger and placed it above the range so the heat could work on the dampness. "Think maybe a pair of snow boots might be a good thing for you to buy next?"

"That's all I've been doing with my pay, buying clothes. I have high shoes. I didn't think there'd be that much snow."

"How about a cup of tea?" She set a kettle on and got a pair of cups from her shelf. "Something happened today?" Maggie queried. "Wait," she looked past Bonnie to be sure Abner was down the steps. She spoke in a low voice. "Have you heard anything about...you know what?"

"Nothing about that."

Maggie nodded slowly while counting on her fingers. She mouthed silently, "seven months."

"Yeah, I can hardly believe it," Bonnie said.

"So, tell me what happened," Maggie said.

"Mom took a lot of pills and went back to bed this morning after Dad went to work. When I tried to wake her up, she told me she had taken a bunch of pills. I think she wanted to kill herself."

"How many did she take? What kind of pills?"

"I didn't ask her. Probably aspirins. There isn't much else for her to take."

"So, she had you kids get her up and give her black coffee, walk her around till she woke up, right?"

Bonnie was amazed that Maggie knew the whole thing. "How do you know?"

"It isn't the first time she's done it. She did that once to Carol and Roger. Didn't they ever tell you about it?" A hint of disbelief was in her voice.

"No, I'm telling you the truth, Maggie."

"It was years ago. I heard about it through the grapevine. And when you hear things that way, they can be messed up. It sounds like the same thing."

"What was she trying to prove?"

"Good question. Did something happen that upset her?"

"I upset her. She expects me to take over buying all the clothes and shoes for the other kids because I have a job. I mouthed off about it."

"Mmm," Maggie said. "You said something that made her feel low down?"

"It wasn't much. I told her at the supper table. Dad was right there. I thought he would say something about it, but he didn't."

"Did he hear what you said?"

"He had to have heard enough to know it would make her mad."

"So, what did she say when you mouthed off?"

"Nothing at the table. Later on, when it was only me and Beth, she let me have it. The same thing she has said to us a dozen times. How hard she works, not just now, mostly back when they farmed. Stories about crews of men helping to thresh and how she'd have to cook a table full of food for all of them. How hard it is to take care of us all. She usually says, 'I'll go downtown and get hellish good and drunk.' And then she goes and gets drunk. Except, this time, she didn't go.

"Oh, god," Bonnie said, realizing she had left out a key part. "She's gonna have another baby. That might be why she got so mad this time. With all the fuss when she took the pills, I completely forgot about it."

Maggie patted Bonnie's hand. "You poor thing. There's so much you don't understand." Maggie looked away into the woods, wishing it were still autumn when the scenery was rich with color, a metaphor of how there was beauty to be found, even in the sadness of life. The midwinter gloom made her want to weep, knowing that it didn't matter how much she told Bonnie, how well she might explain it, the chaos and want in the girl's life would never leave her entirely. She had seen it before. The proverbial line, 'As the twig is bent, so grows the tree,' came to her mind. She could teach, help, sympathize and encourage. That was all. It wouldn't be enough.

"She doesn't want another child," said Maggie. "She's tired and feels trapped."

"Why does she have babies she doesn't want?"

"It's hard not to get pregnant."

Maggie couldn't ignore the quizzical look on Bonnie's face. "Bonnie, we've talked a little bit about sex and all, but people have a lot of wrong-headed ideas. Your mom and dad are gonna have sex. They're gonna screw, you know. As long as they do, there's a chance they'll make more babies."

Bonnie blushed and dropped her eyes, giggling. "'Screw,' I thought that was the word kids used. Can't Mom just say no?"

"I get it. Since I'm an adult, I gotta say 'marital relations.' Would that make you feel better, Bon-Bon dear? Is that a more dignified phrase?" They were both giggling now.

"You like being called 'Bon-Bon.' I think I'll start using that for you. Abner says you're sweet. Course, he thinks any girl younger than me is sweet. He talks like that to make me jealous, the scamp."

"Better watch out, Maggie. I could see myself getting my first kiss from an older, wiser man, someone like Abner."

"Sorry, Bonnie, you didn't come back here to talk playful." Her voice took on her usual sober tone. "Women aren't all the same. Some will say 'no.' Some don't want to. Some, their husband won't listen. There are ways to keep from getting pregnant, but none guaranteed to work. Just like you started your monthly, someday you'll stop. All women do. After that, no more babies. Ward Metts is a hard man to say 'no' to. They say that drinking will make it hard for a man to have sex, maybe not every man. And beer makes people careless."

"Why does it make it hard for a man to have sex?"

"We'll talk about that later," Maggie said, feeling herself blush. She couldn't explain the 'hard to have sex part' with a straight face.

"Can't they use rubbers?"

"So, you know about rubbers?"

"My friends at school tell me a lot."

"Half of what you'll learn from your school friends will be wrong. To answer your question, they can use them. They don't always work. Sometimes, they break or slip off at the wrong time. It doesn't take much. Your mom must be quite fertile. Some women are. Some women never get pregnant. God knows why. Your mom knows there's another nine months of carryin' the extra weight and the birthing, which, by now, she's pretty good at. A lot of women have a hard time having babies. Some even die. Your granddad had two wives, didn't he?"

"Yep, that's why Dad has some half-brothers. I don't think any of them live around here, though."

"Your granddad's first wife died having a baby. Your dad only has one sister and one brother; his dad had six kids with his first wife."

"Nobody ever told me that."

"You should know too, that all of your dad's brothers and sisters were born right there in that house, like you kids all were. If a woman has trouble these days having a baby, she is in a hospital. Fewer mothers die nowadays."

"I remember Richard and Mary being born, but not Jack," Bonnie said.

"Your mom's never had a problem with birth. That's not to say she won't. It's a scary thing to have a child. She might be afraid she's due to have trouble."

"Maybe she could go to Clarion to the hospital for this one." She looked at Maggie. Neither of them said it, but they both knew that Ward and Dorothy wouldn't be going to a hospital.

"You've had two babies, right Maggie?"

"I would have had three. I lost the last one."

"A miscarriage?"

"That's what they call it."

"Did it hurt?"

"Some. Mostly, it was sad."

"You said that it's hard not to get pregnant. It can't just happen. Not the first time you have sex, right?"

"Here we go. Remember how I told you about the wrong stuff you'd hear from your friends?"

"Yeah."

"That's one thing. You can get pregnant anytime you have sex. There are times when it's less likely. Even so, you never want to take the chance. Some boy will probably tell you that it can't happen to you the first time you do it. He'll be lying."

"What other lies will boys tell?" Bonnie asked.

"Let's see. I guess the biggest one is, you have to let me do it to prove you love me."

"Did you do it before you were married?"

"That's none of your business, young lady," Maggie said, chuckling. She knew Bonnie would take that as a yes.

"Come on Maggie. I tell you all my secret stuff."

"We waited until we were married. I was a good girl."

"I heard a lot of couples did it right before the guy went off to the war."

"You mean the last war, not this Korean thing?"

"That's what I meant. Probably some for this war too."

"This thing in Korea isn't anything like the big war. World War Two, they call it. In the days right after Pearl Harbor was bombed, a lot of men left, and their girls were scared they might not come back. There were a lot less virgins in 1943. When a couple is in love or cares about each other a lot, they get to where they want to have sex. The desire can be too strong. There isn't anything else that's like it."

"What can I do? I want to have a boyfriend someday."

"I'll tell you how it will be. Some boy will kiss you. That's nice, you'll like it. Pretty soon, the boy will want to touch you under your clothes. He'll want to feel your breasts. He'll want to put his hands in your underwear."

"Is this when they play baseball?"

"What do you mean? Maggie said.

"They talk about getting to first base, second base, you know?"

"Oh, yeah, yeah. I didn't get it at first. I haven't talked that way for a long time. With boys, it's a lot like a game. They'll talk with each other about how far they got with you, and they'll lie about it. Don't believe what they say once they get excited. The thing is, they want you to get excited. They want you to want to keep going further and further, and if they're a nice guy, you're gonna want to please them. It's the way women are.

"Once a woman is married, she's always a little bit afraid that her husband will get involved with another woman. Have you ever been to a wedding?" Maggie asked.

"No, I guess Carol will get married sometime. Maybe I'll get to be one of her bridesmaids."

"Well, you'll hear in the marriage ceremony that the couple promises to keep themselves only unto the other. That means you can't fool around outside of your marriage. It still happens. Men can be tempted easily. So, us married gals feel like it's our job to keep our man satisfied. Besides that, sex can be a lot of fun. Put all of that together and sometimes you get more children in a family than you plan for."

"What about when you have your monthly?"

"Well, you don't do it then. Men gotta go without. Even though it's probably the one time you won't get pregnant."

"Isn't it messy?"

"You mean during your monthly? Of course, it is."

"I mean, all the time."

"Well, you can say it is, sort of. It's the kind of mess you don't mind."

Their tea was finished, and the conversation lagged. "You want to know why your mom is so crazy, don't you?"

"If you can help me understand. It's hard to think another baby is the whole problem."

"Maybe it's the straw that broke the camel's back."

"A lot of little things over time?" Bonnie asked.

"I don't really know, Bonnie. I won't pretend I do. Lots of people claim to understand things that they have no idea about. I'd rather tell you I don't know than bullshit you. 'I don't know' is an honest answer, and I am not afraid to say it. People don't do well when all they have in their life is work. Even God takes one day a week off.

"Some people, people like Pat Hughes, can work like mules their whole lives, because it's all they've ever known. Your mom had dreams at one time. She was raised in a town. She probably saw folks living in town with easier lives. Who knows, nicer clothes, tea parties, church socials, and most of all, company, company of women her age who share the same kind of life.

"When you have a farm, you don't own it. It owns you. When you have a family, it kind of owns you. The more kids you have, the harder it is. Not everyone can live with that much strain."

"But they don't farm anymore."

"I know. Life has to be easier for her now. There's more to it. The other thing is the beer. Did you ever hear about Prohibition?"

"What is that? I have heard people talk about it."

"When I was about your age, the government made alcoholic drinks illegal: beer, wine, whiskey, what have you. For several years, you couldn't get beer. There were places in big towns that served it. They made a lot of money from it too. I never cared for the stuff, but lots of folks were willing to defy the law and drink it anyway. In a lot of places, the cops looked the other way. Anyway, drinking was kind of fashionable. Rich and classy people drank. It's always fun to think you're getting away with something."

"Good history lesson, Maggie. What does it have to do with my folks?"

"Prohibition created more problems than it solved. So, they ended it. About the time your mom and dad were dating, drinking became a fad, the latest thing to do. The beer joints were one place Ward and Dorothy could go to get away from all that farm work. Some people have hobbies, things they enjoy that take their minds off their misery. Abner hunts and fishes, even does a little trapping when fur prices are up. Some people have card clubs and gardening clubs. Some like to read a lot of books or play music like piano or guitar. I go to church and Sunday School. It gives me a lot of time with my friends and doesn't hurt my soul. In fact, it makes me want to help you out. Kinda prompts me to do good deeds. For Ward and Dorothy, the beer joints are it."

"I wish they would go to church instead of The American House," Bonnie lamented.

"By the way, Bonnie," Maggie said. "I don't think your mother wanted to kill herself. She wanted you to think she wanted to kill herself."

Chapter Eleven

The winter dragged on, the groundhog saw his shadow, and Bonnie continued her job at Carson's, becoming more and more competent and strong; "mature past her years," Martha Carson observed. "Old before her time is more like it," Joe Carson insisted.

Bonnie worked two evenings each week and all day on Saturdays. If possible, Maggie would shuttle her to town and back, sometimes taking Abner to work so the car would be available. In nasty weather, Tom Carson would make sure she got safely to and from his store. Bonnie assumed Tom's generosity was largely inspired by Maggie's, as if he had to keep up with her. Maggie lost her fear that the Mettses would resent her for being so close and supportive of Bonnie. She still avoided contact with Dorothy, and it wasn't hard to do.

Bonnie continued to make sure her siblings had clothes. Many times, there were plenty of shirts and jeans available at the rummage sales to fit Jack and Richard. Things like socks and underwear had to be store-bought. Carter's wages working on the Hughes farm left much to be desired, but he would not ask Bonnie for help with the things he needed.

When Roger finished naval training, he immediately went to sea. His letters home were sporadic; sometimes two or more would arrive on the same day due to the nature of mail service from a ship. As time went on, the letters got further and further apart. Bonnie wanted to write and tell him how the mysterious disappearance of Luther Banks had largely been forgotten, but she stuck to the idea that the less said about it, the better. Bonnie envied her older siblings. They had escaped. She would escape too, at her first opportunity. She became even more determined on a Friday night in May when a car she didn't know came up the lane.

Typically, the Mettses would tell whoever had brought them home to blow the horn. That was Bonnie's or Beth's signal to go to the car and help carry to the house any goods they happened to bring home, often a couple of sacks of beer in quarts. Bonnie liked to stay up late, so waiting for her parents was no burden. When the horn blew, she went down, assuming it was them. Instead, there were two young men in the front seat. "Is this the place Luther Banks boarded his horse?" asked one of the men as he came around the car.

"No, that would be Clint Hughes's farm. It's across the valley." The mention of Luther brought Bonnie up short. Her hesitation allowed the two guys to get her hemmed in. One was behind her with his hands on her shoulders, and the other faced her. "Why don't we take you for a little ride tonight, sweetheart?" The voice was familiar, but she couldn't put a name to it. She squirmed quickly, but the hands tightened, and the man in front took hold of her wrists. She could taste his beer-soaked breath, and the sense that her father was absent overcame her. She was powerless against these two. She struggled, but the pressure of the two men only increased.

There was a brilliant flash, as lightning cast the briefest instant of clear vision to the scene. "Omigod, we are in the wrong place. This is the girl that handles my account at the store! We're getting out of here." He hustled the other fellow back into the car, and they took off.

Bonnie felt her knees buckle and she sat on the damp ground with tears rolling down her cheeks as she watched the taillights of the car get farther down the lane, the tires stirring little clouds of dust that blurred her vision through the tears. "Can't wait to get out of this hellhole," she murmured.

Her tears dried, and Bonnie looked up into the sky, shaking her fist. "God, I don't like you, and I don't like this world you made. I will never have anything to do with you. I don't care how much Maggie likes going to church."

The summer was a continuing routine of work for Bonnie. When not busy at home, she was at Carson's. She knew which customer had tried to force her into the car. There were only eleven single men who had charge accounts at Carson's. The guilty man stopped showing his face when she was working. She could tell from the account sheet when he had come in. Her consistent schedule made it possible for him to avoid her.

Nearly the whole summer went by; her mother got too heavy to make the walk to Parker, and there was about a month when she consumed no beer at all. Jeffrey was born in August. By the time school started again in September, Dorothy and Ward were back to their drinking routine. The newborn was cared for by Jack and Richard when they weren't in school.

Carol came home for Thanksgiving dinner in the company of Frank Parks. It took Bonnie and Beth about three seconds to notice that Frank was the best-looking man they had ever seen and that Carol had a little chip of diamond on her left hand. They did not give her a chance to announce the good news. "Look, look. Carol, you've got a ring," Beth spouted.

"Saw it right off," Dorothy said. "I figured this was coming." Ward's sister Polly had written her about how serious the couple was. Frank had spent four years in the Marine Corps and by some stroke of good fortune, avoided going to Korea. He had a good job at the mill in Grove City, and his family included a sister who befriended Carol. He owned a motorcycle and a new Buick Special Convertible. While Frank was a prize in the eyes of the girls, Dorothy had doubts. She could sense his disgust when a few roaches appeared on the table next to the turkey platter. "What's the matter? Don't you have any insects in Grove City?"

"Sure, we have bugs. Not like these though." He looked around the table, smiling and tried to be nonchalant. Bonnie and Beth both blushed as he made eye contact with them.

"They must be country bugs. I saw some like 'em at Parris Island. That's in South Carolina. Big bugs down south. Fine turkey, Mrs. Metts. My mom is a good cook mostly, but her turkeys are always dry for some reason." Carol was impressed at how easily he changed the subject.

"When will you two tie the knot?" Ward asked.

"Next summer. Frank's folks have a house they rent," Carol said." The lease will be up, and we can move right in. It's far enough from the mill so there's no noise. Real quiet little neighborhood. Close to the park."

"Where do you ride that motorcycle?" Ward asked.

"Out here in the country mostly. But I joined a club, the A.M.A. They hold rallies and tours. It's a lot of fun. I'll bring the motorcycle down once the weather gets nice again and take each of you for a ride. Have you ever been on a cycle, Mrs. Metts? How about you, Ward?"

"You won't get me on one of those contraptions," Dorothy said.

"How about a ride in your car, Frank?" Jack asked. "That's here now."

"Jack, you mind your manners," Dorothy said. "Frank can't fit all of us in that car."

"Ah, come on Mom. I never rode in a convertible. Besides Mom, I'm not askin' for all of us. Just me."

"Oh, it's only you that wants a ride, Jack," Frank chuckled. What about your baby brother here?"

"Jeffrey's too little to know what he's missing."

"Tell you what," Frank said." I'll take you, Mary and Richard for a ride once this big meal settles down in my belly. But the top stays up. Okay?"

"Can I go too?" Beth pleaded, hoping she could sit in the front seat. The Buick was big enough.

"It isn't that cold," argued Richard.

"Not when you're standing still, Rich. Get going forty or fifty miles an hour and you'll freeze your ears off," Bonnie said. "On a warm day, they'd have the top down already, don't you think?"

"Have to be a short ride in this chilly air, Jack," Frank said. "Just wait till spring. We'll take a nice, long ride then. I'll even bring my Harley-Davidson down. It's better than a convertible, trust me.

"I was away at the time, but two years ago today, a huge snowstorm hit this part of the country. It was some kind of record. My father showed me some pictures from the newspaper. It would have been over your head, Jack. You never know when that might happen again. It isn't good to get far from home this time of year," Frank said.

"It was a big snow," Ward said. "Not so bad here, but over toward the state line, things were buried for a couple days. A lot of power lines were down too. It took a week to get everything back on."

Beth imagined herself behind Frank on the motorcycle. The wind in her hair and her arms around his strong shoulders. She imagined pressing the ample breasts she did not yet have against his back. She knew it wasn't right to have those thoughts about her sister's fiancé, but Carol didn't have to know. Frank was dreamy.

When they finished the meal, the adults sat around the table while Bonnie, Beth and Jack took care of the leftovers and washed the dishes. Ward asked about the Marine Corps and wondered about how many ports Roger might get to while at sea.

"Carol tells me you tried to enlist after they hit Pearl Harbor," Frank said.

"That's right. They wouldn't even talk to me. They said they needed my farm production. I think it was more about havin' a house full of youngins. I gotta admit it. Dorothy would have had a hell of a time on her own. I didn't know how little they paid soldiers. Even if we'd sold all the cows, she would have run out of cash before the war ended. Then again, if I'd gone to war, we wouldn't have so many pups to feed."

"We're not pups, Dad," Mary said. "And it ain't you that has the babies."

There were laughs around the table, except for Richard and Mary.

The humor gave Frank an opening. He looked toward Beth, and their eyes met wistfully. She felt a sweet, wonderful longing, something new and mysterious that foretold bliss. She didn't want it to end. Frank winked at her quickly, careful not to betray his thoughts to the others with even the hint of a smile.

The six Mettses who were big enough to go piled into Frank's Buick, and he started out on the back road that went past the farm and wound around the township. Bonnie sat in the front seat by virtue of being older, and Beth was jealous.

"There must be something better to see than fields and cows. Doesn't the Clarion River wind through here somewhere?" Frank asked.

"Take that next dirt road to the left," Bonnie advised. "It's only a mile or so to Grass Flats. It's where we like to go swimming in the summer when we can get a ride. It's too far to walk."

"It's great to go swimming on a hot summer day. Get all cooled off. But after an hour of walking back home, you're hot and sweaty again," Carter said. "Now, if we had somebody to drive us to the river and back..."

The road curved gently through the bare trees of the forest, a rich bed of dry leaves carpeting the ground. They spooked some deer, and their footfalls made a staccato rustling sound as they loped away.

"See any horns?" Frank asked. He was hoping to get a day or two off work to hunt in the next couple of weeks, and if he spotted a nice buck, it might help him decide where to go afield.

"That last one had forks," Jack said.

"You see horns on every deer," Carter responded. "Mostly your imagination. I didn't see any."

"How many were there?" Carol asked. "I only counted five."

"I love Pennsylvania. When the trees are thick with green, it's beautiful. I've been around the country enough to see some other places. I think every state has its own unique beauty, but you can't beat summertime around here," Frank said.

"We pay for it with five months of dreary skies and bare limbs. Nothing pretty this time of year," Carter observed.

The road sloped slowly downward, and soon, they saw the river beside and below them. Frank eased the Buick downhill, careful to miss the high spots on the roughening road. "They don't plow this in the winter, do they?" Frank asked.

"No, the bridge down here is old and not safe for traffic. But you'll see, it makes a great place to swim," Carter said.

The road turned sharply to the right, opening to a wide spot large enough to turn the Buick around. The bridge had a rail gate across its threshold that barred any vehicle. They got out, ducked under the gate and walked across the heavy wooden planks, stopping halfway to admire the scene.

"Like I said," Carter remarked. "It's a lot prettier in the summer." The river, dappled with rounded stones of varying sizes with water roiling and cascading around them, created a symphony of soothing music, and for a while, they all stood there quietly.

"A river is always nice to come and watch. Don't ya think, Frank?" Jack asked.

"I do, Jack. Let's see if I can remember." He eased his head back in thought and drew verses from his memory. "*I come from haunts of coot and hern, I make a sudden sally. And sparkle out among the fern, to bicker down a valley. By thirty hills I hurry down, or slip between the ridges, By twenty thorpes, a little town, and half a hundred bridges. Till last by Philip's farm I flow, to join the brimming river. For men may come and men may go, but I go on forever.*"

"Wow, he knows poetry," Beth gushed, even more enchanted with Frank now.

"Yeah, so what's a 'thorpe?'" Carter asked.

"Don't know what a thorpe is. I think the guy who made up the poem had to make do once or twice. Maybe he made up a word. Shame to have a nice poem or song end up in the trash because of one silly little word now, wouldn't it?" Frank asked. "And what's a 'grass flat' anyway? Looks like a river to me."

"No idea why it has that name," Bonnie said. "I never heard anyone ask that."

"I think it has something to do with fishing," Carter said. They went back to the road and down the steep, sloping path that swimmers used. Directly under the bridge, as if it were planned that way, an enormous smooth sandstone boulder sloped into the water. A steel cable hung from the bridge with a crossbar just right for swinging out over a deep pool. Carter jumped enough to grab the swing, and he backed himself up the rock, picked his feet up and let go, swinging out over the water.

"About here, you let go," he hollered as the arc of his swing reached its far point. "Try it, Frank."

Frank took the swing and went even farther up the rock to begin. He went out and back a dozen times, marveling at the nearly perfect combination of water, rock, and swing.

"I'll come back here when winter's over and it warms up. We'll bring your mom and dad too, the whole family, even if I have to make two trips. We'll spend a whole day."

"That's a good plan, Frank. You should know, it gets pretty crowded here on a hot day. Especially when school's out," Carol said.

"Maybe so, but I won't be happy till I do a flip from this swing into that water," Frank said. "I'm tempted to do it now, even in the cold water."

Winter's first snow came two days later. They closed the school on Monday. Smaller snows came every other day until the middle of January when things thawed enough for the ground to show through in spots. A letter came from Carol, announcing that the date of her wedding had been moved up and that she and Frank were, in fact, already married.

"No fair," Beth whined. "I thought we might get to be bridesmaids in her wedding."

"Your father and I don't have any extra money to pay for a wedding, so there's no reason to wait, since there won't be any big shindig," Dorothy said.

Bonnie indignantly rolled her eyes. "Yeah, like they ever expected that you guys would help pay for her wedding."

"Shut up, Bonnie," Dorothy said. "Look on the bright side. Now that they're married, they'll have a baby this year. I'd just about guarantee it. You'll get to be an aunt."

The thaw meant that the path to Maggie's house would be an easy walk. Bonnie seized the opportunity. It was muddy in a lot of spots, but Maggie gave her a brush and a rag to clean her shoes.

"Do I see a cloud on your face again, Bon-Bon?" Maggie asked, once they were seated together with cups of tea.

"I told you about Carol's fiancé, right? Well, they jumped the gun on their wedding day. Up and got married, about a week ago."

"I bet they jumped the gun on more than their wedding, Bon."

"You mean you think she's pregnant?"

"I bet she is."

"That's what Mom says too. Wait, does 'jumped the gun' mean they had a shotgun wedding?"

"Silly girl. A shotgun wedding is an old expression. Imagine a pregnant girl's father taking his shotgun and pointing it at the boyfriend, making him stand up at the altar and say, 'I do.' Generally, when you hear the words 'shotgun wedding,' it means the girl is in the family way."

"I don't think Dad even knew they were getting married until it was over and done."

"Well, let this be a lesson for you, Bon-Bon. When a girl gets pregnant before she's married and ready, it changes a lot of things. She kinda loses control of her life. Don't let that happen to you."

"I ain't even got a boyfriend."

"Yet," Maggie said. "Believe me, it won't be much longer. Chances are, it'll happen fast. A girl can go along mindin' her own business, doing her schoolwork and her job, not thinkin much about boys, and some cute guy will start flirting, and it'll be off to the races with you. Once one guy takes notice, all the other boys will too. That's why you need to stay quiet and shy as long as you can.

"You might not see it now, but girls get fascinated with boys. I did. There were times when boys were all I thought about. My dreams, while I was sleeping, might be about all kinds of crazy stuff, but my daydreams, the deliberate dreams I enjoyed, were all about boys."

"I can believe that," Bonnie said. "Frank is something. He's good-looking, he's well-mannered, he knows poetry and lots of smart stuff. He's manly and refined. He's been places in the world. Watching him walk and move and smile makes me feel good. I hope I find a guy like him someday."

"I get it, Bon. I remember that feeling. Frank puts stars in your eyes. Just be patient. You'll see other guys as sharp and attractive as him, and you'll want one for yourself. When the most important thing was boys, I'd have done anything to get and keep a boyfriend. We girls think about holding hands, hugging, and kissing. Boys think way past that. For them, kissing leads to touching, and it's touching under clothing that they want. You're gonna want it too, and that's where the danger lies. Everything you dreamed about boys, gets wrapped up in making the one you want happy. Things go further and further. Before you realize what's happened, you're doing it.

"The fact is though, that you can't undo it once you've let it happen. You feel ashamed about it because you can't tell anybody, because they'll make you feel worse. And if you get pregnant, you're stuck. You have to fess up and tell somebody. The whole world will know pretty soon. That's when the shotgun wedding happens."

"But Frank and Carol were engaged to be married," Bonnie said. "I don't understand."

"You mean you don't understand why it's a shame for a girl to be pregnant before she's married?"

"Yeah. Why is it a shame?"

"Bonnie, there is a right way and a wrong way to do things. You've heard the word 'bastard,' right?"

"Sure, we call each other 'bastard' a lot."

"You don't know what a bastard is, do you?"

"I guess not."

"It's a child that's born before a girl is married. Since a girl is only supposed to have sex with her husband, there's no way of knowing for sure who the father is. A bastard is a person nobody intended to happen. A man doesn't want to raise another man's child. Bastards are usually looked down on."

"It doesn't seem right to me," Bonnie said.

"It isn't right. Lots of things in this world are not right. You can question how things are your whole life. You might think they aren't right. Too bad. You aren't gonna change it, or if it does change, it will be a long, slow process. Let some guy get you pregnant, and you'll feel bad about it your whole life. People will talk about you behind your back, and they'll whisper about the kid behind his back. Some kids like that end up adopted. They can wonder where they come from, wonder where they belong. They see themselves as orphans. You have enough family. You might wish they were different people, but when you look at your brothers and sisters, you know that you're part of something. It might be run down, but that farm is where you come from. A part of you will forever be linked to that land, even when you no longer own it. Someday, you'll understand it. Someday, you'll say, 'I'm a Metts,' and it will mean something."

"But Maggie, we are always saying how we can't wait to leave that hellhole. You talk as if we are something special," Bonnie said.

"All you can see is what's right in front of you, what's happening day by day. There's more to you and your family than your circumstances." Maggie let her words hang in the air, hoping they might sink into Bonnie's heart. "I'm not able to describe it in a helpful way, but you aren't just a young girl trying to make her way in the world. You are promise and potential. You aren't just what you know now; you're what you can be, what you want to be, what you will be. Remember the story? You are a swan, Bonnie. You just don't have eyes to see it yet."

Bonnie sensed that what Maggie had just told her was a big deal. But to take hold of the idea was out of reach. Something in Bonnie's spirit was crushed, pressed to the earth and flattened like oats after a hard rain. The dreamlike notions Maggie offered were for other people. They sat quietly then, both sensing the weight of it. Chagrined, Maggie backtracked through her thoughts and resumed talking about the baby.

"Whether this baby Carol's gonna have is a boy or girl, make sure you don't ever bring up the fact that she was in the family way before they got married. Chances are the kid will figure it out for themselves one day. All they need is their birth certificate and their parent's marriage license. Trust me, many a marriage license has gotten lost or been hidden away so that people can lie about that sort of thing. Your life will be a lot less messy if you stay away from boys for as long as you can."

Chapter Twelve

When spring came, the Mettses were eager for the day that Frank and Carol would come again for a visit. But weekend after weekend, they didn't show. When the rainy part of April ended, Pat came on a Saturday with his plow to turn over their turf for the vegetable garden. Dorothy called Bonnie into the kitchen. "Do you remember what I said about getting Pat back for his dirty tricks?"

"I remember," Bonnie said.

"I made this pan of fudge. He likes it, and you can offer him a nice piece. We'll put something extra special on his chunk." She held up a small spice can, and Bonnie read the lettering. It was Cayenne pepper.

Bonnie's eyes brightened, imagining her sweet revenge. "Too bad Roger's not here to see this. I'll have to write and tell him about it."

"Don't sharpen that pencil; we haven't pulled it off yet. These tricks are easier to talk about than to do. We'll push a good dose of pepper down in the fudge and use these crushed peanuts to mask it. We'll make the pieces small so he won't bite into them. He'll pop the whole thing in his mouth. You can serve it to him, but don't you crack a smile, or he'll know something's coming."

They arranged a platter with squares of fudge and put the loaded pieces on a little patch of waxed paper. Pat had finished plowing one patch of ground and was sitting on the stone steps of the springhouse with Ward, talking about something. Bonnie approached and casually offered the plate to Pat.

The man never hesitated. Taking a piece from the platter, he opened his maw and laid the sugary, chocolate treat on his tongue. Bonnie had to turn away and grit her teeth to keep from smiling. Ward gave Bonnie a quizzical look when she covered a few pieces with her hand while serving him.

The shock of a burning sensation on Pat's tongue was doubly rank. He'd expected something pleasant. He stood up like he'd been stabbed in the ass and retched the fudge from his mouth with a string of profanity that was vulgar, even by his standards.

Ward was near to tasting his piece when Pat's mangled mouthful hit the stone steps between them. Shocked by Pat's reaction, having no knowledge of the trick, he saw the satisfied expression on his daughter's face and raised his hand to slap the mischief from her. He paused long enough to say, "What did you do, Bonnie?"

"He gave me a sandwich one time made with cow flop. I almost took a bite. He thought it was funny. I think this might be even funnier. Don't you think so, Pat?"

Ward's face turned from rage to radiant good humor. He saw the whole thing for what it was. He laughed and grinned at Pat, who knew he'd been bested by a teenage girl. He walked away, humiliated. He mounted his tractor, placed a heavy wad of Cutty Pipe in his mouth to cleanse his palate and started the engine.

"Go ahead, Dad," Bonnie said. "Your piece is good." She separated the remaining spiced fudge from the pure samples and tossed them into the weeds.

"Don't worry about him, Bonnie. He'll get over it soon enough. He knows he had it coming." Ward smiled at his daughter. This was a side of her he didn't know existed. He felt proud.

Bonnie got a better job offer on Tuesday. George Tyner, the well-known owner of The Honky Tonk, a café in Foxburg, came into Carson's. Bonnie had never been inside the restaurant, but her friends at school talked about it. Teenagers hung out there on weekends, and some even spent school nights there.

"I don't think it's right of me to hire you away from the Carsons by coming into the store like this, but I don't know another way to make contact. Please get off the school bus at the stop sign and come on in.

I'll see to it that you get home as soon as you want. But look at the place and see what I need you to do. Fair enough?"

"Okay," Bonnie said. "I can come in tomorrow. I only work here two nights a week."

Excited with the possibility of a different kind of work, she reasoned that if it were not a better deal for her, the man wouldn't have asked. She decided right away not to ask Maggie's opinion about it. Maggie would see some hazards or drawbacks. Walking home that night, she realized she wanted the job for the same reason Maggie would want her to refuse it. Boys. Lots of the popular guys talked about getting hamburgers and Cokes at the Honky Tonk. It was the place where things happened, the center of the after-school social scene. Most of the steady couples Bonnie knew met there or had their first date there. She wanted the job as soon as she heard the offer.

George was watching for her as she got off the bus. He met her at the door and introduced her to Amanda, his wife. "I've heard a lot about you, Bonnie. My sister shops at Carson's. I've asked her to keep a sharp eye for somebody who presents well. She says you're smart and friendly."

"Wow. Thank your sister for me. But isn't waiting on people hard?" Bonnie asked.

"I'll let you in on a secret. It could be hard; it would be if we had a big menu. We serve hamburgers, hot dogs, french fries, Cokes, and shakes. Oh, ice cream cones too, but we don't sell many of those. George is open for breakfast, and that can be brisk, but the crowd that comes here after school, well, let's say that food isn't their first consideration. It's where they come to get away from home and school. They want to talk and flirt with each other. There's only nine seats at the counter and three booths. If you stick around, you'll see. The place gets busy by seven, and we close at eleven. Half of our customers are standing because the seats are all full.

"We can start you at twenty cents an hour, and the tips you get are all yours. Six dollars a night for a waitress is not unheard of. You'll probably average about four in an evening. More on Friday and Saturday nights."

"Do I just wait on people?"

"That's the main thing. Let's get you started by learning where everything is. Knowing what the kitchen is like will make you a better waitress."

"If you work here all you can this week, we'll know if this is a good fit for you. If you're not happy, at any time, I'll take you home, and there will be no hard feelings. If we decide it's good for both of us, you can give Carson's notice. I think two weeks is more than enough."

"The bus doesn't run," Bonnie began.

George cut her off, "Free rides both ways when you can't ride the bus."

"No walking home after dark. I could get used to that," Bonnie said.

Her first week was worse than she'd imagined. Overwhelmed by the demands of customers, who had no patience for a novice waitress, and the distractions she felt every time a cute boy smiled at her, Bonnie almost bowed out. When the shift ended Saturday night, the cash she took home made the decision to stay easy. The work was harder; every customer expected her sole attention. Getting more hours and tips meant more money.

Carson's were disappointed when she announced she was leaving. "You're gonna work yourself to death," Martha cautioned. "Two school nights a week is plenty for a girl."

Chapter Thirteen

And so it went, as the months rolled by. Nothing but work and school and homework for Bonnie. She earned more money than her mother knew about. More and more independent, Bonnie stopped calling on Maggie. There was no extra time. Beth took over Bonnie's job at Carson's. It seemed like the natural order of things. The Carson's had become used to the help and were happy when Beth offered to work the same way Bonnie had. They even offered Carter a job. Joe Carson offered to teach Carter to drive so that, once he got a license, he could begin delivering groceries. The lessons began as soon as Carter turned sixteen.

On the first Saturday of lessons, he walked to Parker. Right near the spot where the shooting had taken place, he noticed the sun reflecting something bright from the ground. He stooped and found a belt buckle with the AMA symbol and "Gypsy Tour 1950" stamped on it. He knew A.M.A. stood for American Motorcycle Association.

He brushed the dirt from it and stuck it in his pocket. He thought it was made of brass; it was green with corrosion. One edge was still yellow enough to reflect sunlight. That was what caught his eye. He didn't know how it attached to a belt; that part must have broken somehow. Maybe he could make it decorative, if not functional. He wondered why some biker would stop on a hill to relieve himself unless maybe the guy were desperate. He had that problem himself sometimes. The junction of the path and road made a place large enough to park a motorcycle and get out of sight quickly. He decided to keep the buckle so that when Frank Parks came again, he could ask if he was the rider who lost it, though that seemed doubtful.

It crossed his mind that Luther Banks could be the man who lost the buckle. It was possible that it came dislodged when they were dragging his body. Although the memory was more and more distant, it made him shudder a little.

Nobody in the area rode a motorcycle. If Luther had one, it would have been common knowledge. Still, to play it safe, he would keep it hidden until the next rummage sale; he could claim to have bought it there.

Things changed completely for Bonnie the day Jason Long walked into the Honky Tonk. Bonnie knew who he was, but little about him. He had graduated a year before and was not a regular. His first words to her were different from any she had heard. "I take it you're a busy girl. You work another job?"

Shocked to find him so perceptive, she nodded. "I work at the school during lunch and some study halls. It's a special arrangement. Principal Davis gave me the job for as long as I keep my grades up."

"Surely you're not the only girl who has a job like that, are you?"

"The only one I know of." She moved away, having learned to maintain a dialog while doing her regular duties. The place was small, after all, and she knew enough to act aloof with this guy. Something about him sparked her interest. No other boy ever had.

"You move like you've got a dance routine. It's like your motions are practiced. There's something about people who are good at their jobs. My old man taught me to watch for it."

"Every move I make is done a hundred times a day, pretty much the same way. If it looks practiced, well, it is."

"Same way at the school?"

"No. That job varies some."

"He gave you the school job, because?" His question hung in the air.

"Falling asleep in class. Working too many hours and not sleeping like I needed to."

"Wait. You were working too hard, so he gave you another job?"

"Now I don't work as late here as I used to. I go home at eight."

"That gives you a couple of hours to study, right?"

Bonnie tried to suppress her smile but couldn't, "I don't need to study."

"I knew it. My old man says that people who are truly smart work more easily than people who only think they're smart."

"Guys use compliments to flirt," Bonnie said. "That's better than most."

"You can take it as a compliment. I'd prefer that you did. To be honest, it's just an observation."

Not sure how to take that, Bonnie moved away more deliberately than usual. She stepped into the kitchen and checked her hair.

"Is there a cute one out there?" Amanda asked. "I never see you look in the mirror."

Bonnie blushed. She felt undone, like she didn't know what she should do next.

"He must be cute," Amanda gushed, her face twisted up excitedly.

"Oh, stop it," Bonnie said. "Just keep the food coming."

Other than routine politeness, Jason said nothing more to her, and he left after finishing his food.

Jason smiled to himself as he started his father's Oldsmobile and drove away. Bonnie Metts was the prettiest girl he knew about, and he thought he knew exactly how to bait her. One of those females that guys naturally think are out of reach, it was rumored she had turned down many dates, saying she did not have the time. He knew better. His dad had taught him so much.

That guidance came easily to his mind. "We are a higher class than the working folks here in Foxburg," his father said. "You must carry yourself properly. Class struggle is real. Denying that you are aware of class can be tricky. It is a matter of consciousness. By that, I mean understanding what is really going on and being able to work within it.

"There is a real difference between what people think goes on in the world and what actually happens. What the newspapers report and what is true, rarely match. You must learn to wear our success well. You might not understand that yet. I will teach you as we go along. The most important part of this is never saying or doing anything the townsfolk might see as condescending. As Chief Engineer and Production Manager at the refinery, I have a powerful position. You don't know it, but if I quit that job, we would not miss the income.

"This is how the world works. I know all the important people in the county. I am in the lodge where all the lawyers and judges are. Not everyone gets in there. Most men can't afford the dues. I can get people hired into good jobs, sometimes in return for favors. I can get their kids into better colleges. Most of the time no power needs to be used. And it is always better when power is used subtly. I tell you this now because, in your youthful zeal, you could easily botch things up. Please, be better than that. Real power is not loud or intimidating. It always has self-control. Youthful pride is the enemy of self-control. Self-control is the key to using power. The truly powerful people know who they are. They do not brag about it; they pretend they do not have it.

"Say you began to raise hell around here. The first thing people would say is, 'Those Longs think they can get away with anything. They think they're big shots.' That's why it's important that we stay low-profile around here. For example, I drive an Oldsmobile. I could easily afford a Caddy or Lincoln. My next car might be a Chevy or Ford. Showing off is not for us. Our power is too important to jeopardize for something trivial.

"Back when you were in grade school, there was a terrible accident. Two boys, whose fathers were friends of mine, took their girlfriends for a ride and had a wreck. All four of them were drunk. They plowed into a tree on route thirty-eight. The boys were fortunate and survived, not even seriously hurt. However, both girls were killed. It was quite tragic."

"I remember," Jason responded. "That was the Shepherd girls. People still talk about it."

"Yes, but what you don't know is that the girls actually had not been drinking. The notion that they had mitigated the guilt of those hell-raising boys. Reporting that they were all drunk was an easy thing to make happen; it was believable. Telephone calls were made. No charges were ever brought against the boys. By rights, they should have been in big trouble. You see, that's the sort of thing real power can do. That is why you must learn to wear it well, to use it well. If you abuse it, you will lose it. Can you understand that?

"You have been told all your life that it's hard work and good grades that make the difference for young people. Good habits and behavior, staying out of trouble, and all of that. Who you know doesn't make much difference."

"That's what they say at school."

"It's only true to a point. Grades and all that matter, of course. For a man, it's who he knows. Now, an exceptionally bright man might get ahead on merit alone. Not a woman. For a woman, without exception, it is how she looks. You don't have to take my word for it. Pay attention, and soon enough, you'll see it for yourself."

Jason knew his father ranked among the influential. He rarely spoke it outright, but his dad had invited him into those ranks, if he were willing to pay the dues. Jason was willing.

Jason waited a full three days before entering the Honky Tonk. He smiled big at Bonnie and could tell she liked it. He let her open the conversation.

"It's good to see you again. I'm hoping to hear more of your observations."

"I observe that you, Miss Bonnie Metts, are a most attractive girl."

"Thank you, kind sir. Can I get you a burger?"

"I'll come right to the point. I saw right away that you were unusual, and they tell me you don't have a boyfriend. For a girl as sweet as you, that is hard to believe."

"No boyfriend."

"That is so fortunate for me. May I have your address?"

"I thought you'd want my phone number."

"No. I want your address. Seriously."

"R.D. #1 Parker, couldn't be easier." In truth, the Metts house never had a telephone. Self-conscious about it, she wondered if Jason knew. Was he toying with her? Of course, wasn't she toying with him by implying she had a phone number? She felt unsettled and defensive, the way she felt when a cockroach appeared from her lunch bag at the school cafeteria. She did her best to avoid eye contact with him while he was eating, and she breathed a little easier when he left.

Later, when George was driving her home, she looked away from him, silently staring out the window into the dusk. Tears drained slowly down her cheeks. She had expected Jason to ask her for a date. He had more than hinted that something like that was coming. Yet, she had been disappointed. George could tell she was in a somber mood. That was not unusual for a teenage girl. He didn't ask for an explanation.

The following Monday, when Bonnie got home from work, Dorothy handed her a strange-looking envelope. It contained a monogrammed card with a note from Jason.

Dear Bonnie,

I find myself enchanted by your personality. I hope you will allow me to spend some time with you and get to know you better. Could I take you to a movie sometime soon? I did not want to ask this in the Honky Tonk because I wanted you to have time to think about it in case you needed to. You can answer the next time I come in.

Respectfully,

Jason Long

From the moment she saw the envelope, she was in another world, the combination of every dream and fairytale she'd ever heard. The envelope was not what they bought in the dime store in town. It was thicker paper, more square than rectangular. It was stationery, the stock that wedding invitations and graduation announcements were presented on. The flap bore a raised letter L, with the flourish of calligraphy. It looked expensive and so out-of-place in the Metts house. Every fiber of her body and mind struck a positive note. She felt like some great door had opened. Beyond it was another life. Something different and better, the thing she had been waiting for.

"So, who wrote to you, dear?" asked Dorothy. She knew who the Long family was, and she had seen the name on the return address, but she had never heard of Jason. The letter was impressive.

"He lives in Foxburg. He wants to take me out." Like someone else was speaking, she felt separated from herself. Something distinct was taking shape, and it would take getting used to. One thing was certain: the next big event in her life—greatly anticipated—would be when next she saw Jason Long and told him, "Yes!"

"Bonnie, I figured you'd start getting dates when you started working there," Beth said. "I never thought it would be someone as cool as Jason Long." They were sitting at the table in the out-kitchen, putting their hair up in tight curls. They typically slept all night with the curlers in. They chortled endlessly about boys, especially Jason. The chatter annoyed Carter. There was nothing romantic going on in his life.

"Why do girls torture themselves with curlers?" Carter asked. "It's like gripping a pinecone. Are curls that important to being beauteous?"

"Beauteous?" Beth said. "Don't you mean beautiful? Do you think we're beautiful, Carter?"

"I think it isn't the roaches that keep the rats out of our house. You look like twin porcupines."

"You don't mean that," Beth said. "I should know better than to ask you."

"So where is the 'Long fellow' going to take you parking?" Carter grinned, thinking an allusion to the poet witty.

"He's not taking me parking," Bonnie insisted.

"Maybe not on the first date. But it won't be long. You and he will be steaming up the windows in his car."

"Not this time of year. We'll have the windows rolled down." She gave her brother a mischievous smile to shut him up. "Where do people go to park?"

"Lots of places. Up behind the high school is supposed to be good. You can see any headlights coming in plenty of time. If they come up one side, you can go out the other way and not get caught. You don't want someplace that's a dead end. You need a way out. I can ask around if you need some other spots. I think most guys keep their spots secret, but I'll help you get together a list. Jason will appreciate a girl who is prepared." Talking about this to his sisters gave him a strange, excited feeling. It felt forbidden, naughty. He wondered how far he should press it.

"How did you get to be such an expert? You just got a driver's license."

"You know guys talk, right?"

"Talk about what?" Bonnie asked.

"About what they do with girls."

"You mean kissing and stuff."

"Mostly stuff."

"I don't think we should talk about this with our brother," Beth said. "Go find something else to do, Carter."

"No, stay," Bonnie said. "I need to know what to expect."

"Well, I'm no expert."

"Trish Myers told me, 'All boys talk like they know everything; they all say they have gone the whole way,' but it's bullshit," Bonnie said.

Carter had learned long ago that he could not bluff his sisters. "I guess that's true. I don't believe most of what my friends at school say. It's fun to talk about that stuff. Are you gonna let him kiss you on the first date?"

"Do you think he'll try?"

"All you have to do is stand still and face him when you think he might try it. He'll either try it or he won't. You stand for it, like a cow does."

"Cows kiss?" Bonnie asked.

"Oh brother. You mean you never watched cows breed? You've lived in the country your whole life."

"Who pays attention to cows?" Bonnie rolled her eyes. "You're the one who spends all your time at Pat's. When would I ever see that?"

"Okay, well, when Pat wants to get a cow fresh, he puts her in the shed and turns the bull out. If the cow is ready, she will 'stand for it.' The bull comes up and puts his thing in. Sometimes, she moves away, and he can't do it. When she is ready, they call it 'bulling,' she stands and lets him get it in. People don't do it on their feet like cows, on the other hand, cows don't kiss. Anyway, if you want to be kissed, stand and look at him, and let him do it. If you don't want to kiss, look away, move away a little. He'll get the message."

Carter saw giddy excitement on Beth's face, eager for every word on the forbidden subject. It was the same thing he'd seen with some of his girl classmates on a day when their teacher had been called away, leaving the classroom unattended and trusting the students to behave well. Instead of mayhem, several kids circled his desk as he told them dirty jokes. The intense interest of the otherwise prudish girls made him realize that under the veneer of manners, girls had the same desires as boys.

"Do you know Jason?" Bonnie asked.

"Not well. I know who he is. I guess he knows who I am. His dad is a big shot at the refinery. His folks have money. That's what people say. Roger would have known him."

"You mean Roger knows him," said Beth.

"You think we'll see Roger again, don't you?" Carter asked.

"Sure. Why wouldn't we?"

"Would you come back here after what happened? If you were him, I mean?"

"I thought we weren't gonna talk about that."

Chapter Fourteen

"So, where do you live exactly?" Jason asked. Bonnie saw him pull in to the Honky Tonk and walked outside to meet him.

"I'll go out with you sometime. My folks were impressed by the way you asked me."

"That was my mom's idea. She thinks the ways kids date these days is too casual. You're only the second girl I've asked out. The other one liked it too."

"Who was she?"

"Does it matter? We go to Chautauqua every year for a few weeks. That place is full of teenagers in the summer. You can meet a lot of people. I'll probably never see her again. She lives in Rochester or someplace."

Bonnie felt stupid. She knew better than to act jealous. She hardly knew him. Her head had been so full of dreams she couldn't help it. In her mind, they were already engaged. "Are we going to a drive-in?" Bonnie asked.

"I thought we'd go to the one in Chicora. I don't know what's playing, though."

"Who cares?"

"You didn't answer. How do I find your house?"

"Do you know where the R.E.A. is?"

"Just up from the Parker Bridge, right?"

"Yep. Turn left when you get to the crossroads. I'll meet you at the end of the first driveway you come to."

"Seven-thirty, Friday night, okay?"

"That's perfect."

"What if it rains?" Jason asked. "Can I call you?"

Bonnie wanted to lie. She couldn't think of one quick enough. He'd find out sooner or later anyway. "We haven't got a phone at my house."

"Oh. That's okay. Lots of people out of town don't have phones. It's funny though, don't you think? Out of town is where you need one most."

"I better get back to work. See you Friday." She put on her biggest smile and stepped back, Carter's advice about getting kissed ringing in her ears. She was eager to kiss him. Too bad it couldn't happen then and there.

When she stepped back inside, George was grinning at her. "What night do you want off?"

George took Bonnie home as usual and returned to the restaurant. The pace slowed in the late evening, and one person could keep up. He popped his head into the kitchen, and Amanda shook her head, indicating there was nothing more to take care of. "Can you believe that?" Amanda asked. "You know as well as I do that the Longs will never allow their boy to run around with a Metts."

"Nope. Jason wants to slum it a little so he can brag about his conquests when he goes to Penn State."

"She's not going to be anyone's conquest."

"If she falls for him, even a little bit, he'll feel like he won something."

"I guess you would know."

"What's that supposed to mean?" George asked defensively.

"You guys are all the same," Amanda snapped.

George puffed loudly. He knew the attitude. She'd need some time to cool down.

After a while, Amanda softened. "Sorry George. I've just seen so much heartbreak with these girls."

"Nobody ever said you had to act like a mother to all these teenagers. They come to our place to get a taste of freedom. Freedom brings pain. It's all part of growing up."

"She's weaker than most, don't you think?"

"No. I think she's stronger than most. She may get hurt, but she'll bounce back."

"Let's hope you're right."

Jason wondered, as he drove home from the Honky Tonk, why Bonnie wanted to meet him at the end of the driveway. He decided not to ask her right away. She might explain it on her own. He told his folks that he had a date with a girl he met at the Honky Tonk, nothing more. He had dated a lot of girls, both around home and at Chautauqua. He had never been turned down. He was a gentleman, and even more than that, he was good-looking and had a nice car to drive. Not every guy his age had those assets.

He kept track of how many girls he had kissed and the ones he had partly undressed. His father had warned him not to get carried away by all the notions about true love in popular music. He knew how quickly his feelings for a girl faded when another pretty one came along. His father's warning, "The way things seem in the world is not how they really are," had proven to be valuable advice.

An enormous barn dwarfed Bonnie's house, or houses. He saw two, one needing repainting, the other bare wood, like the barn. It was not what he'd expected. Bonnie sat on a little bench, under one of those spreading trees, maybe a chestnut. He didn't know much about trees. Nobody else was in sight. Most times, when he picked up a girl, her parents at least took a gander at him from a porch or window.

Bonnie tingled with anticipation as she saw the car approaching, the inarticulate sense that a handsome boyfriend would increase her status in the world, that dating a guy like Jason could lead her to a more desirable life and away from the "hellhole" she and her siblings were stuck in. After that, the mysteriously enchanting idea of romance.

She had been ready for a long time. Her first date being the threshold of a new life, she had washed every inch of her body twice. Beth partnered with the other kids to fuss over every aspect of Bonnie's appearance. Dorothy shook her head, knowing that the boy's eyes wouldn't get much beyond her cleavage.

Jason got out and walked around to open the door for her. She had been reaching for it, but stopped when she saw what he had in mind. She didn't want to appear too eager.

Bonnie was the total package, Jason mused. Utterly feminine in dress and demeanor. No hint of the fear he had seen in many girls. With a radiant smile, her face projected openness, warmth, and comfort. Immediately at ease, he felt something new. His admiration clashed with his feelings about her house and barn, like the two were mismatched somehow.

"I didn't know your family had a farm," Jason said.

"It isn't hardly a farm, not anymore."

"That's a big barn. Maybe the biggest one I've seen."

"What I mean is, we don't farm anymore. My dad works there," she said, pointing to the R.E.A. building. She hoped her dismissive tone would settle his curiosity, but it didn't.

"Somebody works those fields."

"The guy up the road does. It's some kind of lease or rent thing he has with my dad. We still have a cow and chickens and pigs." She hesitated to say 'pigs,' almost apologetically. Jason sensed her discomfort with the word.

"Nothing wrong with pigs." He grinned at her. "What's the difference between a pig and a hog?"

"Beats me," Bonnie said. "I think they're the same thing."

"So, what is an R.E.A., anyhow?

"You must not have been listening in school, Rural Electrification Administration."

"I may not have been." He grinned cheerfully at her.

The car moved down the hill toward Parker. "So, I knew Roger Metts in school. That's your brother?"

Bonnie froze. The car was precisely at the point where Roger killed Luther Banks years earlier. She wondered if any trace of the man's body remained in the culvert. "Roger is in the Navy now."

"Good for him. Does he like it?"

"I guess he does. We don't get many letters from him."

"What kind of ship is he on?"

"Hmm, am I supposed to know that?" Bonnie said in a flirtatious, I'm-just-a-dumb-girl tone. She needed something light-hearted to ease the conversation away from her family and home.

"Maybe not. Guys care more about that kind of thing. So, let's talk about music. Do you like The Platters?"

"They're okay. I like Elvis Presley better."

"My dad thinks rock and roll is cheap and bad for people. He says music is art and that art changes the way people think."

"Really? I've never heard anyone say that. Old people don't want us to have fun."

"My dad is different than most people, I think."

"Wait, your dad runs the refinery, doesn't he?"

"I guess so. He's the Production Manager."

"So, he's a big shot."

"I guess so," Jason said. "Is that okay?"

"Why wouldn't it be?"

"You kind of sound like, I don't know, as if you don't like "big shots.""

"People complain a lot about the big shots who run the factory."

"You mean the glass plant?" They passed by it and were moving up the hill and away from the town and the river. Bonnie rarely got that far from home and loved the sense of freedom when she did.

"Yeah. Most people around here work there."

There it was, Jason realized. The class struggle his father talked about. He couldn't remember how to handle it. For now, he wanted to enjoy Bonnie. He figured she would let him kiss her during the movie. He wouldn't say anything to make her uncomfortable.

"I saw in the paper that the movie is '*Giant*.' James Dean, Rock Hudson, and Liz Taylor. It should be good," Jason said, trying to sound cheerful. "Unless you already saw it."

"No, I heard about it though." Bonnie had never seen any movie except newsreels shown at school. She didn't want Jason to know that. She and her siblings had never even gone to the theater in Parker. Ward and Dorothy never had money for things like that. Now she had her own money and used it for essentials. Maybe she should spend some on fun things. She had seen a few Western movies at Trish Meyers's house. She could not let Jason know there was no television in her home, not if she could help it. All her classmates talked about what they saw on TV.

"It got quiet all of a sudden," Jason remarked. "Do you get lost in your thoughts sometimes? I know I do."

"Sort of," Bonnie said. "I should tell you, I've never been to a drive-in." She surprised herself by saying that and wished she could take it back.

"Well good," Jason said. "It'll be a treat for you."

Bonnie smiled at him. She had heard girls say that drive-ins were all about "necking." That meant a lot of hugging and kissing, and she was eager to try it. She remembered Maggie saying that boys want to get a girl excited and get under their clothes. Surely, Jason wouldn't do anything like that on their first date. On the other hand, the car was a private place in the dark.

When they got to the drive-in, the sun was still up. People could see into other cars. Jason would not expect her to get close until dark. With the movie showing, she would not have to look at him much.

"Do you like popcorn?" Jason asked. "Maybe a Coke too?"

"That would be nice."

"Be right back."

She watched him walk briskly toward the little building where the popcorn and hot dogs were sold. She was so nervous that she had to do something. Sliding over to the middle of the seat, she checked her makeup in the mirror. The light was quickly fading. Soon, the makeup wouldn't matter. The idea that she might get her first kiss made her tingle. She had no experience with kissing and had never asked Trish or one of her other friends about it. Girls were supposed to have "tender lips." Her own lips were thin, maybe too thin to be tender. She pressed the side of her hand to her mouth and did her best to make her lips feel tender. She stopped quickly, looking around in case people in the other cars were watching her.

She wanted him to kiss her, maybe even do a little petting. How far could she let him go without him thinking she was a tramp? She determined to only let him touch her boobs through her blouse, not her bare skin.

A cartoon began on the screen just as Jason came back with a big box of popcorn and two bottles of Coke. She opened his door since he had no free hand and took the bottles from him. She did not slide back to her side, but stayed close enough that their legs would be touching when he got seated. The scent of his cologne was thrilling. If this was all there was to a date, she would be satisfied. Sitting close to such a nice boy, one who had asked her out was the most pleasing thing she had known.

"I got us a Hershey bar too," he said. "We can share it."

"So romantic," Bonnie said, immediately wondering if that was too forward.

The cartoon made them laugh, and they sat through previews of movies to come. The feature turned out to be a Western. Though Bonnie loved anything she had seen on a TV screen, she was not interested in the movie.

"That's James Dean," Jason said. "He was killed while they were making the movie."

Bonnie had heard of James Dean. She didn't know what he looked like. "How did they finish it if he got killed?"

"Good question. He must have done enough for it to work out. I like to watch movies, but I don't know much about how they make them. My mom said it might not be true. They may have said the filming was still going on to get people interested and sell more tickets. He is dead though."

Bonnie hoped that going to the movie was Jason's way of getting her alone so they could neck. He gingerly placed his arm around her shoulder, pulling her a little more snugly toward him; that seemed to be a limit for him. She felt disappointed that he hadn't tried to kiss her. She slowly turned her face toward Jason's and tilted her head back a little. She wanted him to get the message. After a while, he did.

"Is it alright if I kiss you, Bonnie?" Jason said.

She nodded and waited, trusting him to know how. She made her lips as soft as she could. When his lips met hers, the whole world faded away. His lips were moist, and he held the contact for several seconds. When he pulled away, Bonnie looked back at the screen, knowing that good girls at least waited for the date to end before allowing a kiss. She had crossed some kind of line, and she didn't care.

"Have you ever been kissed before?" Jason asked.

"That's the first time."

"Aww. Thanks for letting me be your first."

"Jason, do you think I'm loose?"

"What do you mean?"

"Well, most girls don't let a guy kiss them on the first date. I didn't even make it through the movie."

"I don't know who makes these rules. Do you?"

"No. It's what I've always heard."

"Look, both of us thought about kissing tonight. I'm glad you made it easy for me. I don't see any reason for us not to kiss. Can we do it some more?"

Bonnie tilted her head as she had done before. This time, it was smoother and longer. Bonnie felt like she might melt right there in the car. Whatever James Dean and the other actors were doing and saying on the screen no longer registered to them.

Jason felt the glow of desire. As his body reacted, he felt the familiar discomfort in his jeans. He reached his hand down to his belt to put some slack where he needed it. By shifting his buttocks a little, he eased the strain to a tolerable level. He slowly rubbed his hand up and down Bonnie's side. With each upward motion, he drifted a little farther until he felt the bulge of her breast against his hand. He let it linger there and heard an encouraging sigh as Bonnie broke their kiss.

Soon, he was cupping her breast with his hand and squeezing it gently.

"As much as I like that, I need you to stop. Okay, Jason?"

"Sorry, Bonnie. You are so soft and nice to touch. You're so beautiful."

"Thanks. I think you're pretty swell too."

As if Jason's apology were a license to continue, he did so. Gradually squeezing and lifting her breast. The stiff fabric of her bra made the sensation increasingly pleasant for Bonnie. She wanted him to go on. She wanted to open her blouse and unhook her bra so he could touch her. She began to sense warmth in her crotch, and it scared her. "We better stop," she said.

Jason took his arm from around her shoulder. He was relieved because he had never expected to get that far so soon. He could tell that in no time at all, he would get a lot farther. He couldn't help but smile, feeling victorious and confident.

Chapter Fifteen

Carter enjoyed delivering groceries. The work was painstaking, though. Some people had their stuff delivered to avoid the labor of carrying them from the car to the house. Joe Carson told him there would be tips, but they were few and far between. Rural poor took hard work for granted; he worked for wages, after all. He liked seeing the inside of other homes and getting some evidence about what people other than his family were like. He usually took groceries into the kitchen, so he began scanning for roaches, curious whether other homes were infested like his own. He found none.

There were some regular customers. The preacher from the Methodist Church dropped lists off at Carson's for some of his members, saving them the trip to town. Not everyone had an automobile. Charlotte Timko's home was one of many secluded from view by woods. Quiet places to live where privacy was taken for granted. The Timkos were childless. Since the disappearance of Luther Banks, loneliness had driven her nearly mad.

"I never knew this house was here," Carter said cheerfully as he approached the front door. "I knew you guys lived around here. I never knew exactly where."

"You're getting to know Parker and Perryville really well, I bet," Charlotte said.

"Yeah, but Joe doesn't give good directions. I drove past your lane twice before I realized where it was."

"Maybe that's because he's never been here. I'm trying the new delivery service. You're the first delivery boy Carson's have had."

"They helped me get my driver's license so they could start this. They don't know if it will work out. I'd like to join the Air Force or Navy maybe, but I kind of feel like I owe them."

"I heard your brother went into the Navy."

"Yeah. He might never come back home."

"Do you miss him?"

"I do sometimes. But things have changed for me so much since I got this job, being able to drive and all. Besides, I'll probably leave before long too."

"It's such a hot day. You should sit for a few minutes. I have some iced tea."

Something about her eyes and vulnerable tone pleaded. Carter thought she needed some company. "Kenny works away, huh?"

"Yep. Probably won't see him until Friday evening."

"Where does he drive to? Where's the job?"

"Someplace called 'Connequenessing,' I think. I don't know where that is."

"Or how to spell it either, right?"

"Or how to spell it. The pay is good though."

"They say Kenny is a good shot. I know he shoots groundhogs."

"Yeah, he has an expensive, custom-made rifle. The scope is as long as the barrel. Would you like to see it?"

"Would that be okay?"

"I'll just get it," Charlotte said. She went into an adjacent room, and while she had the gun cabinet open, and her back to Carter, she undid the top button on her blouse. A wave of apprehension came over her, quickly displaced by a wave of possibility. She held the rifle just under her loose button. Carter could not help but see. He had no problem with the signal either.

"It must be custom-made. I've never seen one like that."

"Take a good look," Charlotte said.

Carter knew she clearly didn't mean the rifle. He felt scared, not knowing what to say. Charlotte was not as old as his mother, but old enough to be his mother. His breath got shallow. What he felt was forbidden and powerful. Her knowing eyes fixed on his. He was not prepared to respond.

"Thanks for showing me that. Thanks for the tea. I'd better get going."

"Maybe you'll come back next week, huh?" Charlotte asked, her own breath shallow.

Carter nodded vigorously. "Be sure to order some groceries."

Charlotte watched the young man move as he walked out her door and across her porch. He radiated the masculinity she hungered for, and she imagined how dynamic his body would feel when holding her tight. She felt guilty for what she wanted but reasoned that her long relationship with Luther had kept her sane while it lasted. Her husband had no interest even when he was around, and she lived in frustration. She cajoled him to make love on the weekend simply because he was better than nobody. If she became pregnant by Luther or someone else, she would need cover. She had short affairs with several men since Luther disappeared and could not continue any of them. Her cravings were too strong to ignore. She would help this lad become a better man.

Though her home was hidden, Luther would never do it there. Carter expressed no fear of her husband. She would have to be careful with Carter. Young men were impulsive and likely to share any sexual escapade with their friends. Most women did not hunger for a man the intense way she did. She sat down and began her grocery list for the next week.

Cecil and Connie Long, Jason's parents, agreed not to allow Jason to delay going to college any longer. In that regard, dating a local girl was no wise move for him.

"How was your date, Jason?" Connie asked. They were sitting at the table languishing over breakfast, an ideal time for family conversations.

"It was great," Jason responded, his face beaming uncontrollably.

"What is this girl's name again?" Cecil asked.

"Bonnie Metts."

"That Metts family from Perryville, the couple who walk downtown to get drunk?" Connie asked, nearly shocked.

"Now, mother," Cecil interjected, "he knows better than to get involved with someone like that."

There was a long, awkward pause. Both focused their gaze on him.

"No, Dad, that is her family," Jason deadpanned.

Cecil used his most disappointed face as he looked at his son. The evening before, while Jason was on the date, Cecil had called a friend, a lodge brother, the superintendent of the electric co-op where Ward Metts worked. His friend confirmed there was only one family in the area with that surname. He recited a long list of trashy and chaotic behavior witnessed by the community, including the incident where Ward shot up the bar in Parker.

"Ward Metts is a good and faithful employee, though. He doesn't miss work, but we have never been able to promote him. He is still on the crew where all new people start. We can't have him going to homes or working in hazardous situations. He's seen a lot of men work with him and move up to a better job with higher pay and responsibility. He's never complained about it as far as I know. Our linemen need to be respectable people. You can understand that."

"So, what, he drinks on the job?"

"No, no, it's just that too many people know his reputation."

"What are his kids like?"

"Well, let's say they are wild. Not exactly wild. They're mostly not supervised. They come and go from home as they please. A lot of our people live close to the shop. We need them to get here quickly when the power goes down. If you see a kid that's poorly dressed and dirty, it's a safe bet their last name is Metts. None of them get involved in school sports or extracurricular activities. They aren't stupid; they could get better grades. For some reason, they don't. They all carry sack lunches to school and shed roaches from time to time. Ward has never added plumbing to the house. They carry their water from a spring in buckets and still use an outhouse. Any trash they can't burn gets piled behind the house. There are other families with problems, I suppose, but this household has more than its share.

"My wife and some of the other ladies from the church called on Dorothy Metts a few years ago, while Ward was in the insane asylum. They offered boxes of food and household stuff the family could have used. Dorothy threw them off the place, saying they should mind their own business, that they were phonies and hypocrites, the usual stuff.

"I'll tell you something else too. With their track record, people say things about them that probably aren't even true."

"Such as?" Cecil asked.

"Dorothy was a prostitute, and still is, except that she's too old to get much business. A couple of the kids don't look like the rest. Who knows? The boys shoot deer, rabbits, and other game year-round, and they don't get a hunting license. That one is easy to believe with the woods on their place and farm crops. Let's see, they steal anything that isn't nailed down. A couple of the younger ones are so skinny the school nurse thinks they don't get enough to eat. Wait, that last one is probably true."

"Ward still farms?"

"No. They leased the grounds to Pat Hughes a long time ago. Ward and Dorothy drink any extra money they have. What they don't drink, their friends do. The family is a lost cause, in my opinion. Their oldest girl had a shotgun wedding. Their oldest boy went to the Navy or someplace. Dorothy keeps crankin' out kids. They have nine now, seven under their roof, which probably leaks." Cecil had heard enough. He thanked his friend and hung up.

He had been up late, pondering what to say to Jason. "Son, we need to have a long talk. What do you say we take a walk down the tracks?"

"Okay, Dad. It's a nice day."

The Long home sat on a street that overlooked the railroad track and the river. Walking up or down the picturesque river on the road beside the tracks was pleasant. Trains rolled by several times each day, and no one minded the sounds. Fishermen frequented the road. Mostly empty and quiet, an idyllic setting, a customary place for the Long family to get serious.

"So tell me about this girl," Cecil asked his son.

"She works at the Honky Tonk. She has a job at the school as well. Everyone likes her. She hasn't dated anyone before, until me."

"I suppose she's pretty."

"The most beautiful girl I know."

"You sensed your mother's reaction?"

"Of course."

"You probably know the story of Romeo and Juliet, don't you?"

"Not really."

"Well, every time parents oppose two young folks getting together, someone will bring it up. In the story, the families try to keep the couple apart, and it leads to a lot of misery and heartbreak. The story has inspired other tales about parents trying to run their children's lives. The sentiment always leans against the parents, as if it's wrong for them to keep the two lovers apart."

"Yeah, I guess I knew that much."

"Remember how I've always told you that how things appear in the world are not always true?"

"Sure."

"Shakespeare's stories are good to know. You'll probably learn a lot more of them in college."

"It sounds like you're gonna tell me I shouldn't be dating Bonnie."

"Most young people, around here anyway, end up marrying before they have seen much of the world or learned much about people. There are a lot of unhappy married people, especially among the working class.

Remorse in a lifelong commitment is a bitter thing. So, deciding who to marry is a serious undertaking."

"You talk like I've already proposed marriage to Bonnie."

"At breakfast, your face said, 'I am already smitten.' Your tone now says. 'Mind your own business, Dad.'"

"I'm sorry, Dad. I know you want the best for me. I feel like I'm old enough to make my own decisions, especially with girls."

"Well, how should I put this? We don't talk about it much. At your age, all I thought about was getting laid."

"Dad!"

"Look at me, Jason," his father said. "Look me straight in the eye and tell me you don't want to bed this girl."

"Okay. You're right. I'd be the same with any girl. Well, most any girl."

"I understand, son. It's nothing to be ashamed of. Men are sort of made that way. There's nothing to be gained by pretending you don't get excited when you're with a pretty girl. It's human nature."

Cecil altered his tone, sounding arrogant, "Human nature, Mr. Allnut, is what we have been put here to overcome."

"I've heard mom say that," Jason responded.

"Yes. It's a line from that movie *The African Queen*. You'll learn in time that your human nature is what makes life worthwhile. At the same time, you must keep it in its place. Successful people master it."

Jason was pensive, taking in what his father said.

Cecil continued, "A lot of people have been undone by temptation. They give in to their lust and lose control of their lives. When a young man like yourself has as much potential as you do, it is essential that he understand the dangers.

"We are in a strange time. The way people have done things for generations is being called into question. You'll see it when you get to school. You're going to be with many different people. Some of them don't care about self-control. Being careless is coming into fashion, and colleges are the easiest place to get crazy ideas started.

"The guys who won the war are too busy making money and getting ahead to pay much attention to how things are changing or what their kids are doing. You can't blame them hardly. Those years before the war were hellish. They're making up for what they lost. They don't realize the road our society is on."

"Youthful pride is the enemy of self-control. Self-control is the key to using power," Jason recited.

"You were listening," his father said, smiling.

"So why shouldn't I date Bonnie?"

"If it was only dating, I wouldn't care. And she might be a fine person, all things considered. There is a lot more to it."

"What more can there be?"

"Well, there are two things I am concerned about. First is the reputation her family has. I've done some checking, and her folks are not good. They don't take proper care of their children. They get drunk all the time. They don't pay their bills. Her dad has been in the state hospital and should probably be in jail. He's reckless and violent."

"What's the second thing?"

"The girls who come up in families like that tend to be easy."

"You mean...?"

"Sexually easy, promiscuous, slutty if you like. She's smart enough to see you as a good catch. Most girls her age are looking for a husband. Getting pregnant guarantees marriage."

Jason looked down, avoiding eye contact with his father.

"Tell me, did she let you kiss her? On your first date?"

"We kissed a lot. She let me, you know, touch her some."

"She hardly knows you. That should tell you all you need to know. Remember that girl from Vermont you dated at Chautauqua? Caroline? Did she let you 'touch her some?'"

"I didn't try," Jason said.

"Were they small?"

"No, they were prodigious," Jason replied with a grin.

"I know. All the more reason you would want to. I would have wanted to. Men don't stop noticing things like that when they get married. But think, Jason. Why didn't you try? You were alone with her enough."

"Would being married to Bonnie be so bad?"

"Wait. Answer my question first. Why didn't you try to get a handful of those tits?"

Jason had never heard his father use crude language. The tone of their conversation shifted. "Maybe I saw Caroline differently than Bonnie."

"Of course you did. The Mettses don't go to places like Chautauqua. Could it be that something about the setting made you give Caroline more respect?"

Jason slowly nodded. His father's insight never ceased to amaze him.

"You asked if marrying Bonnie would be so bad. You know that you wouldn't just marry her; you would be marrying her family as well."

"That isn't so."

"Sure, it is. The habits and lifestyle she saw growing up were normal to her. Her brothers, some of them anyway, will be deadbeats. They will embarrass you. They will want to borrow money from you and not pay it back. You will try to keep your kids from being influenced by them, and she will be insulted by that. You won't like her family, and ultimately you won't like her."

They walked for a few minutes in silence. What his father told him had the ring of truth. Bonnie had not allowed him to walk her up the lane to her house. He could tell she wouldn't be comfortable with that. He had not dared to ask her why. He supposed the place might be too much like a farm. Farms were never neat, with well-kept lawns, not like the houses in town that he saw daily. But that didn't justify her shame. There had to be something about her home or family she didn't want him to see. Maybe something that would scare him away?

"I understand she's pretty and shapely and desirable," Cecil said. "You understand, don't you, that beauty is only skin deep. The bitterness of her low character will remain long after the sweetness of her face and figure are spoiled by her trashy background.

"Your mom was not the best-looking girl in my circle. You see, I had an old-timer warn me that the prettiest girls don't feel much need to please men, because their appearance draws them and keeps them hanging on. He said I'd be happier choosing someone that doesn't rely on her looks. He made a lot of sense."

"Mom is pretty. She must have been prettier back then," Jason objected.

"She is. She's pretty enough. Good grief, she's your mother. Every guy loves his mother. I wouldn't have it any other way. You see her through eyes that have always sensed warmth and acceptance. You don't see rightly. Trust me, there were other girls that made her look plain. But too many girls like that are vain. Haven't you thought that sometimes?"

"I hear you, Dad. But couldn't I enjoy Bonnie's company for the rest of the summer? When I go to college, she'll understand if we break up."

"Will she? Will you? The longer you date her," his father continued, "the more you kiss her and let her heart get wound up with yours, the harder it will be to break it off. And, unless she's different than most people like her, and there's good reason to think she isn't, I see a shotgun wedding, and along with that, your plans for college going down the drain.

"I hear the radio you kids listen to. Lots and lots of love songs. Real life isn't like that. It just isn't. You and she might have something sweet and romantic going on. The difficulties will come when it becomes clear that your life is on a separate path from hers. You're going to meet a lot of people in college that are like us. There will be lots of opportunities to meet girls that are like us.

"Besides that, you need to understand that sexual intimacy is like a trap. It is the same thing, only different. That's why society forbids it before marriage. Sex is how children are brought into the world. Once you have sex with a woman, it becomes like a glue. The two of you will feel like you are meant to be together. Maybe that's the best way to think about it. Before marriage, it's a trap. After marriage, it's a bond.

"It's kind of like sand. If it has too much water in it, you can't walk on it. It's treacherous. You've heard of quicksand, right? Well, try standing still on the beach as the waves come and go, and your feet can get trapped in the sand. But mix that sand with some stone and cement and you have concrete. Then you can build dams with it." He doubled both fists together for emphasis. "Maybe there's a better illustration; I can't think of one."

Jason looked at his father, his face resigned and sad. Then he pursed his lips in acceptance.

"Bonnie's family built their lives on sand," Cecil said. "They are so deeply into it; they may never get out. Please, don't you step into that sand."

Chapter Sixteen

Beth waited up for Bonnie. She could tell by the glow of headlights that a car had turned in, sat still for a few minutes and then backed out and gone toward Parker. She heard the scuff of Bonnie's shoes coming quickly up the gravel lane. Her pace seemed lively and light-hearted. She could see the smile on Bonnie's face as she came close to the porch light.

"Don't you dare say you're tired. You are not going to bed until I hear every detail," Beth declared.

"Yes."

"Yes, what?" Beth asked.

"Yes, he kissed me. A lot. You know you were gonna ask that." They both giggled heartily. "Oh Beth, he is a dream. He's got real manners. He's different. I mean, I thought that from the beginning, and now I know. I don't know how to describe it. He's, he's...sophisticated."

"Whoa, we think Frank Parks is cool, but sophisticated, that's an even higher level. Are you sure you can handle a man like that?"

"I don't know. I'm sure gonna try."

"How was the movie?"

"About people in Texas getting rich and soaked with oil. I don't know much besides that."

"What did you talk about?

"Lots of stuff. His dad is a big shot. He runs the refinery in Emlenton. They go to Chautauqua for two weeks every summer. He's going to college in the fall."

"That his car?"

"His dad's. Nice though."

"What's it like being kissed?"

"Well, it's gentle and sweet at first. When you keep it up, it gets different. I got all warm and excited. I wanted to pull him in closer to me. I didn't want to let him go. What Carter said about steaming up the windows? I get that now. But, of course, the windows were down."

"Are you going out again? Are you gonna go steady?"

"He didn't say anything about that. Don't make too much of this. He didn't offer me a ring or anything."

Ordinarily, Bonnie would have slept in on Saturday. Now, the happy feeling she had would not permit sleep. She bounded from bed and got dressed. Dorothy had already left for Parker. Ward sat on the porch, drinking coffee. He said nothing to her about her first date and didn't ask the boy's name. She lamented her strange family. A huge event had taken place, and her parents had no more interest than if she had spent the evening sitting on the couch.

She knew from what she picked up at school that most parents were actively involved in their kids' lives. She remembered a few years earlier when she, Roger, Carter, and Beth had gone on one of their long walks, encountering a family of raccoons. They had topped a rise in the dirt road and surprised a mother and two babies. They believed that wild creatures protected their young at all costs.

Upon catching sight of the Metts kids, the mother raccoon made a beeline for the woods, disappearing with no apparent thought for her young, who ambled around in a circle until Roger knelt and tried to pick one up.

Whether bitten or scratched, he could not tell, he began bleeding from several places. Carter tried too, while the creatures growled and hissed so defiantly that he soon thought better of it. It became obvious that they were not cute little furballs, but lightning fast, all tooth and claw. The idea of taking them home for pets dissolved. Maybe, if they had a net or some kind of box to capture them in, it might have been possible. But not with bare hands. The baby coons had to fend for themselves. The Metts kids were much the same.

Carter hadn't been able to concentrate since his first delivery to Charlotte Timko. The creamy skin forming the valley of her cleavage came unbidden to mind. The sight of it and the look in her eyes were an exhilarating gift. He had heard tall stories of older women seducing guys. He never imagined they were genuine.

His father sometimes brought wrinkled, second-hand men's magazines home from work. His crew sometimes sat in the truck, waiting out the rain. Apparently, that is when the magazines came in handy. They usually had a story about some guy rescuing a beautiful woman from bad men. The beauty would insist on rewarding the hero with sex. As exciting as such things were, Charlotte's advance made them seem silly.

He approached her house right after lunchtime. She sat on the porch wearing a naughty smile. She opened the door and directed him to put the groceries on the kitchen table. Desperately hungry, alone with an eager, available guy, she took him by the hand before he even straightened up. He thought he knew what to do but was clumsy and hesitant. He took her in his arms, and their mouths met. Her mouth was warm and eager, her skin a little sweaty.

He ran his hands down her back and felt nothing where her bra should be. He hesitated, shocked that something he had been longing for, something forbidden to boys his age, was happening so easily and quickly. He planned to be deliberate and take mental notes until he discovered she wasn't wearing underpants. He nearly exploded. The excitement pulsed like the sudden, frantic strike of a catfish, unlike anything he had ever known. Masturbation, whether dreaming or reading the men's magazines, produced nothing as intense and overwhelming as the feeling of this mature woman's desire, expressed through the warm sensations of flesh, lips and probing hands.

Careful of his ego, she led him subtly, until her need became too insistent. She took over. While she knew she should feel ashamed about it, she had no room for shame at that moment, or any other thought, only the coupling, the merging of her body with his. She climaxed at once, so much sooner than she'd expected. She gritted her teeth lest she cry out and scare him.

"Was that your first time?" Charlotte asked as they were getting dressed. "It didn't seem like it."

"Yes. Did I do okay?"

"You did very okay."

"Are you sure? I've heard it takes longer for a woman than a man."

"You can't spend too much time on a delivery. We can't waste time getting warmed up. You'll need to take it slower if you get married. You'll have plenty of time to go slower. For now, at least, fast works for me." The whole thing had taken less than five minutes, she thought.

"I've been warming up since last week," Carter said.

Charlotte tried not to smile. Carter was more than refreshing. She had ached to know a man desired her, wanted her, the way Luther had. She was grateful; she wanted to thank the boy. That wouldn't be dignified.

"Are you sure we can get away with this?" Carter asked.

"Watch me when you bring groceries. I'll let you know; you won't have to ask."

"Okay. That makes sense."

"We should be able to spend more time on it if you come when you're not working. I'll figure out some signal at the end of the lane to let you know when the coast is clear. My husband is predictable."

She had a lot more desire. An available male stirred her repressed appetite; she held back. She didn't know what Carter might think if she moved on him again so soon.

So, just like that, Carter had a mistress. He had no girlfriend, but he had a mistress, didn't he? He mused on the matter as he drove slowly back to Parker. Supposedly, only married men had mistresses. Clarence swore that married men in France and Spain were expected to have a mistress. Clarence claimed to know a lot of questionable stuff. One thing was certain: Carter was grateful for what Charlotte had given him. He would not have the burden of romancing her, no candy, movies, or flowers. None of the usual boyfriend stuff. He felt no hint of shame. Apparently, neither did she.

Chapter Seventeen

Jason had a problem now. Bonnie would expect another date. He hadn't said anything to encourage her. Their first date had gone so smoothly. A second would be expected. Guys his age were supposed to rebel against their parents, but he could not. His father had never steered him wrong. He could not tell Bonnie the truth.

He knew enough about the way things worked that if he took another girl to a movie soon, he wouldn't need to say anything. Word would get back to the Honky Tonk, and while Bonnie might be hurt, she would have no good right to feel that way. There were other girls he knew, and the first phone call he made produced a drive-in movie date for Friday night, like the one with Bonnie. Nothing like his time with Bonnie, except the same film was showing. He watched *GIANT* the whole way through and enjoyed it.

Bonnie thought Jason would stop by the Honky Tonk, at least to say hello. It didn't happen. The weekend came and went, and she began to despair. On Monday evening, while waiting on two girls seated in a booth, she heard, "He's nice, and *GIANT* was great. The date was dull, though. We couldn't find much to talk about. To be honest, I think he's trying to get as many dates as he can before he shoves off for college."

Bonnie got a sinking feeling. She knew the girls well enough. "So, who took you to see *GIANT*?" she asked.

"Jason. Jason Long. Do you know him?" The girl had a catty tone. Both girls knew Bonnie's sights were set on Jason. They knew about her date with him.

Bonnie could not answer. She felt like someone had wrapped a rope around her throat. She turned away, pretending she remembered something important and had to hurry off to tend to it. She entered the kitchen and burst into tears.

"Uh-oh," Amanda said quietly to George. "I think we saw this coming." George shook his head, agreeing with his wife.

"Come here, honey," Amanda said. She pulled Bonnie into a hug.

"I feel so stupid. What am I gonna do?"

"You're going to pull yourself together and go on like nothing has happened," Amanda said. "Don't give him the satisfaction of knowing he hurt you."

"We were afraid of this," George said. "We knew how much the date with Jason meant to you. We were hoping we were wrong about it, though."

"You sit back here and get yourself settled down, honey," Amanda said. "Tonight, I'm gonna drive you home." She made eye contact with George. He nodded.

The Tyners let Bonnie stay in the kitchen the rest of the evening. She sat, weeping and brooding silently. They closed up briskly; George began cleaning. Amanda and Bonnie got into Tyner's Ford.

"I understand how you feel, Bonnie," Amanda said. "I've had my heart broken a time or two. You'll heal."

"Isn't there more to it?" Bonnie asked, through sniffles.

Amanda didn't expect Bonnie to dig into things like this. She had no good response. She knew better than to hem and haw; Bonnie would not settle for that.

"Tell me what you mean by 'more to it.' You guys said you expected something like this. Did you expect Jason to treat me like a queen one day and trash the next?"

"He didn't treat you like trash," Amanda said, her tone uncertain.

"You're trying to make me feel good. Why did you 'see this coming?'"

Amanda felt trapped. Bonnie deserved an answer. "Honey, sometimes people don't talk about things because they know they can't change them. Some things you just live with, or maybe put up with until you can change them."

"Keep talking. I think I know what you're gonna say."

"We know your friend Maggie Porter. She's a good lady, salt of the earth."

"She is. I love Maggie."

"Well, she cares about you and your brothers and sisters. She does whatever she can to help you guys. Didn't she help you get the job at Carson's?"

"Yeah, she gave me the idea and got me started. She even lent me some money to get clothes."

"Did you know she told us about you? Said you would be good for our business."

"She did? I thought you guys were looking for someone."

"It's true. Running even a small restaurant takes a lot of time. Having help makes a big difference. We've had girls work for us who didn't make much difference. There's help, and there's good help. You're good help."

"Thank you. You appreciate me. Yet, you didn't answer my question. According to you, Jason dropped me because I'm 'good help.'"

Amanda, annoyed that Bonnie wouldn't accept her vacillation, gave it up. "Damn girl, you're smart enough to know what happened with Jason."

"Is it about my family?"

"Your mom and dad mostly. A lot of people, hell, most people, look at your folks and think that all of you kids are like them. Maggie is different. She knows you don't have to be like them, and she figured that she'd give you a chance to be your own person. And she's right. You have so much going for you. You don't deserve the reputation your family has.

"You were a shining star working at Carson's. She knew that the job would be good for you. Moving on to another job where you could shine for more people to see and where you could make more money, get more confidence and experience, it's been good for you. Don't you think? And Beth, kind of following in your steps. Your other brothers and sisters will see you doing well and know they can do better too."

Bonnie had never imagined anything going on behind the scenes in her life. She hated it. It was late; her fatigue and anger were too heavy for her to think clearly. She had nothing more to say. She thanked Amanda stiffly and left the car.

"Hear anything from Jason?" Beth whispered, as Bonnie slipped into bed. She didn't want to wake Mary, who slumbered between them.

She heard no response.

"Bonnie. Bonnie," Beth pleaded. "Are you okay?"

"No, I'm not okay. Why can't people mind their own business?"

"What is it, sis?" Beth had heard that angry tone enough times to know she should let it go until the morning. Bonnie rarely got mad. When she did, it got ugly for those around her. "Good night, Bonnie. You better now, maybe?"

Silence.

Dorothy made pancakes for breakfast. Always a cheerful morning when pancakes were on the menu, the kids saw them as a treat. Usually, they had oatmeal or cereal.

Bonnie came last to the table. The older kids respected her mood, and one useful thing their mother had taught them was to respect others when they were not themselves. Jack, not so mature, asked, "Did you get up on the wrong side of the bed?"

Bonnie looked seriously at him. "Did you know we are a charity case, Jack?"

"What is a charity case?"

"That's people who need help to make it in the world."

Dorothy caught the tone. "Who says we're a charity case?"

"Not you and dad. Just us kids."

"All right then. Who says you kids are a charity case?"

"Never mind," Bonnie said. "I should keep my mouth shut."

"Have those busybodies at the church been offering you stuff? Surely, they know you have a job."

"Does Amanda Tyner go to the Methodist Church?"

"Now, how would I know? What did she say?"

Bonnie let the matter drop. Whatever came from her mother's mouth would be unfair. Bonnie wasn't being fair to Maggie and Amanda to begin with. She didn't need her mother making a federal case out of it.

Her school day dragged on. She wondered if any of the things she counted as successes in her life were legitimate. She wanted to ask Principal Davis if the cafeteria work he gave her was prompted by people outside of the school. Did every generous thing come her way out of pity?

She remembered a vocabulary word from junior high and realized that it described the way she felt. 'Patronized.' She was being patronized like a small child allowed to hit a home run because all the older kids deliberately dropped the ball instead of tagging him out. It made her sick. Were other things in her life phony? Were the good grades she got even real?

She did not care anymore about having the job at the Honky Tonk. She didn't want to face Amanda. She stepped off the bus as usual, and as it pulled away, she regretted not staying on it to go home. She went inside so frustrated that she turned back to the door when she saw George.

It surprised George to see Bonnie upset and more so when she didn't give him time to say anything. Once outside, she started down the road toward Parker, intending to hike the three miles home.

"Wait, Bonnie," George called. "I can give you a ride."

She didn't turn back or indicate she heard him. He went back inside. "Amanda, what's going on with Bonnie? Did she say anything to you last night?"

"Oh boy," Amanda muttered. She looked out the window to see Bonnie walking down the road, more like a march than a normal pace. "I know her feelings are hurt, but why is she taking it out on us? Did she say anything to you?"

"Not a word. Should I go after her?"

"Beats me. How long does it take to walk to Parker and up over that hill?"

"Hour-and-a-half, I bet. Maybe the walk will do her good. It's harder to be mad when you're tired."

"George, why don't you let her get part-way home and go after her? Offer her a ride and be kind to her."

The road to Parker followed the river and had a gentle bend not far downstream. Bonnie was out of sight in a few minutes, feeling foolish for taking off from the restaurant. People would be wondering about her and talking about her. They would think it was because of Jason, she supposed. Her actions would only make the situation worse. She considered turning back. That would be even more foolish.

Postcard-perfect trees and huge rocks, interspersed with open sections that framed the smoothly flowing water, lined the river road. Visitors marveled at the beauty. She had seen it her whole life. It didn't impress her. After all, the shaded banks and steep hillsides were an ideal place to stash dead bodies. She began to regret her impulsive decision to walk home. Wasn't that the sort of thing that got her father in trouble? Maybe. But she'd sooner be damned than turn around.

She heard a car slowing behind her. "Hey, you need a lift?" She turned, expecting to see George or Amanda; instead, it was Allen Carr, a boy from school. He had been in her class and dropped out the year before. She knew him well enough to say "Hi."

She hoped to get home without encountering anybody. While she felt so rotten, he didn't know what was on her mind. "Sure," she said and reached for the door handle. Refusing would be another dumb decision.

"I drive down this road a lot. I work at the factory. How come I've never seen you walking before?" Allen asked her.

"I usually have a ride."

"You still work at the Honky Tonk?" Allen asked.

"I don't know. I am supposed to be there now."

"What happened?"

"It's a long story." Bonnie couldn't describe her behavior in a way that made sense, since it didn't make sense to her. She had acted childishly by allowing strong feelings to dictate what she did. She would not share that with anyone, least of all a cute guy.

And Allen was cute. His white T-shirt had a pack of smokes folded up in the sleeve. All young guys carried them that way. His brown hair hung below his eyebrows in defiance of the popular combed-back style. He brushed it back with his hand and smiled warmly at Bonnie. "So, you walked off the job? Are you on strike?"

Bonnie laughed at the idea of there being a strike among the few girls who worked at the Honky Tonk. "Oh yeah, we formed a union. Gonna demand higher wages and more days off. Bigger tips too." There had been a short-lived strike at the glass factory a few years back, and she picked up some lingo. She hoped levity would prevent him from asking more questions she didn't want to answer.

"I hope that doesn't last too long," Allen said. "There's no place else to get a burger around here."

"We're gonna have 'binding arbitration' to settle the matter. Whatever the hell that is."

They both laughed. Allen pulled a Zippo from somewhere and lit a Camel.

"Say, you live up the hill across from the R.E.A., right?"

"Yep."

"I know Carter and Beth too."

They were approaching the bridge. Allen began to slow the car. She could smell his armpit sweat among the Camel smoke.

"You can let me off at the bridge," Bonnie said.

"I can take you up the hill. It ain't that far."

"That'll be sweet of you. You don't have to, though."

"I don't get to drive many pretty girls around. I want it to last as long as possible."

He turned the corner, and when they got to the end of Metts' lane, Bonnie wanted to tell him to let her off right there, as she had insisted that Jason did, but she didn't care if Allen saw the house. He drove up the lane to the place where cars turned around and stopped.

"Thanks for the ride, Allen."

"Say, Bonnie, before you go, is there any chance you'd let me take you out?"

Bonnie had not expected that. The idea instantly appealed to her, despite the armpit sweat. "Yes," she said, without hesitation. "Can you stop by the restaurant tomorrow? If I still have a job there, I'll need to see what night I can get off."

"It'll probably be Saturday night. I work the second shift all this week."

"Okay. Thanks again for the ride."

George Tyner drove the whole way to Parker Bridge and didn't see Bonnie. He turned around and headed back, and then thought better of it. He reversed course again and went the whole way to the Metts farm. He assumed someone had picked her up. That didn't mean she had been taken home. He had to know. He left his car running and went up to the porch. Bonnie came outside. They looked at each other blankly. "Are you okay?" George asked gently. A radio newscast and a stale odor he could not identify emanated from the house.

"I think so. Can I have tonight off and come back tomorrow night?" The offer of another date had picked her spirits up a little and besides, she wasn't mad at George, just Amanda and Maggie.

"You certainly can. Bonnie, you aren't mad at us, are you?"

"I'm not myself right now. I'll come in tomorrow, I promise."

"I'm glad to hear it. We love having you with us. Really." George smiled, got back in his car, and drove away. Females were hard to understand.

Bonnie's mind had stopped racing on the ride home with Allen. And the pain of Jason's rejection got softer. It allowed her, for the first time, to sense the gap between how she saw herself and how she was. She once thought that someday she could be her own person. No more. Whatever guiding star she had been following had gotten drunk like her father and lost its place in the sky. She had only been kidding herself; she was nothing but a dirty girl from a run-down farm. She lacked even a clean mirror to see herself in. The neighbors shook their heads, talking about her with pity. The idea that she had begun to rise above hid in a dank culvert under a rough, coal-drizzled railroad track, and nobody, not even she, cared to search for it. She would never be more than an extension of Ward and Dorothy.

High school graduation came. For her classmates, it was a big deal. She and Carter graduated, and no one in the Metts household made a fuss. Most families held a gathering of uncles, aunts, cousins, and close friends. The Mettses did nothing. There were no questions about what Carter might do next. He was bringing in some money delivering groceries, and everyone assumed he would join the Navy or get hired at the glass plant. Bonnie, Beth and Carter knew their parents were not interested. Bonnie and her siblings were not dreamed of nor planned for. They had simply happened.

Chapter Eighteen

Carter woke with a start. His eyes focused on the floral print wallpaper in Charlotte Timko's bedroom. He'd fallen asleep, despite the still, hot Sunday air. Kenny had left early in the morning, driving to Indiana for a week of training on some new equipment. Lying naked on her bed, their bodies were not touching, partly because they were sticky with sweat from their coupling and partly because of the aura of guilt that descended on them once their desire had flagged. An oscillating fan washed air over them intermittently. He turned toward Charlotte. Her eyes were wide, drinking in the sight of his body, studying it like a work of art. Astonished, he never imagined a woman could be fascinated with his physique. When their eyes met, her gaze shifted.

"How long was I out?" Carter asked.

"Not long. A few minutes."

"Did I snore?"

"No, young guys don't snore much."

Now, it was his turn to stare. He let his eyes roam across her contours. He knew her skin was not as tight as it once was, and where her breasts sagged; there was a hint that the part behind her nipples was fuller than the rest of it. He'd heard that an older woman's boobs resembled half-empty feed sacks. Charlotte's were relatively youthful.

He reached out and took a nipple between his thumb and forefinger, squeezing and twisting gently. "Like combination locks. A little to the left and a little to the right. Pretty soon, everything opens up," he said.

Charlotte felt a twinge of remorse. Despite all she had shown him, he still had an adolescent mind, immature and raw. "Where did you hear that?" she asked, with an annoyed-sounding laugh.

"Clarence told me that. He says it's a surefire way to seduce a woman."

"If you get the bra off, aren't you halfway there?"

"I think that's called second base. So yeah, maybe."

"Do you think Clarence knows anything after what I've taught you? If you want to know more about women, just ask me."

"Okay, I will. Are they all like you?"

"Like me, how?"

Carter hesitated, hoping to be tactful. "Do they all like to fool around?"

"No. Well, I think they might want to. Mostly, they don't think they should want to."

"And you're not like that?"

She didn't know how to answer. If what she did with Carter became known, she would be branded a shameless slut. She wondered if he thought that of her. No way he would say it, not while getting laid twice a week.

When she didn't respond, Carter tried another tack. "Are you this randy when Kenny comes home?" He almost bit his tongue. Not a good question, but it was out. He waited, certain she felt saddened, maybe ashamed.

Charlotte chafed under his curiosity; he had a right to ask, she having initiated their relationship. "Kenny is a good man. He doesn't care about this stuff anymore. We tried for years to have a baby. Once we gave up, he lost interest. It doesn't make sense to me. I guess disappointment is powerful. He feels foolish for trying. He feels like a failure anytime we make love, and I don't get pregnant."

"You must have tried to talk him out of that."

"Yeah, it never worked."

"What will you do if I get you pregnant?"

"There's not a big chance of that. I might be the one who can't get pregnant. The doctor doesn't know if it's him or me. I have a diaphragm. Even so, I make him do it most weekends. I tell him I need it for my nerves, and that's true."

"So screwing calms you down?"

"When it works right, it does. The hunger builds up inside me. Can't you tell when I release it?"

"Yeah, I can. I get it. Sometimes, you release it more than once."

"It's not easy for most women, they say. I've never had a problem getting the release."

"Will it be okay with you if I get a regular girlfriend?"

"Let's go out and sit on the back porch." She swung her legs off the bed and put her dress on. It slipped down over her body like the curtain closing on a play. Maybe his thought of getting a girlfriend was another stupid thing to say, and she intended to end the play. Carter got dressed and followed her out, desperately trying to formulate an apology.

"Want some iced tea?" she asked.

Carter nodded and watched her go into the kitchen. She seemed to be nervous all of a sudden, despite getting the release. It had to be his dumb question. He sat on a chair and surveyed her backyard. It wasn't much. Maybe thirty feet of grass before the woods took over. Someone could be in the woods spying on them, and they might never know it.

Charlotte returned and handed him a glass of tea. Water condensed on the side from the humid air. Carter drained his glass quickly and set it down on the handrail. Sipping the way most people did seemed silly to him.

"You should get a regular girlfriend. If you and I are getting together, you can be a perfect gentleman with her."

"What does that mean?"

"It means you won't try to get in her pants. Never twist those combination locks. I will keep you satisfied. No shotgun wedding for Carter Metts."

"Charlotte, can you tell me something?"

"Probably."

"I know my family isn't well thought of."

"You shouldn't worry about that."

"Just how bad is it? What do people say?"

"They all say it isn't the fault of you kids, the way your parents are. Why are you asking me this?"

"Did I ever tell you that Bonnie's first date was with Jason Long? That was a while ago. She was excited, thinking they were gonna go together. As it turned out, he never came back or even talked to her again."

"Does she think it's because of your family?"

"We both think that's the reason."

"The Longs have their noses in the air. You guys are better off she didn't end up as his girl." Charlotte wasn't being truthful with Carter. Most people in the area did see his whole family as being trashy. She could remember saying that sort of thing herself more than once. The Metts bunch was a standby subject for conversation. They were used for comparison whenever anyone felt low down. Everyone looked decent next to the Mettses. Hardly a week went by without some ugly rumor circulating about them.

"You don't have to be like them. You know that, don't you? You can move away some time to a place where nobody knows your family. You can start fresh and make a new reputation. Look at me, Carter. Tell me you know it's true."

He repeated her words, but it was not convincing. What she was doing with him would add to his feelings of being low. She may even be holding him back from becoming his own person. It was warm, refreshing, and joyful while they were together; she felt alive and vital. Old enough to be his mother, she hated herself in the still hours of the night. She missed Luther, a man her age at least.

On the Fourth of July, Frank and Carol finally got around to visiting the farm. The Buick convertible had been replaced with an older Ford.

"Where's your motorcycle?" Jack asked.

"Had to let it go, Jack." Frank offered with a tone of regret. "Babies cost a lot of money."

"We finally get to meet this baby girl," said Dorothy." I thought you would at least come for Thanksgiving again. Do you realize it's been nineteen months? It's not like you live a long way off."

"The doctor told me not to ride a long distance if I could avoid it. And raising a baby is hard, Mom," Carol said. "Packing up to travel is no fun either.

"Really? It was easier twenty-two years ago when I had you?" Dorothy asked sarcastically.

"You didn't have to take me anywhere, though."

"I didn't have anywhere to take you."

The others were making a fuss over the baby, whose name was Deborah. Dorothy had never heard a doctor say a pregnant woman shouldn't travel. But, she had not gone to a doctor at all when pregnant with Carol, Roger, Carter, or Bonnie. She wouldn't tell them that.

"Maybe I'm not showing as much as I used to when I was thinner. I'm gonna have another myself," Dorothy said.

"Oh, Mom, really? When are you due?" Carol asked.

"Sometime in November. A week or two before Thanksgiving, I think."

"I thought Roger told you guys to quit making babies."

"When would he have told me that?"

"He said he told you that in a letter. We write each other, you know."

"Well, our sailor boy never writes to me. So, he never gave me any such order. He isn't my boss, anyway. Your granddad had nine kids.

Your dad wants to do him one better. I'm quitting after this one, mark my words."

"We were hoping the four of us could go to the American House later," Carol said. "The girls won't mind watching Debby."

"I'd like that. I think your dad would too. He's never been able to show you off, or your good-looking husband."

Beth looked at Bonnie, whose eyes reflected the same astonishing truth. After many times repeating the line about escaping the hellhole, probably herself the author of it, their oldest sister had allied with their common enemy, beer.

"Are they having fireworks this year?"

Carter handed little Debby to Jack and turned around to face Frank. "Take a look at this." Carter dug into his back pocket and produced the A.M.A belt buckle.

"Gypsy Tour Award," Frank said. "Is it for me?"

"No, sorry Frank. It's cool, don't you think?"

"It is that. Where did you get this?"

Carter almost told the truth; he had some lingering doubt. "They have these rummage sales in Parker every couple of months. People go through their stuff and donate it to these sales. The fire department gets the money. I paid a dollar for it."

"You know it's busted, don't you?"

"It is?" Carter asked.

"It's supposed to have a square link where the belt goes. Must be why the guy sold it."

"I thought it clipped on."

"I don't see a clip," Frank said.

"Can you show me how it goes on?"

"I bet if I had an old coat hanger and a good set of pliers, I could fix it for you."

"Come on. Dad has some lineman's pliers. I can find a coat hanger."

Frank cheerfully helped his brother-in-law repair the belt buckle. "It isn't as good as new. Find some Bon Ami or rubbing compound to shine it up with. It will look real spiffy. Be careful not to scratch your girlfriend's tummy when she cozies up to you."

Carter wanted to tell Frank about his secret girlfriend. Instead, he smiled like a man with a secret. Frank looked at him curiously as if he sensed Carter was holding out on him. Frank had more important matters to tend to. Repairing the lad's belt buckle would get Ward's approval, he was sure.

The American House had large windows in the front, facing the street and the river. The party could sit at tables and watch the show while enjoying the beer. By the time the fireworks were soaring into the air, Ward, Dorothy and Carol were feeling no pain. Frank surprised them by how well he held his booze. "You know, Ward, I lost that nice Buick I had because I lost the good job at the mill."

"I figured you'd have a sad story," Ward said. "That's why so long between visits, right?"

Frank nodded gravely. "The mill foreman blamed me for some damage to equipment. They took me to court, and I have to pay the bastards. They say they'll put me in jail if I don't come up with it."

"How much is it?"

"It was $1100. I paid some of it." Frank answered, swallowing hard.

"Whew. You could buy a nice car for that much."

"Why do you think I had to let the Buick go back?"

"I wish I could help you, son," Ward said. "I got no money."

"Actually, you can help me. The bank says they'll give me a personal loan if I get a co-signer. I can get enough to settle with the mill and work it out by the month. I hate to ask you, but I got nobody else." Frank looked down at the table and held his breath.

They endured a long silence. Frank knew that the one who spoke first in such situations usually conceded.

Ward took a long slug of beer and set his glass down decisively, "Where's these papers you need me to sign?" he asked, never taking his eyes off the grand finale popping in the sky and draining bright, colorful embers into the water.

"They're in the car. You'll sign it for me, really?"

"Go get them."

Dorothy wanted to object, but she knew better. Ward saw an opportunity to be a hero for his oldest daughter. She couldn't risk him getting mad, maybe letting her have it, not when she was five months pregnant. Ward liked to declare proudly that he would never hit a woman. Dorothy had doubts. He had come close to punching her while drunk many times. Frank had better get another good job. Eleven hundred dollars was a lot of paychecks if it came down to it.

"Don't look at me like that, mother. How's the boy supposed to feed Carol and little Debby if he goes to jail?"

Carol said nothing, trying her best to be invisible. Her husband had twisted and stretched the truth.

There were two spots for co-signers on the papers. Frank laid them on a table away from the beer glasses and the wet rings on the tabletop. Ward signed carefully and looked impatiently at Dorothy. "Come over here, mother."

She obeyed. The whole thing seemed fishy to her, even in her addled state.

Once the papers were signed, a more festive mood came over the group. Frank slapped Ward on the back. "I knew I could count on you for help, Dad. It means a lot, and I won't forget it."

"Let's get some quarts and go up the hill," Dorothy said.

The four of them were soon seated around the table in the out-kitchen. The kids—with no thought of going to bed—stood close by or sat on the old bench they used for meals. Beth and Bonnie had begun cooking hot dogs as soon as they saw headlights coming up the lane. A small fire lit up the yard above the out-kitchen. It was the same spot where the Mettses burned their household rubbish. Fire was fire.

Sometimes, the kids loved their father's late-night, beer-fueled festive mood. He would sing old-time songs, nothing from their school songbooks. His favorites were *The Racoon in the Simmon Tree and the Possum on the Ground,* and *We'll Hang Jeff Davis from the Sour Apple Tree.*

"Jack, go out to the barn and bring me that coil of rope." Ward spouted cheerily. "I want to teach Frank to tie the hangman's noose."

"Do you have to, Dad?" Beth asked. The girls remembered the last time their father had tied a noose. He had put Dorothy's head in it. The coils of the noose hung down across her shoulder. The boys thought it funny; the girls thought it grotesque.

"Good thing I know where the rope is. The flashlight batteries went dead," Jack said. He handed the coil of rope to Ward, inwardly resolving to always keep extra batteries once he got old enough to work and have a flashlight of his own.

"No, Jack, give me the end. Keep what you can coiled up. We're not gonna hang anyone tonight, just learn how." Ward's warm breath smelled like beer and mustard from a hot dog he had eaten. He took the rope and began the knot on the kitchen table. "This is the easiest way to start." He took an end and began the winding.

"Looks like an S," Frank said. "Now it's like a bow."

"You can do it with the rope loose, a flat surface works best. I've seen guys try to tie it without the double loop. That's not the real thing. Looks like it, but it's not. You need a large enough knot to push against the head when the man drops. That's how you break his neck. Single loop is too thin. And this rope is barely big enough. One-inch diameter manila rope is considered proper."

"Thirteen times around, right? Frank asked.

"It don't matter. They always said there were thirteen steps on a gallows too. That don't matter either."

Ward never explained where he learned so much about hanging. Dorothy saw it as a bluff. Men liked morbid subjects, especially Ward.

"You never actually hung anybody, did you, Dad?" Frank asked.

"No, but my friend Judson saw it once when he lived in Kentucky. There were thirteen steps on that gallows, he said."

"They put people in the chair these days. Bzzzt, bzzzt," Richard gushed.

"That'll be enough, Richard," Dorothy said. "Isn't nothing funny about people being put to death. Even when they deserve it."

"They fried the Rosenbergs, didn't they? Bzzzt, bzzzt," Jack said. Soon, all the smaller kids were chanting, "Bzzzt, bzzzt."

Ward tried not to chuckle. "You kids settle down. Mind your mother." The buzzing ceased abruptly.

As the girls expected, the noose went around Dorothy's head. Snugged up, with the coil resting on her shoulder, Dorothy sat with a bemused smile on her face, Camel hanging from her lips, and a glass of beer in her hand. Intending to be comical, Ward had degraded his wife. If that bothered Dorothy, she never let on.

Ward captured everyone's attention with the noose. Knowing he could do better, he peeled his T-shirt off, revealing a flat stomach, rippled with muscle. He balled his hand into a fist and brought it solidly into his belly. "When I was in the fight game, these muscles were even harder than they are now. Carol, give it a try. Hit me in the old breadbasket."

"Daddy, I can't hit you."

"Don't be scared. You can't hurt me."

Carol wanted to suggest that her father let Frank hit him. She was sure Frank could make him regret his bluster. But Frank and she had worked together to incite comradery among the two men; it wouldn't do to jeopardize it. Carol pulled back her arm, made a fist and began to deliver a punch. Ward immediately snatched her by the wrist. "You know better than that. I taught all of you kids how to make a fist. Where does the thumb go?"

Carol had made her fist wrong on purpose, knowing her dad would correct her. It was all part of stroking his ego, though it didn't matter so much now that the papers were signed. She gave him a sharp blow in the stomach and was surprised at how hard it was.

"I'm sorry, did you hit me? I didn't feel it," her father crowed. "Try it again."

Carol gave him another and he only laughed. "John L. Sullivan said I could lick any son-of-a-bitch in the house."

Determined to make a showing and driven by alcohol, Carol put everything she had into her next punch. When her knuckles made contact, she felt a sharp pain. She cried out and turned away from her dad to bend over in agony, sheltering her right hand with her left. Tears flowing.

"Did you hear that crack?" Jack asked. The other kids all said they heard it too.

Carol's hand was swelling. "Boy, Ward, you've done it now," Dorothy said. "Frank, I hope you're sober enough to drive her to Clarion. Bet she'll need a cast."

Chapter Nineteen

Four hours later, Frank and Carol left the hospital emergency department, and Carol was indeed sporting a heavy cast. She had broken the proximal phalange of her right hand. The medical terminology sounded graver than "little finger."

"Did you hit belly muscle or belt buckle?" Frank asked. "I don't believe his stomach is that hard."

"All I know is it hurt like hell; it still does."

"You didn't hit squarely. By the way, I think your old man made up that business about John L. Sullivan."

"Was this Sullivan guy a fighter?"

"He was. Back in those days, boxing was mostly bare-knuckle. I think Sullivan was dead before your dad fought. There is a history book about sports. I'll look it up sometime if I get near a library. The thing is, your dad's a phony in a lot of ways."

Carol had never heard anyone call Ward a phony. A drunk, rude, impulsive, brutish maybe, never phony. She didn't like Frank saying that about her dad. In the painful reality of her broken finger, she found something she denied before. Frank was the phony, a pretender.

She'd helped to defraud her dad. She knew nothing about this supposed debt to the mill. It made sense if Frank had been fired for destroying some kind of expensive equipment. She didn't think the mill could do more than fire him for it, but what did she know? He always had a sad story about why they were short of money. First, he sold his motorcycle, and then some stranger drove the Buick away. Their neighbor told Carol it had been repossessed, an entirely new word for Carol. It turned out that the house they lived in did not belong to Frank's family after all. They had been told to pay the rent or move out by the first of August.

Frank had stopped leaving the house to work on a regular schedule, and he came home smelling of beer more than once. When she questioned him about work, he got angry, and she felt threatened.

"I'm going to leave you and Debby here with your folks for the rest of the summer. With your big mitten, you're gonna need help taking care of Debby. That way, I can concentrate on making money. I'll work overtime, maybe get a second job. My buddy Mike needs someone to stay nights with his grandfather. I get free room and board. All I gotta do is sleep there and be available if the old guy needs anything. He's senile, and they think he might do something dangerous."

"Why didn't you tell me this? I didn't bring extra clothes, and I need stuff for the baby."

"Your mom has plenty of baby stuff. Richard and Mary do most of the baby care anyway. You have two sisters that are the same size as you. An extra hand working in the garden is always helpful. You'll be fine."

"I can maybe go back and stay with Aunt Polly."

"Maybe before you had a baby to care for," Frank said. Something in his tone said there would be no further discussion. Carol's head was spinning. Things weren't supposed to work out this way. Life was moving backward, not forward.

Dorothy rolled her eyes when it was announced that Carol and the baby were staying. She was not surprised though, just disappointed. Frank jumped in his old Ford and took off before Ward could weigh in on the matter. "We'll set up a bed upstairs of the out-kitchen," Dorothy said. "You'll have to make do with that. We've never had eleven people live here. It is tight enough already.

Carol began to weep, now being exiled to the lowest place. The upstairs was dingy, bare wood. Dust and soot, still present from long ago when the place had been heated by a coal stove, covered everything. It was stale smelling with only one window, so there was no way to cross-ventilate the place. Crammed full of old cardboard boxes, teeming with yellowed books and other worthless items, no lights, and unbearably cold in the winter despite the gas heat. The out-kitchen had spaces between the wall planking. Unlike the farmhouse, it was not built for full-time occupancy. Only the roaring gas flames made it habitable. The second floor, however, was tight enough so little heat made it upstairs. What did, flowed out the eaves that were open to the wind. The kids had all played some in that place, mostly on rainy days. There was nothing pleasant about it. Surely, Frank would take her back to a decent house in Grove City before the cold weather came. He would have to. The terrible truth gripped her that she had escaped the hellhole only to find herself back in it. And now her precious baby daughter had joined her there.

Charlotte Timko remembered what it was to be in love. It had happened again, with Carter Metts. She could never say the words to him, that didn't matter much. It was the substance of a beautiful life, the positive feelings she had when she woke every morning and imagined his youthful visage sleeping beside her. One day soon, she would let him stay overnight.

The dreary existence that had plagued her when Luther disappeared had slowly been occluded by the gentle touch of her virile stud. They could not go on forever; it wouldn't be fair to Carter. He would, in time, be paired with someone his age. There would be children and all that went with it. Since she could not have that, she was determined to squeeze all of the happiness she could from life for as long as possible.

She had often wondered about those who had nervous breakdowns and ended up in the state hospital or worse. A man hanged himself in a barn a while back. So many had wondered why. Charlotte knew. Loneliness drove him to it. On the other side of the township, an old farmer had shot himself after a long life of living alone. Her own life was so empty. Kenny had been laid off sometimes in the winter, and so, for a few weeks, was with her every day. Life was tolerable then. The war had drained something out of him, a convenient explanation. If his ordeal in Europe were dreadful, he kept it to himself. He was simply a dull person. Not mean or hard to get along with, just dull.

Her affair with Luther was wrong in every way, like her affair with Carter. She knew it. While no admirable man, Luther was lively. She needed that. Carter's youth, innocence and openness were a never-ending treat. She was using Carter, but she was teaching him as well. No question, he liked it. There was zest in her world while knee-deep in an affair; the planning to meet, the great care she had to take to ensure nothing suggested unhappiness with Kenny. She had come to know that it wasn't only the sex and companionship she relished; the clandestine nature of it gave desperately needed color to her world. Let most women be satisfied with the humdrum existence of rural life, gardening, housekeeping, watching the wildlife, cooking, canning, and sewing that filled up so many hours for people like her. She had to have more, something unique, or she might go crazy.

When Carter wanted it to end, she would thank him for what he had given her and wish him well. It would be followed by months of gloom, like when she lost Luther. That was in the future. Today, her young lover would bring her groceries and pleasure. Some day, he would not show up. Some other kid would take his delivery job, and he would move on without saying goodbye. If it ended that way, she could accept it. She had no claim on his heart, even if he had hers.

Carter parked the wagon in the lane. In her eyes, it belonged there. She realized that they were getting comfortable with what they were doing. That could not be good.

She opened the refrigerator door, and he put the bag inside. They had begun doing that regardless of whether the contents needed refrigeration. Such expedience meant they could move immediately to pleasure. Even with adequate time, they rushed through as if their iniquity were milder if it happened quickly. He would turn away from the cold air, take her into his arms, and they would kiss, tingling with anticipation. She had coached him so well. He knew how and where to touch her. He knew what demeanor worked best for lovemaking, and how to make her feel precious.

"These are all things that will make you an unforgettable husband," she had assured him. "The girl that snags you will do whatever it takes to keep you coming home to her bed. You will be a well-loved and happy man." She knew that most women were not wanton like her. She could be setting him up for disappointment when he did get married. She thought it was better for him to know what was possible than to settle for dull the way she had.

They had danced to the bedroom, Charlotte shedding what little garments she was wearing and jumping up to wrap her legs around him so that he could ease her bottom down onto the sheets. He backed away like always and dropped his pants. There was a curious thud when his jeans hit the hardwood floor. "Are you carrying rocks in your pocket?" she asked playfully. She had even taught him to be playful with her because that was part of a good relationship.

"No, that's my new belt buckle. You can see it later." He moved to cover her quickly and gently. Their foreplay had become routine, and routine was better for a couple with limited time. She had taught him to hold off and to let her peak twice before he climaxed himself. It was asking a lot of a young man, but that skill would serve him well when he married.

With a long, guttural moan, Carter finished. Charlotte smiled against his cheek, so happy to feel satisfied yet still hungry and entirely pleased to know he was the same. They chatted for a while, their voices stark against the silence.

Carter sat up and pulled on his underwear and T-shirt. He pulled the pants up and swung around proudly to display the A.M.A. buckle. She was leaning on one elbow, and the sight of it caught her at eye level.

Their mood turned awkward as her facial expression changed from lighthearted and happy to morose in an instant. She shook her head slowly from side to side. Her eyes were fixed on his belt buckle.

"Wha...what's the matter?" Carter said.

"Where did you get that?" Clearly, she meant his buckle.

"At the rubbish sale," he said, trying to be playful, saying "rubbish" instead of "rummage."

He dropped his face, hoping she could not read his lying eyes.

Chapter Twenty

"So, are you a good swimmer?" Allen Carr asked Bonnie. He had brought her home from a date. They had gone to Clarion and seen a movie.

"Don't know how good, but I can swim," she replied.

"How about I pick you up around one o'clock tomorrow, and we go to Grass Flats?"

"Sounds good. We always have a Sunday dinner. They expect me to be here to help with it. It's always over by one."

"What's going on there?" Allen asked. He could see somebody shining a flashlight inside the barn.

"It's probably Jack and Richard catching chickens."

"Wouldn't they be easier to catch in the daylight?"

"No," Bonnie laughed, "they run too fast."

"They don't run at night?"

"No, silly. They roost. Come on, let's go watch. You'll see."

They stepped quickly to the barn, Bonnie leading the way. "Watch where you step. The cows are in and out of this shed all the time," she said.

"What, you can see cow pies in the dark?"

With enough moonlight for Bonnie to avoid the muck, Allen did his best to put his feet where she stepped. Soon, they were close to the boys. "Wait up, guys. I want you to show Allen how we catch chickens."

"Hey, we'll even let him catch one if he wants," Jack said.

The four of them were gathered in the shed. Jack shone the flashlight on the hay rack. At the top were horizontal boards, and the chickens were all roosting quietly. "They think that up that high, they are safe from foxes," said Richard. "I guess they are too. But they're not safe from me."

"I thought chickens were kept in coops or hen houses," Allen said.

"Some farms do it like that. Our chickens kind of run free," Bonnie said.

"Do you gather eggs?"

"Every couple of days. We usually get enough that we don't need to buy any."

Jack turned off the flashlight and stepped directly under where the chickens were roosting, and climbed the hayrack like a ladder. He handed Richard the light. Richard held the light so that Jack could see where a plump chicken's clawed feet grasped the edge of a board. He shut off the light, and Jack grabbed both lower legs of a chicken in one hand. It squawked and thrashed a little. "Got her," Jack said triumphantly. He brought the bird down to ground level, and Richard looped some twine around its legs.

"All this talking doesn't scare the chickens away?" Allen asked.

"It never has," Richard said. "Chickens are stupid."

"Do you keep roosters with your chickens?" Allen asked.

"It would be too much trouble to separate them," Bonnie said.

"I don't get it," said Allen. "I'm not a country boy."

"What don't you get?"

"Don't some of the eggs have peeps in them?"

"Oh. I see your problem. Peeps only happen if a chicken decides to sit on her eggs. If one of them is sitting, we leave her alone. We get more chickens that way."

"What makes them decide to sit on eggs?"

"I don't know. I never asked a chicken, and they've never told me."

"Now, who's being silly?" Allen asked, playfully.

"You want to catch the next one, Allen?" Jack offered.

"No. Don't they ever scratch you?"

"I don't recall anybody getting scratched," Bonnie said. "If you surprise a hen with a bunch of peeps, she will flap her wings and come at you, peck at you, try to hurt you. We run away, let her raise her babies so we can eat them."

"And the eggs they lay."

"And the eggs they lay," Bonnie smiled.

"You should stay over, Allen. Watch mom butcher these in the morning," Richard said.

Allen whispered into Bonnie's ear, "What a great idea. I'll sleep in the barn. You can tuck me in. Maybe even snuggle in and keep me warm."

Bonnie liked the idea of getting alone and naked with Allen. No prize as far as men went; she could not help comparing him to Jason Long, who was, unfortunately, long gone. Allen had a crude, masculine way about him that she found stimulating. He was a rough-handed, flannel shirts and steel-toed boots kind of guy. He smoked Pall-Malls and drank Koehler beer when he could get someone older to buy it for him, declaring that he would get as much as he wanted when he turned twenty-one. Something about him was reliable and productive, a be-at-work-on-time, pull-your-weight kind of guy, like her dad. Despite his faults, he had virtue. Allen's family was even poorer than hers, but only if you count having land as wealth. He was as good a catch as most of the guys in the area.

In her time with Jason, she had raised her sights to expect more out of life. She could no longer imagine what more might be. She had no lofty vision anymore. What would she do besides get married? Every girl married soon after high school. Being practical made more sense than being a dreamer. The abandoned raccoons dreamed of their mother coming back, but she hadn't.

"You have your two chickens, Richard. Give me the flashlight," Bonnie said.

The boys took the now-tethered chickens toward the house. Bonnie and Allen watched them go. "Did you ever lie down on hay, Allen? It's itchy."

"Let's try it anyway," Allen said.

Sneaking into the barn by flashlight was exciting; the hay was indeed itchy. Too itchy for the kind of action Allen wanted. Bonnie let him get to third base. If she ever went any further, it would have to be someplace more comfortable than a hayloft. She liked getting worked up. She liked getting him worked up even more. Could there be anything better, she wondered, than wrapping her man up in her arms and enjoying all the sensations of kissing and touching? The less clothing, the better. She could tell by her body's response that intercourse was the most natural thing in the world. Only Maggie's admonition about losing control of her life kept her from yielding to Allen's desire. She remembered what Maggie had told her about sex, that a woman wanted to make her man happy, to satisfy him. She understood that now. She wanted to give Allen what he craved. Maybe that meant she should marry Allen. If they were going to be married, going the whole way wouldn't be as big a deal. Shotgun wedding or regular wedding? Did it matter? And Maggie had it right about sex. Nothing else was like it.

"Can you believe it?" Richard asked. "Carol has been here a week, and I can count on one hand the number of diapers she has changed. Why do we have to take care of Debby? It's hard enough taking care of Jeffrey."

He had just finished changing the child's diaper and given her a bottle. Deborah was nestled in a laundry basket with a bottle. They enjoyed watching her with her bottle because when she had drained it, she would throw it straight away from her into whatever space there happened to be, an unusually sassy gesture for a tot.

"I thought you liked taking care of 'Debby, Debby, Debby,'" Beth said. She was mocking Richard's usual sing-song handle for their beloved niece. He would spout the tune whenever he picked the child up. Her delighted, smiling laughter was his reward.

"I change her and make sure she's fed because if she had to wait for one of you to do it, she'd be dirty and hungry all the time. Taking care of babies is women's work. Everybody knows that."

"I'll bet Carol would say you beat her to it most of the time," Beth said.

Richard didn't respond to her comment, supposing that Carol would agree. He dropped the matter. He did most of the work for the two babies in the house. It made him feel good to shoulder a burden that nobody else wanted. Nobody picked on him for acting like a mom. They were happy to let him do so much.

"We've always done whatever is needed," Beth said, realizing something about it seemed unfair. They were in the out-kitchen, busy with the usual mid-day chores, drying dishes with a worn towel, now as wet as the washrag. There were only three small towels in the household to wipe dishes with. They rarely got washed, but were simply hung up on the oven handle to dry between uses.

"They had us kids so we could work. That's the way it is on a family farm." Jack said.

"Ask the other kids at school," Beth said. "They'll tell you their mothers do most of the housework." She wasn't sure about that, but it validated her resentment. "A couple of ladies were talking at Carson's yesterday. One mentioned that the five-and-dime got in a shipment of linens. Bed sheets, towels, and stuff like that. One of them said she needed at least ten dish towels, and she would buy all new ones before they sold out."

"When we were at Aunt Polly's house, I saw her shelves," Jack said. "I bet she has six bath towels, and there's just her and Uncle Curt."

The trio of siblings counted silently in their heads. There were only four bath towels in the Metts house, and one of them had a hole in the center that grew larger every day.

They were normally silent about the lack of things in their home, poverty being more manageable if they didn't focus on it. Beth wondered why Jack cared about bath towels. He often went for two weeks without a bath. She couldn't say that to him. Not long ago, she had been the same way.

Chapter Twenty-One

Sunday afternoons, once or twice a month, Aunt Polly and Uncle Curt would visit. Always in their Sunday best, they went to church and drove to the farm in the same clothes. They normally brought some kind of treasure, candy or baked goods from Polly's kitchen, old magazines, or newspapers for Ward to read, and best of all, a genuine interest in the kids.

Curt would always look one of the boys straight in the eye and speak for a few minutes as if they were the only person on earth. He made them feel valuable for a shining moment. Nobody in the Metts household ever said it, but Curt and Polly were the decent kind of people that they were not. Everything about them graciously implied that a better lifestyle could be had. They all remembered how Carol had been given the opportunity to move in with them so she could get a housekeeping job. Bonnie had assumed that her turn was coming now that Carol had married. Carol's moving back in, coupled with Bonnie now having a boyfriend, put the matter in a different light.

"I was wondering, Aunt Polly," Beth said, working up her courage, "if maybe I could do like Carol did."

"You mean come and live at our house? Maybe get a job?"

Beth nodded, carefully looking around. Her gaze settled on Bonnie, who she thought might balk at the idea, seeing that she was next in line for the opportunity.

"Our spare rooms are always open, dear. Our children, Ralph and Barbara, live so far away. I'm sure we could find you a place to work. You know, they opened a diner only a block from our house. You could probably work there. If not there, maybe one of the businesses on Broad Street. Come to think of it, the one grocery store is a lot like Carson's. You would fit right in there."

"What about graduation, Beth? You still have a year," Bonnie asked.

"Roger quit. So can I."

"It would sure help out if we had one less around the table," Dorothy interjected vigorously. "Maybe Jack could take your place at Carson's before too long."

"Gosh, Mom, you're eager to get me out of here," Beth said.

"Well," Dorothy said, looking down at her swollen belly.

"November will be here before you know it," Aunt Polly said.

"Why don't you tell the Carsons you're moving away, Beth? When we come in two weeks, you can ride home with us."

Aunt Polly and Uncle Curt had driven away. Dorothy and the girls put a supper of Sunday chicken leftovers on the table and nobody noticed when Carter slipped away. The walk to Charlotte Timko's house only took ten minutes, cross country. He had begun to wear a path.

Kenny had gone already. He preferred to leave home on Sunday evening rather than rise at four a.m. to drive to his work site. The usual signal Charlotte put out for Carter when it was safe to approach, a potted flower in a particular place, was not there. There had been no grocery order to deliver the prior week. Carter did not know what to think. He could tell that Charlotte had been upset when she saw his belt buckle the last time he was with her. He didn't know what that meant. He had stopped wearing the buckle.

He veered off into the woods and eased closer to the house. He could see Charlotte sitting by a window, perhaps reading a book, surely alone. He whistled from the woods, but he could not whistle loud or shrill and she did not hear.

After a while, he approached and knocked. She came and saw him. She opened the door but did not speak.

"Hey, Charlotte," Carter said.

"Hey, Carter," she whispered.

"Did I do something wrong?"

He had her on the spot. She had avoided him by not ordering groceries, but she knew he'd need an explanation sooner or later. She didn't have one, and she couldn't tell what was driving her feelings about him.

"Talk to me, Carter." Her voice was plaintive. She needed something besides his body. "Let's sit on the back porch and talk."

They got to the porch and were seated. Carter looked at her and watched as she slowly began to cry. He felt responsible for her sadness and moved toward her, kneeling in front of her chair like a supplicant, looking up and taking her hands.

"Oh, Carter, I'm so ashamed."

"I'm not ashamed of you, Charlotte." He wanted to reassure her, to be noble and rescue her from whatever dragon had her cornered.

"I got you into something you'll never understand."

"I'm no dummy. Explain it to me."

"Maybe you could understand, but I can't tell you."

"Why not?"

"What you and I do is our secret. They say that two can keep a secret only if one is dead. If three know it isn't a secret anymore."

"I'm not telling anyone about us. I never will."

"That doesn't mean it won't get out. I remember having a secret I thought was safe. It wasn't. This one will get out too. We will be found out somehow. I can't let it happen to you. We have to stop. I know it now. I am so sorry, Carter."

The evening air and the green surroundings were idyllic, it spoke peace to them. Carter chose his words carefully. "It's okay if you're sorry because you think we'll get caught. I understand that. Just don't be sorry for what you've given me. You've been incredibly kind to me."

"There is too much at stake. It could get both of us in a lot of trouble." Then, like an afterthought, "It would be so unfair to Kenny. Besides that, you think your family has a bad reputation? If our secret gets out, the reputation will only get worse."

"But you've been so good for me. Surely you must see that. I don't know why people think you and I getting together is such a bad thing. You're right that I don't understand." With that, he rose and stepped back.

Charlotte sensed his defensive posture and regretted the remark about his family. She softened her tone. "Carter, what we have been doing is wrong. I know you understand that. Having someone to love, to really love, it's supposed to be that way for married people. So often, it isn't, it just isn't. Carter, there is so much about life that we don't understand until we can look back on it. Everybody has some story about how they wish they had seen what they were getting into before it was too late. I have a lot of stories like that."

It was his turn to speak, and the pause got awkward, then a thought dawned. "Maybe they didn't want to see it," Carter said.

Charlotte slowly nodded, looking into his eyes. Her tear-soaked face was serious. The profound wrong she had created overwhelmed her; only absolute candor would do. She gazed into the distance as if there were no thick foliage to stop her vision. He was so right about her not wanting to see. "I don't know how to make my marriage to Kenny be what I need. But that is my problem, my cross to bear. I've been asking you to love me the way I need him to. I can't keep doing that. The world is so full of halfway love, makeshift love, cobbled together love. So many people give up on ever being happy. I've refused to give up, and I've been lying to myself that using you is my answer. It's like I've mixed up the recipe for your happiness with my recipe. What we have here is never going to make something worth hanging on to. If it could, we wouldn't have to keep it secret." A sob escaped. She checked herself.

"Isn't what we have real love?"

"Oh Carter, dear, sweet, honest Carter. Yes, it is. It's real, and I will always treasure it, as I hope you do. It's one of those things in life that has a limit. No, that's wrong. Love might be the only thing in life that is unlimited. But it won't work every place we find it." The wistfulness in her voice was like a prayer. "I dream of a world where it does. I know that you can move on and find someone to love who can give you the whole thing, the right recipe. You see what I mean? I've been spoiling your life for the sake of my happiness; it's a selfish thing to do. I know that now. I'm able to look back."

"That doesn't add up," Carter said. "You tell me the world is full of halfway love, and yet you think I can find the whole thing."

"I'm too messed up to do anything except make you unhappy. I want you to be happy. I want you to find a place or a person where at least you have a chance to get the whole thing. I've been teaching you to make love, and you've learned well. I know now that what I've been reaching for is a child. I want a baby so bad." She began to sob uncontrollably.

"I thought you had a diaphragm."

After her sobbing slowed, she looked up. "No, that's another lie."

Carter nodded. He knelt again. Her having a diaphragm had not made sense to him when she'd said it.

She leaned over him, tears dripping on his shoulder. "Thanks for putting up with me. I know I can tell you the truth."

Chapter Twenty-Two

"I can see that deciding to move out was the right thing," Beth said. "You guys may as well be pushing me."

"We're gonna miss you, big sis," Mary said. Her eyes were misty, her voice on the edge of breaking, the first indication from anyone that her departure might be a sad event. Sad as Mary's face was, Beth smiled to see it. She turned to her younger sibling and hugged her. Something rare, the only hugs in their house were from Mom, and those stopped when a child went to school.

"You can come to visit with Aunt Polly and Uncle Curt. That way, we'll see you every couple of weeks," Mary said.

Dorothy knew that once Carol left home, she did not ride along with Curt and Polly when they visited. Beth would be no different. She kept that thought to herself, letting Mary enjoy her childish ideas.

It struck Beth that Mary did not yet see home as a hellhole, even though she must have heard it enough to understand and know why the older kids said it. It wouldn't be much longer until Mary reached the age where the other kids at school would make her aware of her family's shortcomings.

"It will be so nice to live with Aunt Polly. You'll have nicer clothes and books to read. She even has a piano," Mary gushed.

"You're right, Mary," Beth said. "But the main reason I am going there is so I can get a job and start a life of my own." As if someone else were saying the words, she realized the truth of it. So far in life, she had been one of the Metts kids, like being a chicken or hog or cow, one of the animals they grew to be slaughtered. From here on, she would determine what came next. Now on the threshold of freedom, the promise of it faded some.

"Aunt Polly will know what I should do."

Mary looked quizzically at her sister, not sure why she said that. "Doesn't Aunt Polly have a lot of neighbors? People who live in town like that get to do more stuff than we do in the country." Mary went on. "They have a swimming pool in Grove City that anyone can go to. They have a library and a fire department. You can almost see the college from Aunt Polly's house. Gosh, Beth, maybe you can go to college. Wouldn't that be nice?"

"Well, well, Mary, I can tell you listen when they come to visit. You know more about Grove City than I do. I don't think you can get into a college unless you finish high school, and I won't do that. There is a movie theater there, and I will be able to make money to buy tickets. I'll get to see all the good movies."

Beth didn't say it to Mary, but in a town with a college, there were bound to be lots and lots of boys. She pondered why she hadn't thought of that before. She also realized there was a good chance Aunt Polly's house had a TV set. She told herself to remain aloof about that if she could.

When dinnertime came, Carol sat with Debby in her arms. The child fussed, and Carol became agitated. She glared at Beth, her eyes boring holes in her face.

"Don't think it's gonna be all fun and games at Aunt Polly's. She will expect you to go to church with them. They practically live beside it. It ain't fun sitting through those boring sermons. The church music is nothing like you hear on the radio. And on Sundays, when they don't come here to visit, you have to sit quietly and read a book or something like that. That will get on your nerves. They're particular about their house too; everything has to be neat and orderly, 'a place for everything and everything in its place.' They're not like Mom and Dad."

"Neat and orderly?" Beth asked. "That sounds good to me. Not like Mom and Dad? That sounds okay too." She let her voice trail off lest she offend her mother.

"You'll find out," Carol said. "You've got a lot to learn, missy."

"You did pretty well there. Met your husband and all. Nice guy he is, too."

Carol had no response. Frank's luster had worn off, and they all knew it. Beth's sarcasm hit her like a swarm of hornets.

"You're being a smart ass. I don't need that from you," Carol said.

"No, I'm not. He is a nice guy."

"Oh, I get it," Carol said, "You're jealous."

"I think maybe you're jealous cause I get to go where you're supposed to be."

With that, Carol stood up, her chair fell over behind her. She kicked it away, but there was no place to kick it to in the crowded room. It clattered off the wall and came back to its starting point. "Don't smash up my chairs," Dorothy roared. "You'll have to get a damned milk stool from the barn to sit on."

Carol stepped over the fallen chair clumsily. Her jerky motions scared little Debby, who began crying wildly. Carol stomped to the door of the out-kitchen.

Ward sat like a stone.

"Beth, you should be ashamed of yourself," Dorothy said. "Try putting yourself in her shoes."

"Guess I better keep my mouth shut," Beth said, "since it's obvious I can't say anything right." She felt bad. Everyone knew Carol had been humiliated by her husband. Reminding her was cruel, even if she asked for it.

"Pick up her chair," Ward said with his heavy tone that commanded respect and silence from everyone in his presence. They knew he meant Beth should do it. She complied, even though there were others closer.

The next few days were tense. Carol's unhappy situation punctuated the quarrel between her and Beth. When Friday evening came, Carol joined Ward and Dorothy at the American House, as if leaving her baby for the boys to take care of and coming home drunk were the natural order of things. Carol had jumped a divide the kids never expected her to. They felt betrayed and bewildered. It seemed okay now to say derogatory things about Frank when Carol couldn't hear.

"Did Frank and Carol have a fight, Mom?" Beth asked Dorothy. They were making pie crust on the out-kitchen table; Dorothy's hands were white with flour. Carol was still in bed, sleeping off the previous night's beer. She was not yet a hardened drinker.

"Frank got himself in some kind of trouble. He has to earn money to pay some kind of debt. He can live cheaper while he works if she stays with us. He has some living arrangement with one of his buddies."

"How long will it be until she goes back with him?"

"Frank didn't say."

Since Beth opened the dialog, Dorothy felt free to speak her mind. "You kids were impressed by Frank when he showed up. I had a feeling about him from the beginning."

"Why didn't you say so?"

Dorothy looked at her daughter over the top of her eyeglasses. "You think it would have been helpful? Do any of you kids trust my judgment?"

For the first time in her life, Beth saw her mother through sympathetic eyes. The answer was plain as day, and they both knew it. Beth's mind raced to find something kind to say and came up empty.

"At least you could say, 'I told you so.'"

Dorothy rolled her eyes and went back to rolling out dough.

Jack entered the kitchen and quickly sensed the somber mood. "You guys have been talking about Frank, haven't you?"

"What do you think of him, Jack?" Beth asked.

"I think there's more to the story. Something she didn't tell us."

"What did she tell you?" Dorothy asked.

"That Frank had to pay the mill where he worked because the boss had it in for him and blamed him for something he didn't do."

"Does that sound right to you?"

"How should I know? I've never worked anywhere except for Pat. He blamed Carter once for losing a wrench that Pat didn't put away. It didn't matter until the baler picked up the wrench out in the field. It broke the baler. So yeah, I guess it makes sense. It could happen like that."

"How did this missing wrench get out in the field?" Dorothy asked.

"Somebody, either Pat or Carter, left it lying on top of the baler. It should have been in the toolbox. They figure it fell off and got picked up."

"Did Pat make Carter pay for the damage?"

"No. But he won't let him forget about it."

"Sounds like Pat. He enjoys holding something over another person," Dorothy said. "I've never worked in any factory. Never worked anywhere except as a housekeeper for a few months before I married your dad. But I have sense enough to know that a big company can't make a worker pay for some accident. When my uncle was an engineer on the P.S.& N., he derailed a train. They tried hard to make him responsible for it. It turned out some switchman got drunk and caused the wreck. It took a while for it all to come out. The point is, when something bad happens like that, everybody wants to blame someone else."

"What was P. S...what did you say?" asked Jack.

"The Pittsburgh, Shawmut, and Northern," Dorothy said proudly. "The line was not doing well. Any accident brought it closer to bankruptcy. Even with that, they didn't try to make anybody pay for the damages. They just fired the switchman."

"So, Frank should have just been fired?" Beth asked.

"Right," Dorothy said. "But if he did something deliberately, that's a different story."

"So, you think Frank did something on purpose that got him in trouble."

"I'm guessing. My bet is that he lost his temper, got frustrated and smashed something up. He might have been a little bit drunk too. Or hell, it might all be made up."

Chapter Twenty-Three

When Sunday came, Beth had her things in a few cardboard boxes inside the bedroom door. Doubts clouded the thrill of moving in the direction of her dreams. Carol had left in the same way, and it had not turned out well. The sad-puppy look in Mary's eyes did not help. The three younger sisters shared a bed all their lives. There would be a hole in Mary's life now, and Beth struggled, knowing that the younger kids had always needed something from the older ones.

The life she had grown to hate didn't look so bad. Here, she at least knew how things were. The people she met and mixed with at school and at Carson's were different. She didn't know why they talked about having things, doing things, and going places. Their lives were exciting compared to hers. She could not be like that. It was out of reach. Those people going to something; her getting away from something. Big difference.

Was she like the caterpillar turning into a butterfly, something new and beautiful at hand? No. If a view like that came along, she would not spread her wings and fly. That was too much to hope for. Getting out of where she was would do. She would not end up the way Carol had, like the boy in the old story, who flew too close to the sun and came crashing down. One who escaped had to be cautious.

She opened a window and gazed into the panorama to the west of the farm. Endlessly rolling blue hills. Like lines of poetry, the hills called to her with the mystical promise of a better life. Her soul could not reach them. One day, God willing, her children would get there.

Curt and Polly's visit had a purpose this time. Like they were absconding with Beth, feeling awkward, they dared not linger. The back seat of their Mercury sedan was clean but had a curious smell that Curt told her came from sitting in the sun too long. "Cars that are kept in a garage don't get quite this bad. We don't have room on our lot for a garage." Their home seemed even tinier than she had noted. Seeing it and living in it were different things. Out-of-doors, there was no privacy. In every direction Beth looked, a window or sidewalk or another family's house intruded. They didn't drive anywhere for pleasure. The car went mainly to the grocery store. Curt only drove to work on days with bad weather.

"You need to spend some time getting used to the place before you take on any chores, dear, but I'll take all the help I can get with cleanliness." The tidy, well-decorated room reminded Beth of a dollhouse. She could hang her clothes in a closet for the first time in her life, and Aunt Polly expected it. Not only were there no roaches, they would not tolerate a single housefly. The swatter came out at the first buzzing sound, and Aunt Polly was relentless. It was the first chore that she let Beth help with; the kindly woman took vicious delight in killing pests. "No mice sneak into this house, Beth. They wouldn't dare!"

Beth learned that her favored aunt and uncle were painfully meticulous and thrifty. When meals were served, the portions were adequate, never generous. Second helpings were not available. If Polly baked two dozen cookies, she knew when each one would be eaten and by whom. The couple knew how many pieces of dinnerware they had. Food never left the dining room. The tiny kitchen got back to perfect order when the meals were over. Beth picked up the rules by observing them and never asked for something she did not see them enjoying. Baths were taken before bed and each person cleaned the tub when they finished. A bathroom with a toilet and tub punctuated the lack of it in her family's farmhouse. How her parents could live on and on without that modern convenience bewildered her. Indoor plumbing outranked beer in any sane person's mind.

Carol had warned her that she would be expected to attend church services. It seemed a small price to pay. The next Sunday, she tagged along. Their home sat close enough to be in the church's shadow early on a sunny morning. The people were friendly enough but formal. The inside of the church felt cavernous, and the organ music was truly impressive. She had never felt more out of place. Aunt Polly sensed her discomfort as they were walking home from the church. "Beth dear, I know it is different here than what you're used to. In a town, people must get along with one another. There is a lot of give-and-take. Having good manners is important. And we go to church because the Bible is true."

Her aunt and uncle were like something out of a fairy tale, warm and supportive of her. Beth refused to find the fault that Carol had reported chafing under. After all, the two children Curt and Polly had raised were living in far-off California. Albert had been valedictorian of his high school and college class. He had entered the Army Air Corps after Pearl Harbor and flown bombing missions in Europe. He had survived being shot down and held as a prisoner of war. Then he had gone to a prestigious law school and become became a lawyer. When the war in Korea broke out, he had been called back to active service to train navigators.

They didn't say it so much, but a small town in Pennsylvania was not good enough for accomplished people. Albert had taken his sister along to the West. They were Beth's cousins. She could barely recall a few small interactions with them. They were older, so she didn't really know them. Beth only learned about Albert's heroic life because she saw photographs and asked questions. Beth and her siblings had no chance of becoming what Curt and Polly's children were. Curt and Polly had done something right. Beth wanted to know if they knew some secret.

"You grew up with Dad on the farm, right Aunt Polly?" Beth and Polly were sitting on the porch swing on Sunday afternoon, with Curt napping in an overstuffed chair. They could hear his choppy snoring through the open window.

"Yes, dear. Your grandfather sent me to Normal School in Slippery Rock, and I became a teacher."

"Normal School?"

"Yes, dear."

"Was there an Abnormal School?"

"Yes, Beth, that's where they sent girls like you," Polly tried to hide her smile. Like Dorothy, she was a terrible liar.

"Seriously?"

"Yes. That is what they called them. It isn't normal in the usual sense. It means more like a standard school. They taught teachers how to teach."

"How long did you teach?"

"Only until I met Curt, and we were married. Not long."

"Tell me why you and Dad are so different?"

"That is a hard question."

"What is so hard about it?"

"Well, I know that we are different. Why we are, I don't know. I have never thought much about it. I am five years older than your dad. I can't say we grew up together. We had the same parents, the same house and school. I thought him being male made all the difference until I started teaching. Some kids were easy to teach, some were not.

"So the smarter ones were easy to teach?"

"Not exactly. It wasn't so much their ability to learn as their willingness to learn. Most of the girls were willing to learn. Some of the boys didn't care. They thought school was a waste of their time. The boys cared more about what the other boys thought of them than what the teacher thought of them. Your dad had that problem.

"Ward had to prove himself. Most men are like that. They don't want to prove themselves in school. They always compare themselves to each other. The boy who could run faster, hit a ball farther, things like that. Maybe because your dad had two brothers close to him, he never stopped trying to best them and kept doing it with other men once he grew up."

"Is that why Dad became a boxer?"

"He never became much of a boxer. Lots of young men were trying to break into that. It was a big sport like baseball, if you can believe it. He got a lot of training. He left the farm for a long time. He met your mom in those days."

"So, finding a husband or wife is what changed your life and his?"

"He didn't talk much about his boxing. I think the people who got him into it were looking for the next great fighter. Lots of young men tried it. Only the ones with a lot of talent got to make a living from it. Your dad was always tough, but I think there is more to it than being tough."

"He talks about it when he gets drunk."

"You see, there is a difference between your dad and his brothers. Your dad began drinking, his brothers didn't. Come to think of it, your Uncle Telly almost became an Olympic swimmer. I bet you never heard that."

"No. Dad never talks about our uncles."

"I know. Your Uncle Marvin lives here. You've probably never met him."

"You're right. I have heard the name, but never seen him. Why is that?"

"Him and your father don't see eye to eye. Marvin won't have anything to do with your dad. Maybe you didn't notice, but there is not a single bar in this town. Your folks wouldn't like it here."

"Can I meet Uncle Marvin?"

"It's probably better if you don't."

"Why do you say that?"

"He won't see you as a separate person from your dad. He'll assume you are like him."

"That reminds me of Pat Hughes."

"How so?"

"Pat has something he holds against his sister, so he won't speak to her or let his kids speak to her kids. They live right beside each other."

"You mean Beverly Hooker?" Polly asked.

"Yep, and since we are friendly with Pat, we don't talk to his sister and her family."

"Why are you supposed to feel that way?"

"All of my life, I have heard that the Hookers were no good and that we should stay away from them."

"That's the way kids are. Haven't you seen that among your friends at school? If you're her friend, you can't be my friend, things like that?"

"Yes. I guess I've been that way myself."

"I'm glad to hear you're being honest about it," Polly said, turning on the swing to face her niece more squarely. "I remember them from before they had that fight, whatever it was."

"So you don't know what the problem is either?"

"It must have to do with the land. They both grew up there. I assume Beverly thought she had something coming to her because Pat got the farm."

"That's what Mom thinks too," Beth said.

"I saw that kind of thing all the time when I taught school. It's the way children behave. We expect children to be like that. When people grow up, they should know better."

"I have heard people say that Pat and Beverly probably don't even remember what their fight was about. They hate each other, and they always will."

"You need to see what's really going on there, Beth. It's probably true that the inheritance wasn't fair. Only their dead parents know why Pat got the farm, and Beverly didn't. They should have tried to work things out so they could at least stay friendly. In most things like that, pride takes over. The bad feelings not only go on for the rest of their lives, their children inherit the poison. It's human nature."

"So, it's natural for people to act that way?" Beth asked.

"The pride is the thing. One side feels like they were shortchanged. They feel insulted."

"You mean they take it personally?"

"Yes! That's exactly what it is. You're a smart girl," Polly said, patting Beth on the knee affectionately. "It's the old Mom-likes-you-better-than-me story. Who knows, Pat and Beverly's father might not have been in his right mind when he wrote his will. Who knows if he even left a will? Let's say he did, and it all got left to Pat. Beverly could have said something nasty to Pat. Maybe they never got along well to start with. She says something mean, and so he says something mean, trying to defend himself. They stomp off and never speak to each other again. All the possibilities of being good neighbors and helping each other down through all those years go up in smoke. You see how it might be? Pat maybe never intended harm to Beverly, and she maybe never intended harm to Pat. Years, not just years, generations of hard feelings, because of one small moment of anger."

"Why wouldn't one of them see what their hard feelings would do and say they were sorry?"

Polly shook her head and shrugged. "It's what we call sibling rivalry. Have you heard the term?"

"It's when kids don't get along with each other."

"Yep. It's the oldest story in the Bible. Well, one of the oldest," Polly stated, matter-of-factly. "But it doesn't have to be like that. I think neither Pat nor Beverly knew anything about forgiving. All those years the strongest idea in their heads was that the other had done them wrong. For some reason, hatred takes hold. It doesn't let go. The wrong notions that people have in their heads need to be replaced with better ideas. That's why I became a teacher."

"You mean you taught that stuff? I thought you taught reading and arithmetic and so on."

"The subjects kids learn in school matter. That's what I got paid for. But the worst ignorance that people have is...well, the kind of ignorance that lets a man live next to his sister and hate her for no good reason. You need to keep coming to church with me. It's the best way to learn about that ignorance."

Beth sat quietly, wondering if Aunt Polly knew about her harsh words with Carol.

Chapter Twenty-Four

"You'll have to get over being so touchy about Frank. It won't help things any," Dorothy said. She was sitting on the porch with Carol and Bonnie, enjoying the evening of a pleasant day.

"That's easy for you to say. I might go crazy waiting for him to get things back the way they should be. I shouldn't be eating and living here without paying you some kind of rent or board or something," Carol said.

"You're our daughter. We don't think like that when it comes to you and Debby."

"I wish there were a phone here," Carol said. "Don't you think we should have one, Bonnie?"

"Actually, I was wondering about that, Mom. If I pitched in, say, half of the cost, couldn't we get one?" Bonnie said.

"I think your dad might like the idea. I don't feel all that well, with being pregnant again. Some of the guys your dad works with say babies shouldn't be delivered at home anymore. We have hospital insurance now, so there wouldn't be any cost. Getting there is the problem. A phone might be good for that. We could call someone to take me."

Neither Carol nor Bonnie commented further on the idea. Another sibling seemed outrageous to them. Jeff was still in diapers and might still be when the new child came. Debby could be too. Surely, Frank would have his family back with him before that.

"Tell you what girls, you get the phone in your name, Bonnie, and I will slip you half of the bill every month," said Dorothy. "We'll let on like it's yours alone. Calls to Grove City will be long-distance, so there can't be many of them, and you'll have to pay for them, Carol."

Bonnie already knew that the cost of installation would be around thirty-five dollars. She had thought it over. She would surely be stuck with the entire cost, despite what her mother said. And she could imagine big, long-distance bills if Carol continued to live with them; she would call Frank a lot. But having a phone would make her feel more like other people. Bonnie smiled. Calling Allen would be free.

After breakfast the next day, Polly's telephone rang. After a short conversation, she smiled at Beth as she hung up the phone.

"I told you I could find you a job. Would you like to work in a grocery store or a car dealership?"

"I kind of know the grocery store thing. What would I do at the car place?"

"To begin with, you would do housekeeping. Lots of people come and go looking at the cars. They want the place to be neat and tidy. Lots of window glass, the showroom, and the cars. Who knows what else?"

"It's so exciting." Beth was shifting on her feet, bouncing up and down. "Which job do you think I should take, Aunt Polly?"

Polly smiled, "I'm glad you're so eager. I think if you had a tail, you'd be wagging it. You may be able to get both jobs. I've known the people in those businesses for years. Why don't we start with the market? Once you get settled in there, and if you have the extra time, you can try Long's Dodge."

"I can't wait. Thank you so much, Aunt Polly."

The A & P was only a few minutes down the street. She had walked it before, but now that she would become a part of it, Beth saw the town with fresh eyes. The street contained a series of shops, a movie theater, two cafes, a dentist's office, a legal firm, two barber shops, a hairdresser and much more. Polly introduced Beth to her friend Grace Miller, the manager. She acted formally, like the people at the church. In short order, Beth had a white apron with the embroidered A & P logo across her bosom.

"Be sure you pay attention to what you're doing, don't rush, but work steadily. Smile at the customers," Polly whispered to her before she left the store. Beth spent her first day stamping prices on cans and stacking them on shelves.

Grace seemed to know enough about Beth and didn't bother her. Beth knew enough to face the labels of the cans properly. Grace came by every half-hour or so and nodded her approval. Polly appeared at lunchtime with a sandwich for Beth, who didn't realize she was hungry until she saw her aunt's smiling face. "You can bring your lunch with you from now on. I wanted to come and check on you anyway."

"I'm doing fine, Aunt Polly. Thank you again, so much," Beth said.

The first three days were constant with stocking shelves, sweeping floors, and dusting the less busy aisles where things like school supplies and stationery were kept. Beth seated herself in the little room behind the meat counter, eating her lunch and chatting through the open door with the butcher, a swarthy-looking man they called Louie. He was showing her how to weigh and wrap meat for the customers when she heard the familiar voice of Frank Parks. "Let me have a pound of that sliced roast beef," he sang out.

Immediately, Beth remembered how Frank had winked at her the first day she met him, though it seemed long ago now. He would be happy to see her. She ducked into the bathroom to quickly check her face in the mirror. She straightened her apron and stepped up close to the meat counter, and caught Frank's eye right away. "Hey, stranger," Beth said.

Frank's mouth dropped open, then quickly turned up in a grin. "Well, how about that, Louie, it's my sister-in-law from Parker."

"You Carol's sister?" Louie asked, looking surprised.

Beth nodded, smiling. "I've only been working here since Monday. Do you come in often, Frank?"

"A couple times a week at least. I eat a lot of cold cuts, you know, living by myself." Frank's eyes fell in humility.

"How are things going for you?" Beth wanted to ask about the prospect of getting Carol and him back under the same roof, but it might be hard for Frank to talk about it in Louie's presence.

"I'm working a lot. I suppose you're staying with your aunt?" Frank asked.

"That's right. I plan to be working a lot too. Maybe get a second job even."

"We should talk sometime. Kinda catch-up, you know?"

"I'd like that."

"Okay. Bye for now," Frank said, with an extended gaze into Beth's face that carried a message. Louie caught it from the corner of his eye. Whatever Frank was thinking, Louie did not approve.

After Frank walked back to the front part of the store, turning the corner and out of earshot, Louie made even longer eye contact with Beth. "You should not be friendly with that guy."

"Oh, Louie, he's practically family."

"I don't see your sister and baby in long time. They don't come in with Frank anymore."

"That's because they don't live with him right now. They are with my folks on our farm in Parker. It's only temporary; Frank had some kind of money problem."

"People who gamble maybe have money problems," Louie said in a low voice.

"I'm sorry Louie, what did you say?" Beth tried to listen closely to Louie and ask a question if needed. Louie came from Italy after the war and had an accent. Beth liked the way he talked.

"I say, 'Is not my business,'" with a dismissive and final tone.

Beth didn't press him further. She didn't want anything to dull the fine feeling she got when she talked to Frank. She knew she had a schoolgirl crush on him. Things like that were harmless. Didn't every girl have affection for someone?

Another week passed and Grace Miller asked Beth to begin working Friday evenings and Saturdays. "The weekends are busiest, especially at this end of the store. People get their Sunday roasts and chickens. You'll need to stay and help us close at eight o'clock both nights. I know you mentioned getting a second job, but I can give you more work than you need, and you won't have to bring lunch or dinner, not if you're satisfied with what is available here."

"That sounds good, Mrs. Miller," Beth said excitedly, trying not to act like a happy dog again.

"I hope you like working for Louie; he's your new boss."

"Louie is great; we get along fine."

Beth enjoyed Grove City. She had little spare time, but Aunt Polly thought she should get to know the place. With more to the town than the few blocks between their house on Poplar Street and the A & P, she walked around taking it in. Everything that met her eyes suggested a good life. The streets were clean, and the lawns were well-kept. What passed for a lawn on the farm was a patch of short weeds that stretched into a pasture field kept lower by the grazing of their cattle. The shops were welcoming, and they held a variety of inviting goods that made Parker seem bland. The streets had benches under awnings so that shoppers could sit and chat.

She saw a young couple seated on one of those benches, chatting. They were probably college students. She could see they were enchanted with one another. She imagined herself sitting there one day soon, with an exciting boy who would be her first kiss. The idea of clean romance without the specter of a run-down farm and poor-looking family as her background kept her heart singing as she went about her work. The faces of the men and boys who passed by her on the street signaled unanimous approval. Walking home one evening, a boy she had seen the day before, walking with a girl, nodded shyly. As he passed by, he said, "Wait, wait."

She stopped, and he backed up his steps until he could face her directly. He moved within a few inches of her face, gazed longingly into her eyes, and said softly, as if he were losing his breath, "Wow."

A giggle escaped her. She hoped the dim light would hide her blush. She had no idea how to respond, and the boy said nothing more. She walked on toward Aunt Polly's house. She kicked herself. The opportunity to meet a guy had slipped away because she was shy. She wished Carter was around so she could ask him what to do.

Hoping something like that would happen again, she now walked with eyes wide open for possibilities. The next evening, Frank Parks was sitting on one of the benches, apparently waiting for her.

"Do you have a little time now, Beth?" His voice was a showcase of sorrow, as if he were in need.

"Sure, Frank." She sat down and, assured now that her face had something wonderful to offer, looked straight into his eyes. Frank shifted closer to her on the bench, his knee settling against her thigh. She knew she should move away from the contact, but it was exciting, and just the sort of thing she needed to overcome if she were ever to stop being a bashful country girl.

"It hasn't been easy for me lately. I've been trying to get ahead. Every time I turn around, there's another expense."

"I know you lost that good job at the mill. Where have you been working?"

"At another mill. It's the feed mill. You know, cattle feed, pig feed, chicken feed. That's how they pay me; it's chicken feed."

"You mean, it's not much."

"About the same as you make in the store. It's okay for you, living with your aunt and all. A guy can't support a family on it. Babies cost a lot."

"Aunt Polly knows a lot of people in town. Maybe she could help you."

"I don't think Curt would let her. He doesn't like me."

"I didn't know that. Why doesn't he like you?"

"It's more of the small-town thing. He's got a lot of friends. It's like a club; they stick together."

"I see."

"Yeah. If I don't get a better situation, well…I just don't know." He reached out for her hand, and she gave it to him. He squeezed it, and the message it sent to her brain was unlike anything she had ever felt. "I miss Carol and Debby," Frank said.

Beth could see his eyes were misty, and she feared he might weep. "Oh, Frank," she said. "Can't you get down to see them on weekends?"

"I don't have a good car. It's ok around town here, but it's like twenty-three miles to the farm. I don't trust it to go that far. If it breaks down, how will I pay to get it fixed?"

"Yeah, that's tough. Have you tried to get a better job?"

"You didn't grow up here, so I guess you wouldn't know. In small towns like this, people know each other. If one boss has it in for you, he tells the other guys. I have to take what I can get. I'm gonna keep trying, though."

"What can I do to help?"

"Hey, you've got your own life to live. I can't be leaning on you."

"Frank, we're family. We have to help each other as best we can."

"Have you ever been lonely, Beth?"

"Everyone's lonely from time to time."

"I guess that's true. When you've had the company of a woman, being a father, well, it's different. Having people who depend on you makes you feel like a man."

Beth didn't know how to answer him. She felt annoyed yet honored. Instinct told her that men didn't show weakness. Not even her kid brothers did, because deep down, it mattered whether a man felt like a man. Didn't she want to feel like a woman? Men, her brothers, and the guys in school all acted self-assured, especially when others could see they were not.

"Maybe being around you can help me feel manly again," Frank said. "Remember when I came to the farm that first time? Everyone sort of looked up to me. I had a car and a motorcycle. I felt good then. Not now."

"So, things like that make you feel good?" Beth asked.

"I had Carol, too. That's what did it."

"You still have Carol."

"Sure doesn't seem like it. Not with her so far away."

"I'm sorry about your situation, Frank. I better get home. Aunt Polly will wonder where I am."

"Sitting here and talking to you has helped me a lot, Beth. I'm grateful."

"You're welcome. I want to be helpful."

"Could you maybe hug me before you go?"

"Sure."

They embraced, and Beth let him hold it longer than she thought was proper. She loosened her arms. Frank hesitated, then slowly followed suit. "Thanks again, Beth," Frank said.

Beth felt light-headed as she resumed her walk toward Aunt Polly's place. The delightful sensation of being wrapped up in Frank's arms stayed with her. Maybe it could happen again.

She bathed quietly, getting ready for bed. Even the soap and water didn't remove that warm sensation. The bathroom door had a full-length mirror. As she toweled herself, she took a long look. She noticed her nipples were standing out. They got that way when she was chilly, but she was not chilly. It was the opposite. She wondered what it might feel like if Frank were holding her now, undressed. As she wrapped herself up in the blankets, she imagined being next to Frank under the covers. It was a long time before she fell asleep.

Chapter Twenty-Five

There was plenty of time in the morning for her to talk to Aunt Polly, and she came close to telling her about the encounter with Frank. She decided not to. Frank wouldn't want her to share his plight with anyone. Having Frank on her mind made her unusually cheerful, humming as she helped Aunt Polly take care of the flower bed out front. The postman came at 10:30, and Aunt Polly took the mail straight from his hands. "Oh my, there is a letter for you dear, from home."

It had not occurred to Beth that any of her siblings would bother to write to her. She expected to accompany Curt and Polly when they made their next visit, which was coming up Sunday. She understood why when she read the letter. It was from Richard.

Dear Sis,

I doubt that anything will be said about it when you guys visit, but Carol and Bonnie had a fight. It was bad. Bonnie blamed Carol for flirting with Allen. It didn't look like flirting to me, maybe girls see things differently. Everyone here, especially mom, thinks that Bonnie and Allen will get married soon.

Carol is grumpy all the time. Remember the fight you two had before you left? You should be careful what you say to Carol. Have you seen Frank? She'll probably ask if you have or if you know anything about him. She thinks Frank should hitch a ride with Aunt Polly so he could visit. I don't think Frank likes Curt and Polly. I don't think they like him either. I cannot remember them talking about him any time they visited. They knew Frank and Carol were together, so why didn't they?

Anyway, Carter has a car and a girlfriend now. It's Trish Myers. She is trying to talk Carter into getting a better job. They both say that you won't have any trouble finding a boyfriend in Grove City. You know everyone here will be asking you about that.

Sincerely, Richard

P.S.: Bonnie is getting a telephone put in here soon. She says calling you will be long-distance and that costs too much.

Beth read through the letter several times. The part about Frank and her aunt and uncle not liking each other seemed to be correct. They never said anything about him even though they knew all about the situation.

Polly had been having lunch early so that Beth could eat with her before she went to work. As they sipped their iced tea, Beth gathered her courage, fearing that asking about Frank might be a touchy subject.

"How well do you guys know Frank Parks?"

"He grew up here. We've known his family for as long as I can remember."

"Do you like Frank?"

"Did I say I knew him well? I've known about him since he was born. That doesn't mean I know him."

Polly had never answered her with quite that tone before. Beth got the sense that questions about Frank were not welcome. Polly knew about the letter, but not what it contained. Beth thought that if she asked more questions, Polly would sense that the letter pertained to Frank. Maybe she should simply ask Frank about it.

Beth reported to Louie at noon. "You can watch while I take lunch break," he said. "Every day, we can do that. I like regular routine on job. You like regular routine?"

"I suppose so. I didn't have a routine on my first job, I just did whatever they said. Some days stock, some days check out, always staying busy. Carson's didn't like it if I was idle."

"It's good for person to work hard. Staying busy makes day go by faster. You should tell that to your friend, Frank."

"He's my brother-in-law, Louie," Beth said.

"He was in earlier today. Got some meat. Expensive stuff. I think man having hard time would buy jumbo and wieners. Not Frank. He buys steak, roast beef, ham, Swiss cheese," Louie said.

"Is there something wrong with Frank?" Beth asked.

"I hear things. That not my business."

"Tell me, Louie. I like him. My whole family likes him." Beth said, knowing it was not entirely true.

"He is, how you say, 'good time Charlie.'"

"I've heard that before. What does it mean?"

"Is man always looking for fun and games. Man who not like work."

"He is working at that feed mill by the railroad tracks. I know they carry a lot of heavy sacks there. It's hard work. I was on a farm, you know. I've seen hard work."

"Frank have job at big mill, Cooper-Bessemer. Make good money. They fire him. Loafer."

"Do you know for sure that's true?" Beth asked, sternly.

"I say too much. Not my business. They tell me when I come here, mind your own business. There plenty men like him in Italy. 'Buon Vivere.'"

"Whatever you say, Louie."

"Thing is, Beth. You are pretty girl. Plenty of boys around town. You could find one of them."

"Louie, Frank is my sister's husband. I am not after him."

"Maybe not. He is after you."

"Why would you say that?"

"I can tell you like him. Not just brother-in-law. I hear in your voice."

"Isn't family important? Shouldn't I like my sister's husband?"

"So, you admit you interested in Frank."

"Louie," Beth said, shortly. She turned away when a customer came close. They worked together weighing and wrapping meat and cheese, but Beth's movements were tense, and she knew Louie could tell.

"I am sorry, Beth. I think that if you meet nice boy, one same age, Frank not look so good to you."

Beth knew Louie was right. But it could not be wrong to like Frank. She didn't expect he would ever want to be anything more than a friendly relative. She certainly would not try to kiss him or anything like that.

"Let me tell you something. Girls in my country know something American girls not know."

"Really Louie, what's that?" Beth said.

"You have something make you more beautiful than make up, more beautiful than nice clothes or perfume or jewelry. It cost you nothing. You need to learn use it."

"Tell me, Louie, what is it?"

"Smile," Louie said.

"A smile?" Beth said, skeptically.

"Yes, yes. Strong man get weak like puppy dog when pretty girl smile at him. Smile better than makeup, do more than expensive wardrobe or curly hair style. Not just smile. People all smile when happy. Learn to smile at man you like. Smile say everything."

"I never heard that before." She pondered his idea. People smiled unconsciously, most of the time. To deliberately smile at someone took things to a higher level. She should have known that sooner.

"Trust me. You look in mirror and smile. That good. But not like smile you give man when you want be his girl. That kind of smile hard to fake. You learn to fake loving smile, you be movie star.

"Smile with eyes, mouth and heart. Man know you like him. Be dressed in flour sack, knotted hair, no lipstick, barefoot, smile make you beautiful anyway."

"So, you say if I smile at boys, I'll attract them?"

"If you meet nice boy, you feel too shy to talk, smile. Smile better than talk."

"Thanks for the advice, Louie, I might try that. My mother never told me that. My sisters neither."

"You only girl I tell this to. Some things you only learn by living. Italians very romantic people. We know these things."

The renewed loneliness Charlotte felt since breaking off with Carter was more bearable than what she had experienced with other guys. Besides Luther, which lasted nine years, they had all been short-lived. She enjoyed Carter more than the others and would have been happy to go on with it indefinitely. Turning him loose was the right thing. If Luther had not disappeared, she might never have stopped that affair. The mystery of the belt buckle began to fade. Had she seen that buckle sooner, she would have shared it with Sheriff Wyant. It had been so long. Luther was gone for good. Why she had never questioned Luther about sporting a belt buckle about motorcycles when he didn't ride one was a mystery to her as well. Maybe it was not the same buckle. Maybe he got his from a rummage sale too. Without the shock of seeing Luther's distinctive souvenir, she may not have mustered the strength to end it with Carter.

She was getting used to her lot in life, learning how to cope with it. That Saturday was her and Kenny's wedding anniversary. She made a special dinner for him, mostly because of her guilt, certain that she would not pass up the next opportunity to have sex with some other male. Being unfaithful to a good man like Kenny was doubly wrong.

Her menstrual cycle was a day late, so it was risky to coax him to bed. She did it anyway. On such a special day, he would expect it. She exaggerated her excitement and pleasure, having learned early on that letting the man know you enjoyed him was good for his ego, and she had so much to atone for. As pleasant as their weekend was, Kenny drove off again on Sunday evening. This time was different though. She had heard someone say that if one pretended long enough, they could change the way they felt. She resolved to give that a try. The days Kenny was home should be joyous, not the other way around. It was foolish to carry on the way she had for so long. If she ruined her marriage, she could end up growing old alone. Some people could handle lifelong singleness. She would not survive that. Being childless, she felt invalid. It would be much worse without Kenny. She recalled the suicides that had happened locally.

Chapter Twenty-Six

"You need to behave yourself, Carter," Trish Myers told her new boyfriend. "I like you, and you're a good kisser, but I only share so much." Carter withdrew his hand from the front of her blouse. She had let him undo one button and put his hand inside. He caressed the smooth, warm skin under the bottom of her bra.

They were parked on top of the hill overlooking the farm. The movie they had gone to was not compelling enough to keep them from necking in the darkened theater, and certain that Trish would allow more intimacy, Carter drove to a private spot, a place he might rightly say he owned. Assuring Trish that nobody would bother them there, they climbed into the back seat.

"You're teasing me," Carter replied.

"That's a good one. Teasing you? How am I teasing you?"

"You look so terrific; how can I keep from wanting to touch?"

"Flattery will get you." Trish paused for effect. "Another kiss."

Their lips met once more, and Trish broke away gently. Quickly undoing the remaining buttons on her blouse, she opened it and slid her bra up over her breasts, and twisting a little on her seat, presented them to Carter with all their perky splendor.

"I take it back. You're no tease," Carter said. He cupped them each in his hand, squeezing tenderly. "Very nice," he breathed.

"Have you ever done this with anyone else?" she asked.

"Oh sure," Carter said.

"And I suppose you've gone the whole way with someone too?"

"Many times," he said.

"Uh-huh, with whom?"

"That'd be telling," Carter said. "Just like I won't tell anyone you let me do this, I can't tell you who I did it with. That's kinda the deal."

"I think we both know that guys tell each other what they've done."

"I have not told anybody what I did. I wish I could."

He sounded so sincere and convincing that Trish believed him or wanted to believe him. Saying that he wished he could tell dampened her ardor, and she pulled her bra back down.

"Do you think Bonnie and Allen have done it?" Trish said.

"Probably. The Carrs are a pretty rough bunch."

"Funny you say that. Aren't you Mettses a rough bunch?"

"I don't know. Do you think we are?"

"Carter, you know you guys are. Bonnie knows it. I've heard her say that."

"But you said that you liked me."

"I do."

"You don't know how many times I wanted to ask you to go with me. Since like seventh grade. I couldn't work up the courage to ask you," Carter said.

"Probably a good thing. I might have snubbed you. I didn't start liking boys until eighth grade." They both chuckled.

"What is different now?"

"I am more mature, I guess."

"Do you remember how me and Barb Kinney were such good friends all through grade school and part of junior high?"

"I do remember. I was jealous."

"Jealous of her?"

"Yeah."

"Wow, now you tell me."

"Wait. You liked both of us?"

"I think I have had a crush on most of the girls in school at one time or another."

"Me too. The boys I mean. So, what about it?"

"I went home with Nick Baker one weekend to work for him. We carried firewood into his basement and pitched the manure out of his horse barn, stuff like that. He and Georgia are good friends with my folks. They meet up at the American House a lot."

"Yeah, so?"

"I didn't know where Barb lived. Turned out she lived on the same road as the Bakers. Nick and I were outside working, and Barb came by in the back seat of her dad's car. She saw me. I saw her. I waved, but she didn't wave back. She looked surprised. The next Monday at school, she asked me if I was working for Nick Baker. I told her I did that from time to time."

"And?"

"She snubbed me. She never spoke to me again."

"Never? You're kidding."

"Nope. Just like that, I went from being her best friend to being nobody. I'll never forget how the look on her face changed."

"Aw, Carter, you poor guy," Trish gushed. "What a bitch. I didn't know she was like that."

"I guess she found out that I came from a rough bunch."

"I know what it is. Nick and Georgia aren't married. Not really. It's what they call a common-law marriage. If they live together for seven years, the law considers them husband and wife."

"They had two kids."

"All the same. Decent folks don't live like that. Barb probably figured that if your family were friends with the Bakers, you weren't decent either. Barb's dad is a big shot, a township supervisor, a lodge member. They have their noses high in the air."

"Well, the way my folks drink, is that decent?"

"You are not your folks, Carter." She took him by the chin and glared intently into his eyes. "Do you hear me?"

"I may as well be."

"No. Why would you say that?"

"It's another story. It happened the day I got this car. A guy in town had it for sale. He lived just across the street from Ellie Sims. You know her?"

"Not that well. She goes to school in Lake City. Her house is just over the school district line. We hung out together at church camp one summer."

"Anyway, she was waiting for me as I was leaving the house. I delivered groceries to her neighbor every week for a while. She came out and sat on the porch when I was there. She waved and smiled once or twice. I wasn't that sure she liked me, but there she was with her thumb out, like she wanted to hitch a ride. So, I picked her up. I figured it was her way of asking me for a date. The way she looked at me, even as shy as I am, it was easy to ask. She said yes, and just like that, we were on for that night."

"See, other girls see you as a swell guy. Doesn't that prove it?" Trish asked. "Was she a lousy kisser? Is that why you asked me out?" Trish smiled big and batted her eyelashes coquettishly.

"The date never actually happened," Carter said. He looked out into the darkness as if trying to hide in it.

"Why not? Tell me."

"When I got to her house, she came out on the porch, looking like a million bucks. Hair and clothes really nice, makeup, everything. It made me feel so good. Just like when I come to pick you up. You're fresh and spiffy. I'm almost scared to touch you, you look so perfect. You smell good, and when I take your hand, it's really special. Like a dream come true.

"I never got to take Ellie's hand. Her mother came out on the porch, right behind her. She got her nose right up in my face. She said for me to leave. Said she knew who I was and where I came from. She said I wasn't taking Ellie anywhere, not that night or any other night. She said if I even spoke to Ellie again, she'd have the constable on me."

Trish's mouth hung open. "She actually said that stuff?"

Carter nodded, and Trish saw his eyes were glistening.

"How can anyone be that cruel?" Trish paused, wanting to let him have her breasts again. He needed comfort. Wasn't that what her breasts were for? "So, how did Ellie react?" Trish finally said.

"She started to cry. Said she was sorry."

They sat in silence for what seemed like a long time. It was not uncomfortable for them to sit quietly like that. In fact, it felt appropriate to be silent. Carter took in a deep breath, wanting Trish to hear him, as if the sigh that followed exposed all his counted sorrows. "So, you think I'm decent, Trish?"

"Would I take off my bra for a guy who wasn't?"

"Gosh, Trish, I didn't think of it that way."

They kissed again. "Trish," Carter asked. "Will you take it off again?"

"Oh, you bet I will."

Chapter Twenty-Seven

Dusk fell on a nearly deserted street as Beth stepped out of the A & P and began her walk toward Aunt Polly's house. A block ahead was one lone figure seated on a bench. As she approached, it became clear it was Frank Parks. Louie's advice about smiling at a man she wanted to attract had been ringing in her ears since she heard it. She was eager to try it. She had deliberately smiled at him before. That was before Louie's advice. Trying it on Frank was safe. Carol loomed between them like a stone wall. She gathered her eyes, mouth, and heart and beamed the warmest smile she could imagine right at him. An encouraged look came onto Frank's face, and Beth saw that Louie was right. A man responded to her face. She knew that what she was projecting was more than a smile.

"I hope you don't mind me waiting for you, Beth. I've been feeling lonely the past couple of days. My talk with you before made me feel so much better. Can you spare some time tonight?"

She didn't worry that Aunt Polly might wonder where she was. She had been leaving the store at erratic times, taking on more and more tasks and responsibilities since she began working with Louie. "Sure, Frank. We can sit here and talk for a good while."

"Actually," said Frank, "I thought I could show you my place. I need to know if it's big enough for Carol and Debby to move in. Maybe you can tell me what you think."

Beth could hardly contain herself. She wanted to be closer to Frank, to meet whatever need he had, to do anything that might get Carol and Debby back where they belonged.

"Of course, Frank. Show me where you live. You know what they say about a home needing a woman's touch."

"Oh, and you are very much a woman, Beth," Frank sighed.

It surprised Beth that Frank's place was so close. He had an apartment over a store. There were a lot of places like that in town. The steps up to it were narrow and steeper than most. Frank stepped aside and let her go up the steps ahead of him, acting the gentleman. After a few steps, Beth realized that with the steepness, Frank would be able to see halfway up her thigh. He placed his hand on the small of her back. "Careful now, if you lost your balance on these steps, it would be awful. There ought to be a handrail."

His hand on her back and his protective words about falling telegraphed a warm sensation that her whole body responded to. Her brothers might show concern for her, but not like what she felt with Frank. They reached the top. There was a wide step, a landing, and Frank came beside her to open the door.

"You don't lock it?" Beth queried.

"That bench is close enough that if anyone comes in, I can be behind them before they get three steps up. Besides, most people don't know there's an apartment up here. We've got privacy." Beth thought it strange when Frank turned and locked the door, but she said nothing. Did they need privacy?

"So, what do you think?" Frank asked.

"It is small. I've heard that the apartments in big cities are so little they call them cracker boxes. I think it's more about what people are used to. The bedroom I share with Bonnie and Mary isn't any bigger than your bedroom. To tell the truth, the inside toilet and running water make up for a lot when it comes to a place to live. Carol would be happy here."

"I don't know," Frank said. "It gonna be awfully hot up here in the summertime. I'll have to get a fan." He faced Beth and placed both of his hands on her shoulders. "Thanks for coming up. It means so much. It's like you trust me. A man needs that feeling." He drew her closer to him gently and waited for her response.

Beth remembered Carter's advice about how to get kissed. She looked into Frank's face. She could sense what was coming. No hint of shame intruded into her thoughts. The pleasure of the moment consumed her. She had no experience with boys and had never been kissed. Surely, a guy like Frank could show her how it was done. When his lips moved toward hers, she made them soft and a little gapped.

"You can't tell anyone I did that," Frank whispered. "You make me feel like a man, Beth. I've needed that, seems like forever."

Beth's head spun with confusion. Things had gone too far, but the kiss was so delightful. She did not move away or give any hint of discomfort. When his lips returned, he had an eagerness that sent a shockwave through her. He pressed harder. She moved her head in an encouraging motion. She felt his strong arm slip below her hips. In one smooth motion, Frank swept her up and carried her to the bed. She landed so smoothly on the rumpled blanket she could hardly believe it.

Before she even settled into the softness of the mattress, Frank had her dress up, exposing everything below her waist. A bolt of fear tore through her, reminiscent of the time a vicious dog had chased her up a neighbor's tree. But there was no tree to run to; she wasn't even sure she knew the way to the door if he did let her up.

"Oh Beth, you don't know how much I appreciate this. I need you so bad."

Beth remembered being so terrified in dreams she could not speak or move. She had always assumed that she would do better in a real-life situation. That confidence melted away. Nothing would stop what Frank wanted to do. She should protest, she should fight or run or scream. She did none of those things. Frank expertly slipped his fingers into her underwear and pulled them down. The cool air on her thighs and knees were soon replaced by Frank's knees as he opened her to his desire.

She expected pain, but that was minimal compared to the overwhelming shame she felt. Frank became something more animal than the sophisticated man she had so long admired. She gulped deeply when the worst of it came. Before she could gather her thoughts to say or do anything, Frank got off her. Something warm hit her thigh. She closed her eyes and wept. The weeping turned to sobbing and full-blown crying as Frank gathered himself. He brought a wad of toilet paper and wiped the spot on her thigh.

The strangest thing came to her mind. She had always wanted to see a penis, not merely a drawing of one. Now, one had invaded her, and she had never laid eyes on it, nor would she. That was another shameful thought, the kind of thinking that had resulted in her being here, wishing she could die, anything to escape what had happened.

Frank came and tried to cradle her in his arms and soothe her. Something had left him now that he had reached his goal. No longer clever or good-looking, Frank was some kind of brute, wretched and hideous. She remembered how Louie had warned her. She wished she could apologize to Louie. If she had heeded him, she would not be here now, swimming in regret. This unspeakable event must be hidden, like the body of Luther Banks had to be hidden.

Beth's anger boiled up now. Angry with Frank, even angrier with herself. As the rage grew, it gave her what she needed to move. She pushed Frank away with a force that amazed her. He retreated calmly to the shabby couch in the other room and lit a Lucky Strike.

When she had gathered her wits, she could tell that Frank had no more need of her and would be content if she left quickly. She stood up and looked in the bathroom mirror. It became clear that she would need some lie to tell Aunt Polly. She might get into the house and up to her room without much conversation, but the sticky spot on her dress and the redness on her face was something Polly would not look past. She had an inspiration. One of the meat cases at the store had a water leak. She and Louie avoided it because the mess could soak their clothing. She opened the spigot and splashed water onto herself until the offending part of her dress was drenched. She rubbed her face with the only washcloth she could see, obviously Frank's. As distasteful as touching it to her face was, she could not bring herself to ask him for a clean one. He probably didn't have another anyway.

She stepped as lightly as possible to the door. Clutching her purse under her arm she fumbled to unlock it and exited to the stairs. As she went through the door, she heard him mumble, "Thanks again, sis. I know you liked that as much as I did."

The tone of his voice turned her stomach, and she nearly retched. She held it in check until she reached the street, letting much of it hit her dress. The lie she needed formed in her mind.

"Oh, Aunt Polly, I hoped you would be in bed already," Beth said quietly.

Curt dozed on the couch while Polly was watching Alfred Hitchcock Presents. The room was dim. They watched TV with no other light. Beth liked that.

"It's a little too early for bed, dear. What's wrong?"

"I had an accident. My clothes are smelly. Even worse, I made Louie angry." She held her face down. She tried her best to seem authentic. Aunt Polly learning what really happened was unthinkable. "This piece of meat that I should have thrown away; I forgot about it and covered it by mistake. It sat for two days, starting to rot and mix in with good meat. I tried to clean it up so he wouldn't see, but I couldn't do it fast enough. He's fussy. We spent the last two hours cleaning the mess. He spoke sharply, and I cried. We had to dispose of a lot of good meat. He'll be short of beef tomorrow."

"There, there, Beth. Things like that happen. He'll get over it. It's a good thing you got it cleaned. I smell something a little rancid. You get your bath, and I'll soak the dress. It's not a big deal."

"Louie was starting to trust me. He's been treating me like a daughter."

"Of course he is, dear. He's a sweet man. He won't be mad for long. I'll bet he apologizes tomorrow." Polly said.

"Maybe. Oh, Aunt Polly, promise me you won't tell anyone. Louie says if people hear we let bad meat get out of hand, the A & P will lose customers."

"Let's get you and the dress washed up. We'll forget the whole thing. Poor girl."

Beth was astonished at how easily she had fooled her aunt. She hardly believed the story herself. As the bathwater ran, she sat in the tub, weeping, straining to keep her sobs in check. She found a spot of blood on her underwear the size of a quarter and her monthly two weeks past. Her friends mentioned that they spotted sometimes, so it wasn't likely to alarm Aunt Polly. She would not see the underwear anyway. Beth always hand-washed them.

She remembered how she, Bonnie, Roger and Carter had been forced to pretend they knew nothing about Luther Banks. Success depended on absolute disregard for the incident. They had conspired to behave like it had never happened. As hard as that was, as much guilt and anxiety as they suffered for the weeks following the man's death, they had acted cooly, being as curious as the other people concerning the man's strange disappearance. Such stealthy behavior was possible, she knew.

"Are you alright, dear?" Aunt Polly tapped lightly on the door. Beth had washed herself completely and had been sitting quietly in the water, trying her best to keep her emotions in check.

"Sorry, Aunt Polly. It feels so good to sit here. I almost fell asleep. I'm done. I'll be out soon, and I'm going straight to bed. Thanks for being so kind." She hoped the quiver in her voice would be deadened through the wooden door.

When she pulled the blankets up around her, she felt like a groundhog diving into its hole. She never realized how sacred her virginity was. She wanted to bury herself from the world and sleep for months until the unfamiliar sensations went away; until she could forget who Frank Parks was and scratch a layer of moist earth over her stupidity. She found no refuge. Sleep did not come. Water drained from her eyes as she recalled how Frank had gone from gentle to demanding, as if he had set some trap for her and captured her innocence. Frank's demeanor, when he had finished with her, filled her stomach with a baseball-sized knot. Morning would come, and she would have to pretend endlessly. Worst of all was the thought that she would have to treat Frank the same way she always had, or people would sense that some dramatic thing had come between them. If someone asked her, she would surely cry. She had made up a story about Louie to cover herself. It would be hard to look him in the eye, especially since he had tried to warn her. She ground her head into the pillow. "Oh, Louie," she whispered.

She stayed in bed until ten, letting Aunt Polly think she was sleeping in. She did not feel tired despite the restless night. She needed help with what had happened. She needed her siblings. Carter and Bonnie could help her know what to do. Calling them was out of the question. She didn't know the phone number. Even if she did, the cost of long-distance would not be justified. It was like some kind of miracle to hear Aunt Polly say, "I got a call from Bonnie this morning. She had to try out the new phone. Also, the only way she could tell how much a call to us would cost is to make one and wait for the bill."

"You must have some idea what calls cost, Aunt Polly," Beth said.

"I know the first three minutes are like a flat rate. After that, it goes so much every minute. If all you want to do is exchange information quickly, it's not too bad. Spend time chit-chatting, and you'll regret it. I think a three-minute call to Parker is gonna be less than a dollar."

"I don't need to talk to anyone that badly. Not today anyway. But give me the number. I should keep it in my purse. You never know," Beth said.

On her way to the store. Beth stepped into a phone booth. While she had never used a pay phone, she knew the process began with a dime. The operator took her number and demanded forty cents for the first three minutes.

"I'm sorry, operator, I only have the one dime."

When she hung up, the dime dropped down. She retrieved it and went into a coffee shop. She asked the annoyed cashier for ten dimes from a dollar and went back to the phone booth. She knew that morning would be the best time to catch Bonnie at home. It would have been exciting to make the call if there were some happy reason for it. It was Richard's voice on the home end.

"Hi Rich, how are things? I need to talk to Bonnie. Is she there?"

She could hear Bonnie chastising Richard for being so eager to answer the phone. "Give me that, Richard." Bonnie snapped.

"Hi, little sis, how's life in the big city?"

Beth immediately began to sob. "Oh, Bonnie, something awful has happened. And I don't know what to do."

"What is it, Beth?"

"I can't tell you over the phone. Is there any way you can come here?"

"Carter and I can come. He'll drive me."

"No. Carter can't find out about this. Can you get Allen to bring you down?"

"I probably can. He'll want to know why," Bonnie said.

"Tell him it's private, sister stuff. I can't talk about it this way. It's almost as bad as the other secret."

Bonnie knew the other secret meant the death of Luther Banks. It seemed like a lifetime ago. Surely, her sister didn't kill someone.

"I'll talk to him and see if we can work it out. He's on the day shift. If we come tomorrow evening, will that work?"

"Can you come tonight? I get off at eight."

"I'll see what I can do," Bonnie said. "I can call the plant and ask them to leave him a message."

"Thanks, Bonnie. I need your help."

Bonnie made two calls after Beth hung up. One to the Honky-Tonk, saying she might not make it to work, and the other to the plant, asking them to tell Allen Carr to come to the Metts place when he got off work.

Beth knew she wasn't acting quite normally all day. She did her best to fake it for Louie and Grace. She yawned several times and did her best to stifle them, fearing someone would ask why she hadn't slept. She kept making some excuse to walk to the front of the store, hoping to be there to see Allen's car pull up. She felt that if she shared it with Bonnie, the thing would be manageable, at least. Finally, at seven-fifty, Allen's Chevy pulled up to the curb outside.

When the store closed, Beth went straight to the car and got in the front seat. Allen could see the girls were close to tears and wanted privacy. He reluctantly left the car, bought a Coke from the vending machine, took a seat on the closest bench and lit a cigarette. He didn't like being left out, but he knew Bonnie would tell him everything on the ride home.

The sisters rarely hugged. Now they did. Beth sobbed into her sister's shoulder until Bonnie felt the tears on her skin.

"Start from the beginning, Beth. Tell me everything."

"Frank, he made me, I don't know how to say it. He's strong. I couldn't stop him. He raped me."

Bonnie was speechless. Since the phone call, she had feared something like this. But she could not comprehend that Carol's husband had done it. She immediately knew she needed a talk with Maggie. Too much time had passed since their last one, and Bonnie hoped Maggie wouldn't mind.

"How could that happen?" Bonnie asked.

"He gets his sandwich stuff here. He came in and saw me the first week I worked. He talked to me on the street there a couple times. We sat on the same bench that Allen is on." They waved, and Bonnie smiled at Allen, who didn't respond.

"He told me how hard it was to get ahead since the job he has doesn't pay much. He doesn't have anybody to fall back on in town here. I felt so sorry for him. He asked me to look at his apartment. He wanted to know if I thought it was big enough to move Carol and Debby in. It's right up there." She pointed to a storefront with a small, plain-looking door on the side.

"I was no sooner inside until he kissed me. I knew he shouldn't do that, but I was so surprised, and it felt so nice. I should have left right away. Before I knew what was happening, he had me on his bed. He pulled my dress up and," Beth began sobbing again. Bonnie didn't need to hear anymore.

"Okay. That's enough for now. Have you told Aunt Polly?" Bonnie asked.

"You know I can't tell her. Would you tell her?"

"You know who we really can't tell? We can't tell Carol," Bonnie said. They sat in silence for a few moments, while the shame of the whole thing gnawed relentlessly. "One thing I do know is, I have to tell Allen."

"No, Bonnie, I don't want anyone to know. I want it to go away."

"There is no way I can ask my boyfriend to bring me here for an urgent reason and keep him in the dark. He'll want to know. He has a right to know. And we can trust Allen. He's a good guy. I'm gonna have him get back in the car with us."

"What am I gonna do, Bonnie?"

"You know that what he did was a crime, don't you?"

Beth nodded vigorously. "I'd rather die than let the whole world know."

"For now, you're not doing anything. Not until I get some advice from someone we can trust."

"You mean Maggie Porter," Beth stated.

"Yep." Bonnie leaned past her sister and rolled down the car window. "Hey, Allen. Come on back."

Beth opened the door and got out. "I can't," she said.

"I understand. You go on home to Aunt Polly."

Beth kept her head down as she passed Allen. He felt odd not speaking to her, but it was plain she would prefer that. He settled into the driver's seat while hearing Bonnie release the longest sigh he had ever heard. Looking into Bonnie's eyes, he wasn't sure he even wanted to know.

"It will be late when we get home," Bonnie said. "Let's go. I'll tell you on the way."

Chapter Twenty-Eight

Once they were away from town and night settled around the car, Bonnie felt calm. The whole thing seemed simple to her. She took Allen's hand in hers and told him everything.

"That son-of-a-bitch," Allen said. He clenched his teeth. "I figured it was something like that. You realize he thinks he can get away with it? Beth is not gonna tell Carol what he did. Besides that, Beth had no business going up to his place. People will say she asked for it."

"She's a kid. She didn't know better."

"She's a kid? How much older are you?" His question got no response. "Imagine for a minute if I forced myself on you. How would you handle it?"

"If you were gonna force yourself on me, you would have done it already."

"Sure. How would you handle it if I raped you? How would you prove I did it? I could say you were willing. Did he hit her or anything?"

"She didn't mention him hurting her. I bet she did hurt, though. She was a virgin. He pushed himself in. That had to hurt."

"The more I think about it, the madder I get," Allen said. "He was a Marine. They're supposed to be tough and protect people, especially women."

"Mom thought Frank had a bad side. She was right."

"Honestly though, what can a woman who gets raped do?" Allen's anger gave way to thoughtfulness, "By the way, I always thought it was 'raked.'"

"You mean spelled with a 'k?'"

Allen nodded.

"Really? You chucklehead," Bonnie said. They both laughed.

"I don't know. I guess I never saw it written. It isn't something people talk about much."

"That's true. I bet it happens a lot more than we hear about."

"You know why it's hard to prove the crime of 'rake,' don't you?"

"Is this a joke?" Bonnie asked. She could tell by his playful tone.

"Because a woman can run faster with her dress up than a man can run with his pants down."

Bonnie reached over and cuffed him. "That's not funny."

"Well, it isn't now anyway," Allen said.

"I'll tell you who else better not find out," Bonnie said.

Allen glanced over quizzically.

"Dad. He'll kill Frank if he finds out."

"I get it. I want to kill him, and I've never met the man." He paused again, thoughtfully. "When I think about it, forcing yourself on a woman is about the most unmanly thing a guy could do. Could you even enjoy it that way?"

Bonnie gulped. "Oh god, Allen, what if Beth gets pregnant?"

"That is not likely. Is it?"

"I don't know. Maggie said it can happen anytime you have sex."

"We know it doesn't happen every time, though. Right?"

"Right."

"We'll jump off that bridge when we come to it."

"You mean, we'll cross that bridge when we come to it."

They both laughed again.

"All jokes aside. If Beth is pregnant, she might want to jump off a bridge."

"Good point. Oh, poor Beth. Poor, poor Beth."

Maggie Porter sensed that something had happened when Bonnie appeared at her door the next morning. She had accepted that Bonnie no longer wanted her guidance. She also accepted that the girl would do something regrettable. "How's life treating you, Bonnie? I hear you have a boyfriend. Do you remember the things I told you?"

"So many questions. Maggie, I know I should have come to see you sooner."

Maggie put her hand up in protest. "Not at all, Bonnie. I know you've been busy. I hear the Metts house is fuller than ever. So, fill me in on your life. Amanda Tyner hasn't told me everything, I'm sure."

"Well, I'll tell you all you want to know. First, I need your advice."

"Considering what you've shared with me in the past, you know you can trust me."

"I do, Maggie. You've helped me more than you know. But this is not about me."

"Just grab it by the horns, Bonnie. You know I've heard worse."

"Did you know that Carol is living back with us at home?"

"I heard. Her husband is in some kind of trouble."

"Well, Beth went to live with Aunt Polly in Grove City. She got a job working at the A & P there. She ran into Frank, that's Carol's husband. Long story short." Bonnie paused and drew in a breath. "He raped her the other night."

Both mulled over the statement. Maggie sighed brusquely and said nothing for a while. She felt a headache coming on. Then she began. "Let me fill in the blanks of the long story you shortened. This Frank fellow treated Beth like family, used that to gain her trust, and took advantage before Beth saw it coming."

"That's pretty much how it happened," Bonnie said.

"This rape. It happened in the guy's car, or what?"

"No. He has an upstairs apartment there, a small, cheap place. He talked her into going up there. He kissed her. Her first kiss. One thing led to another. He forced himself on her."

"That sounds like a dozen other stories I've heard."

"What do we do?"

"Well, you could wait ten years or so. Maybe somebody will shoot the bastard for you. It has happened before."

Maggie waited for her statement to sink in.

"You mean to tell me....Luther Banks and you?"

"Yep, and as I look back on it, I see how he got away with it. The same way Frank is gonna get away with it. Beth is too ashamed to admit she let it happen. Just like I was. I had the excuse of being lonely. It happened during the war. A lot of women were lonely. You want some male contact. You lie to yourself that it won't get out of hand."

"So, there is nothing we can do?"

"I can't think of a thing. Maybe in time, you can find a way to give the guy what he has coming. But I doubt it. The only person I know who got paid back for raping someone was Jimmy Brewster. That's the guy your dad beat up and threw in the river. And he did that based solely on gossip, mind you. Jimmy denied it time and again."

"I thought for sure you would know what to do."

"Sorry to disappoint you, Bonnie. I never said I had all the answers. Think about it. If Beth goes to the police and tells them what happened, what will they do?"

"What will they do?" Bonnie asked, seriously.

"First, they will probably discourage her from pushing it, saying it is so hard to prove. Beth will have to sign some report about what happened. He will deny what she said. If it gets so far as him being arrested, there will be a report in the newspaper about it. Your Aunt Polly will know, the people Beth works for will know. Everybody in three counties will be talking about it. If it goes to court, the lawyer Frank has will ask Beth the usual questions, like what were you doing there with Carol's husband, and did you do anything to lead the man on? If they don't find him guilty, it will look bad for her. Unless Frank confesses, it'll be her word against his. He said, she said. Even if Frank has a bad reputation, the people who know him may not be allowed on the jury. Put yourself in Beth's shoes. Would you want to go to the cops?"

"I suppose not. Should I tell Carol?"

"That's a hard question. Who all knows about it?" asked Maggie.

"Me, you and my boyfriend Allen."

"You told your boyfriend?"

"He drove me to Grove City so I could talk to Beth. She had to tell me."

"So, you had to tell him." Maggie shook her head. "Does Carter know?"

"Not yet."

"I don't see how it will do any good to tell anyone else. That has to be Beth's call anyway," Maggie said.

"Let's hope and pray it's over," Maggie said.

"Why wouldn't it be over?"

"Think about it. Beth might be pregnant."

"I have thought about it. What are the chances?"

"Who knows? We wait and see. I do know that anytime Beth finds herself alone with a guy, she's gonna relive what happened to her. That's a damned shame."

They sat for a few minutes. There wasn't much more to say.

"So, tell me about this boyfriend."

Charlotte Timko was on pins and needles. She had been to see Doctor Masters a week before. He had taken a urine sample and dropped it off at the hospital in Butler when he went to see a patient. His nurse had called saying the doctor needed to see her. After so many barren years, her monthly had stopped coming. She had missed her second one and was certain she felt something stirring deep inside, but she was afraid that it was only wishful thinking. The door swung open. The gray-haired gentleman had a broad smile for her.

"Does that smile mean what I think it means?"

"The test was positive. You are with child. In the family way. Pregnant. Congratulations, Charlotte."

Instantly tears formed in Charlotte's eyes. She couldn't wait to tell Kenny.

"When am I due?"

"Do you keep track of your monthly?" Doc asked.

"My last one started August third."

Doc pulled a small, printed object from his pocket. "How does May ninth sound?"

"Oh Doc, I want to hug you." The doctor opened his arms. They embraced.

"I guess you and Ken had given up on having kids, huh?"

"We had. He's gonna be shocked."

"Well, all I can say is, take care of yourself, eat regularly and don't strain yourself physically. It's better not to drink beer or whiskey, none of that hard stuff."

"Kenny and I don't drink."

"Okay. The only thing I want you to do, unless you start bleeding or have some other strange symptom, is come see me every couple of months."

"I am not as young as most women when they get pregnant. Does that mean anything?"

"No. As long as you feel well, there is no difference between you and a twenty-year-old."

She had so much to do. Kenny would come home in another day, and she had been anticipating the joy of telling him that it had finally happened. She was so glad about ending things with Carter Metts. As if the end of their relationship were a new beginning, he had bought a car and begun dating a local girl. If she had ended it a little sooner, she wouldn't wonder who had sired her child. On the other hand, if she had ended it sooner, she might not be expecting.

As she pulled into her home, the trees surrounding the place were intense with autumn leaves. As if her life were now framed in vibrant glory, a new day was at hand, the beginning of a life she had longed for since as far back as she could recall. Not a devout woman, she took a moment to thank God for men, for Kenny, for Carter. She might never know and that was okay.

Chapter Twenty-Nine

Judson Johnson pulled into the Grove City Feed Mill. His brother was a horse trainer and needed a special blend that the mill stocked. The mill had run short of that particular mix. They told him if he could wait twenty minutes, they could fill the order.

Expecting the twenty minutes might turn into forty, Jud seated himself in an out-of-the-way place and lit a smoke. He could hear two workmen talking with their voices raised so they could hear each other over the grinding machines. Consequently, Jud heard their conversation. He missed a word or two but picked up enough to get the gist.

"Her folks live on a run-down farm down in Parker. You know where that is?"

"I've passed through there. It's on the river, isn't it?"

"Yep. The farm is across the river a mile or so. The place isn't worth much, but it was enough for them to cover my debt. I got the old bastard to co-sign for me. Her family isn't too bright. Her old man likes beer, and I had the papers with me. We got my mother-in-law to sign too. I don't think they can take their land. My debt isn't that big. I'll find out soon enough. I got a letter saying that since I was so far behind, they were gonna go to them."

"Is this the same place you took Carol and the baby?" the other man asked.

"It is. They'll be fine there. When it gets cold, I'll bring them back here with me. Summertime is almost over, and I've had a lot of fun. Had me some fine ladies. You know me. I wasn't ready to settle down anyway."

"Now that's real classy Frank," the other man said. "You get in trouble, and you persuade your wife's family to back you up. You stop making the installments and stick it to them."

"Hey, we're not young forever. I have better things to do with my money. And believe it or not, it was Carol's idea."

"Better things than paying your debts? Sure, you do. Don't bother asking me to help you make it to payday anymore."

Jud heard the disdainful tone in one man's voice, while the other man laughed as if cheating a family member were a grand joke. To Jud, family was everything. To a black family, in a mostly white region, surviving meant trusting one another. The notion that a man could betray his family unsettled Jud. To make it worse, the one white man that had proven worthy of Jud's friendship was the victim. A man like this joker should be done away with.

Jud remembered how Ward felt a few years back, when the whole world knew he had been in the insane asylum. Learning that his daughter and son-in-law duped him, Ward's humiliation would certainly come out in anger, but Jud had to tell him. A proverb came to mind that reassured him: *Faithful are the wounds of a friend; but the kisses of an enemy are deceitful.* Letting Ward know about his worthless son-in-law would be a loyal gesture. The Metts farm was on the way to his brother's place anyway. He decided to stop in Parker and tell Dorothy about it. Ward would be at work. Telling Dorothy might be safer. She could decide how much to pass on. If Ward's oldest daughter were living with them, revealing her husband's conniving way could make real trouble.

Dorothy and Ward had never received a registered letter before. It had to be important. The mailbox had a card in it telling of a letter at the post office they would need to sign for. Dorothy asked Carter to drive her to town. She opened it in the lobby and saw that what Judson Johnson overheard was true. The letter was from a finance company demanding over six hundred dollars.

"What's the letter about?" Carter asked, as Dorothy got back into his car.

"It's about money. Money we ain't got. That's all I'm gonna say. Your father's gonna hit the ceiling. I hope he's in a good mood when he gets home today."

Dorothy made no mention of the letter until supper was over and the kids were clearing the table. "Ward, take a little walk with me." She led him to the springhouse steps, confident that nobody else would hear. "Jud stopped by yesterday. He asked me to remind you what he had said about being an underdog and how important it is to think before you act."

Ward could tell from her subdued tone that something bad was coming. She showed him the letter from the finance company. She saw the storm forming on his brow as he read and re-read the letter.

"That's not the half of it," Dorothy said. She repeated what Jud had overheard at the feed mill. Ward did not speak. She had seen him angry many times. This didn't look like anger. What Dorothy read on her husband's face was profound and strange. It overwhelmed her. Tears fell as she came to grips with it. Carol had done something unspeakable to her father. Something no failure or fist had ever done. She had broken his heart.

As Ward's hearing slowly faded through the years, he spent longer periods of time with his own thoughts. That was a good thing. He hungered to thrash Frank Parks. Frank deserved a thrashing. If Ward gave it to him, Frank would heal before Ward got out of the strait jacket. His entire adult life he had pretended that people respected him, when in fact, it had been fear that his demeanor evoked. Now the chickens of his arrogance and pride had come home to roost, and there was no plucking and slaughtering this kind of poultry, not even by flashlight.

The advice of Judson Johnson rang in Ward's ears. Even without that, his time in the state hospital proved to him that power was subtle.

It made a mockery of the cloak of rules and manners it hid behind; they were a pretense. The asylum was staffed by scrawny men who acted mild until they were out of sight from the doctor and nurses, and then enforced their will by sheer numbers and the kinds of blows that no prize fighter could get away with, much less stoop to. If he were put away again, he could lose his job, and another job within walking distance of home would be impossible. He lacked the money and probably the stamina to go back into farming. He recalled from his fight training that when a man's punch missed it cost him more energy than the person who ducked it. Judson had called him an underdog. Indeed, he was the worst kind, a self-made underdog. It dawned on him that he had even bought the beer that clouded his judgment to co-sign the loan papers.

Two weeks had gone by since Beth had been raped. Her monthly was due. She put her napkin belt on, only to be disappointed when the day ended. She repeated the ritual the rest of the week. When Sunday came, she opted to ride to the farm with Curt and Polly. Aunt Polly had been pestering her to go anyway. She let Polly think she was being respectful, but she needed to see Bonnie.

After the initial exchange of information, upon arriving at the farm, Ward suggested that Carol and the other girls go for a walk, maybe find some nice apples that Polly could take home for baking. Everyone knew and accepted that he wanted to speak privately to his sister and her husband.

"Curt, take a look at this letter. Do I understand it rightly?" Ward asked.

Curt took his time reading and re-reading. He knew that registered mail added weight to a threat, as if the government were endorsing the claim in the letter. Wearing his suit when he visited the farm had a dual purpose. No chance they would ask him to help with dirty work, and pinstripes gave a man the look of education and achievement. Curt had little more education than Ward and he was a mere laborer by trade, but his friendships through the church included academics and local politicians. He had picked up a tone or manner of speaking from them. Working men like Ward never looked past the shirt and tie. His fedora suggested a dignity and competence he would never be able to back up, even so, Ward and Dorothy respected his opinion. He enjoyed that. "So, you secured a personal loan for Frank?"

"Dorothy and I both signed."

"I'm guessing you don't have that much money."

"We don't have any extra money. Can they take the farm?" Ward asked.

"This farm is worth considerably more than six-hundred dollars."

"What do you think I should do?"

"You need better advice than I can give you. I would go to the bank and show the manager this letter. He should know what happens in situations like this."

"I don't know the man. I know who he is, but I don't have an account there, and I have never borrowed money," Ward said.

"Didn't your mother leave this place to your children?"

"She did. I am allowed to live here all my life, but I can't sell it." Ward stood and looked around, making sure that Carol and the kids were not in earshot.

"I thought so." Curt said. "That might be your answer. If you have nothing for them to take, what can they do? This letter doesn't say anything about taking your land. My guess is that they never asked about your mother's will. They assumed that since you live here, you own the place. I have heard of a worker's wages being garnished. I suppose they would start with Frank's wages. Of course, they could be bluffing. That's easy for me to say. Maybe you should talk to a lawyer."

"Would Albert know anything about this?"

"He might. But he lives in California and has that state's license. He's not allowed to give legal advice here. Frank is supposed to make monthly payments on this. Obviously, he hasn't been. The interest on loans like this keeps adding up. You might want to start making the payments."

It didn't take long for the girls to fill a basket with apples. Bonnie and Beth wandered away from the others. They couldn't allow Carol to hear.

"You must have run into Frank since it happened," Bonnie said.

"Not yet. There is another grocery store in town. He might be going there to avoid me."

"He should want to avoid you. But it probably won't last. Do you think you can handle it if he shows up to buy a chicken?"

"If I see him coming, I can duck into the back. Louie, my boss, doesn't like him and told me not to be nice to him. I should have listened."

"Don't feel too bad. We didn't know what a skunk he was."

"Louie did." She stepped squarely in front of her sister. "Bonnie, my monthly is late."

"How late?"

"It will soon be time for it to come again," Beth said, nervously.

"Listen, when a girl worries about missing, her nerves will keep it from coming. You must have heard that."

"Nothing, Bonnie, not even a spot." Beth began crying gently.

"You're going to worry yourself to death. Isn't there a doctor in Grove City you can go to for a test?"

"Aunt Polly will find out. I can't let that happen."

"No, she won't. Doctors keep things like that to themselves. Even if the doctor was Aunt Polly's best friend, he can't tell her about you.

That's private and personal. It's part of the oath doctors take. The only way he can spill the beans is if you've committed a crime."

"Are you sure about that?" Beth was doubtful.

Bonnie was not at all sure about it. She plowed on anyway, figuring it better to find out than to worry for who knew how long. "Tell you what. Call the doctor's office and ask. They won't know who you are. Ask about getting a pregnancy test. Tell them you need it to be discreet. I'll bet they will even let you come in the back door. People get venereal diseases all the time. The doctors need to know who the infected people have been with. They keep all that information under lock and key. A girl who is afraid she might be with child is not a shock to them."

"That's a good idea. I'll make a call tomorrow. I'll have to give them my name when I go in. I doubt they will accept, 'cute, brown-haired girl.'"

"Like I said. They keep that stuff secret."

Chapter Thirty

Ward let the next week go by. He gave his situation some thought. He told the other men on his work crew, hoping someone would have some experience with such things. "Isn't that about what you spend on beer in a weekend, Ward?" Johnny McCall asked. Johnny, the newest man on the crew, had a careless mouth. Ward had to admit it; the kid had a point. When Friday night came, Ward did not go to the American House. He forbade Dorothy from going as well. The whole household knew something extraordinary was happening.

On Saturday morning, Ward got up and had his breakfast and walked slowly and deliberately to the upstairs of the out-kitchen. He removed his wide leather belt, doubling it so his hand covered the buckle. The kids all knew when he did that, someone was in for it. His stern voice roused his daughter like no alarm clock could have.

"You get that husband of yours on the telephone. I want you and everything you have out of this house, today." The tone of his voice was controlled, but Carol sensed he was on the threshold of violence. She started to speak, and Ward checked her.

"Don't say a word. Just get out. Don't ever come back here, and don't ever write to me or call me on the telephone," Ward said.

Carol made the call quietly and crept around, mouse-like, as the day dragged on. Frank showed up at three in the afternoon and made no effort to speak to anyone. Ward sat like a stone on the porch, as if defying Frank to question him. They didn't have much to pack up. Carol had gathered a few odds and ends at the rummage sale, that was all. Dorothy and the girls were sad, knowing it might be a long time before they saw Carol. Richard cried outright. He had a strong attachment to Debby, and he kissed the child repeatedly, saying it wasn't fair that they had to go away.

The doctor's office in Grove City handled Beth's query about a pregnancy test the way Bonnie had predicted. Beth got an appointment. When she arrived, the nurse took her quickly to the back, asking her to provide urine in a paper cup. She had to sign a form. "We should know something in a few days," the woman said. "We will call with the results." Beth didn't like the condescending tone the nurse used with her, but it would be worth it. She had to know.

"It would be better if I called you," Beth said. The phone number she had written on the form was Aunt Polly's, except for two digits she changed. She wasn't taking any chances.

The nurse had been told not to call before and had come to expect it. "Call Thursday around one," she told Beth. "Before you go, you should know that if it turns out you are pregnant, we can put you in touch with places that can help you." The nurse's uniform, the sample, the paperwork, and the medical trappings of a doctor's office, gave substance to her fear. Beth worried even more, if that were possible.

What the nurse said made sense. She had heard about girls being sent away to mysterious places where the child would be placed for adoption. That was out of the question for Beth. She had never considered suicide in her life, but what else could she do? With Carol practically pushed out of the family, how would her father react if the truth about her and Frank came out? How would Aunt Polly and Uncle Curt react?

Every person who approached the meat section of the store caused Beth to look closely, fearing Frank would show up. Beth felt like she should apologize to Louie. After all, if she had heeded his advice, she wouldn't be in this trouble now. Though she did her best to hide her anxiety, Louie could tell she had something on her mind. Their conversations felt contrived and formal. They were relieved when the day's work ended.

During the two days of waiting, Beth began to feel like her breasts were fuller, and her nipples were becoming tender. Whether or not that meant pregnancy, she didn't know. It added to her worry. So much so that when Thursday came and she called the doctor's office, she was not surprised when they made another appointment for her to see the doctor. If the test had revealed nothing, they could have simply told her. Why else would the doctor need to see her?

She arrived right on time. She got the feeling the nurse was waiting for her specifically, but that may have been her imagination. The nurse took her to a room where she waited alone, but not for long.

"Do you have a fiancé?" the doctor asked her straightaway upon entering the room. No introduction, no preliminaries.

Beth did not expect that question, and she quickly decided that only a lie would do. "Yes, he doesn't live here in town, though."

"You ought to contact him right away. He is going to be a father before long."

Beth was unable to focus. The doctor and his office, with all its clean spaces and glass cupboards, were detached from her. She got lightheaded. The doctor pulled a chair out and helped her to get seated.

"Can you give me the date when your last cycle began? Your monthly, I mean. That's how I predict when you're due to deliver."

"Yes, thank you," Beth said. She got up from the chair and headed toward the door.

"Miss Metts, please. We aren't finished here," the doctor said.

Beth didn't hear him. She stumbled out the door of the exam room, through the waiting area, and out into the street. Something strange was going on in her mind. She should have been crying, but the usual sadness was not there. She saw herself moving down the street, strangely unable to feel her legs and feet. Just like when Frank had overpowered her, her mind would not work. She moved toward the A & P, and only when she walked by the door did she become aware of her situation.

She rested one hand on a parking meter on the street outside the store. She began to throw up. She leaned over and retched calmly, as if people vomited on the sidewalk every day.

"Beth, Beth, oh dear, are you alright?" It was Grace Miller, her manager. She had watched Beth walk by the store instead of coming in and had stepped out to see why.

Beth came to her senses, drew in a deep breath, and wiped her mouth with the back of her hand. She paused a moment, preparing again to lie about her situation.

"I'm okay, Grace. I ate something that didn't agree with me. Is it alright if I wash up and go to work?"

"Let's get you inside and get you something to drink." She put her arm around Beth and led her through the double door into the market. She sat her down in the office and brought her a bottle of Coke. She pulled an opener from the drawer and quickly popped the cap. "This will settle your stomach, dear."

"Thank you, Grace. I better now." Beth said, trying to sound light-hearted. Instead, she sounded childish.

"You mean you're feeling better?"

"Yes. It's what we say at home." Beth answered.

"Why don't you sit here for a while, until you're sure. Louie will be fine."

Beth would have to call Bonnie again. She needed someone to tell her what to do. She could not tell Aunt Polly. Her mother and father could not find out. She wondered if she could tell Louie. He cared about her. Frank had pretended to care about her too, until he got something from her.

"I don't know what to do," Bonnie said. Allen had picked her up from her shift at the Honky Tonk. Almost as an afterthought, she looked up to receive his kiss. He knew she had bad news.

"This has something to do with Beth, doesn't it?" Allen asked.

"She's gonna have a baby."

Allen exhaled loudly. He quickly felt grateful that, as frustrating as it was, Bonnie had never let his advances get further than they had. This was real trouble.

"Has she told Frank?"

"She never wants to see Frank again. Why would she tell him anything?"

"Isn't it his problem too?"

"He probably doesn't think so," Bonnie said.

"Well, this happened to my big sister, a couple years ago. The guy she was dating did something to help her out. He took her to see some doctor. When they got back, no more baby."

"You mean someone adopted the baby?"

"No, silly. They weren't even gone overnight. This doctor, or whatever he is, does something and, I don't know," he raised his hands off the wheel in a gesture of ignorance.

"I better go talk to Maggie," Bonnie said. "Can we go to her house? I know it's late; I bet she's still up."

"Maybe so. Good time, cause Abner's at work now," Allen said. "Saw him coming on when the shift changed."

One light was bright against the curtain as they approached the house. Maggie heard the car and came out to meet them.

"Hi Maggie. You said you wanted to meet Allen. Here he is," Bonnie spouted cheerfully.

A little too cheerfully, Maggie thought. She tilted her head and smiled at the couple. "I'm guessing there is news from Beth," Maggie said. "Come in and sit down. It is nice to meet you, Allen. I've heard a lot about you."

"What do we do, Maggie?" Bonnie asked as soon as they were all seated.

"You mean," she hesitated.

"Beth is in the family way," Bonnie said. "The doctor gave her a test, and it's true."

"I don't see that she has any choice. There are homes for unwed mothers. I was curious, so I asked a couple of the ladies at church. They say there is one in Erie. That's about a two-hour drive. Not that far."

"If my dad finds out, he will want to know who the father is. He hates Frank; he will want to kill him. He probably will. He threw Carol and her baby out. You didn't know that, did you?"

"He threw his own daughter out of the house? What did she do?" Maggie asked.

"Sometime last year, I think, Frank got Mom and Dad drunk and talked them into signing some loan papers. Frank couldn't make the payments, so Dad has to start paying now. It's a lot of money."

"So, he's taking it out on her?"

"He thinks it was her idea."

"Ooooh," Maggie said. She stood up and began pacing, deep in thought. "So this Frank, he gets the oldest daughter to trap her dad, and to make things worse, he rapes her sister. Good thing you didn't take a shine to Frank like Beth did."

"How did you know Beth liked Frank?" Bonnie asked.

"You told me, after that first time he came home with Carol. You thought it was disgusting."

"I guess I did. I forgot about that. I never thought it would lead to anything."

"I understand. The way things turned out, I would want to forget it too," Maggie said. "There will always be guys like Frank. And there will always be naïve girls for them to take advantage of."

"Tell her about your sister, Allen," Bonnie said, looking toward her boyfriend.

"I get it. I know your family secrets, so now I have to share mine," Allen said. Although he tried to sound miffed, his smile betrayed his real feelings. It felt good to be on the inside of something so grave, serious and personal when he was not the one in trouble. "My sister's boyfriend took her somewhere, and when they got back, she wasn't pregnant anymore. He had to pay someone and promise to keep it a secret, but the problem went away."

Maggie admired Allen for being concise and to the point. She hadn't expected that from him. "It's called an 'abortion.' That's what they paid for. And they had to keep it secret because it's illegal," Maggie stated matter-of-factly. "I don't think you can even get one in Mexico." She looked sadly at the couple. "Remember what I told you about losing control of your life, Bonnie?"

Bonnie wanted to hug Maggie. Her advice, so long ago now, had perhaps saved her from a fate like Beth's.

"How desperate is she, Bonnie?" Maggie asked.

"How would you feel? She wants a way out; she doesn't have any."

"What I mean is that girls in her situation have been known to drown themselves or something worse. You need to let her know that you're willing to help her. We don't want her to feel alone," Maggie said. "Can't she tell your aunt? The one she's living with?"

"You don't understand, Maggie. Aunt Polly and Uncle Curt are not like us. Remember what you said about some people having better manners and habits? Curt and Polly dress up for church on Sunday and stay dressed up all day. They are better than us; we know it. They've never had anything like this happen to them. People like us screw before marriage. Not them."

Maggie caught the shocked look on Allen's face. Their eyes met knowingly. "So when are you going to do it?" she asked.

"We're not." Bonnie said. "Especially not now."

"That is good to hear. I'm gonna hold you to that."

"You go right ahead," Bonnie stated.

"By the way, Bonnie. If you think your aunt and uncle are pure as wind-driven snow, you're more naïve than I thought. They might be neat, combed-down, and proper church-going people, but I guarantee you they have done some shameful things in their lives. That's one reason they go to church." Maggie said. "It's called human nature. It's called sin. You think there's no way out; that's not true. Sometimes people get in terrible situations; sometimes it's their fault, and sometimes it's not. It would be better for Beth to go ahead and let the baby come. She can go to one of those homes. She won't have to pay anything. I know some women who have done it. They leave it in their past. They move on with their lives. The baby gets to live, and the child has a chance. God forgives people for the mistakes they make."

"I think what Bonnie means," Allen said, "is that Beth would rather be roasted over hot coals than confess to her aunt that Frank had had his way with her."

"She would." Bonnie paused for effect, "She'd throw herself in the river first."

"Did she let Frank have his way?" Allen interjected, "Or did he force her?"

"Did he force her to go to his apartment?" Maggie asked.

Allen looked at Bonnie.

"He tricked her into going, saying he needed her help," Bonnie said.

"You know that was his way of getting her alone," Maggie said.

"Beth didn't know that." Bonnie shuddered in frustration. "What difference does it make? Even if she asked him for it, she's in trouble.

He's not gonna admit he did it, and he's not gonna help her. Even if he would admit it and be willing to help, what could he do?"

They stood quietly for a long moment. Finally, as if accepting the inevitable, Bonnie asked, "Allen, can you find out where your big sister went?"

"Look, as bad as I feel for Beth, going that route is not good," Maggie said.

"I think we're out of good ideas, Maggie," Bonnie said.

Maggie chafed with the desire to make a fuss, to scream and insist and cajole. It would only be noise. These kids would come to regret getting rid of the baby. It might even be dangerous. Maggie had no advice to outweigh the shame threatening Beth. She had helped Bonnie grow up, hoping what she taught would spread to her siblings. Now, it seemed, they were independent before their time, maybe independent before they were mature. She had tried to free them from the shame that wound through their hearts like a poison vine. What good was shame anyway? She pondered. It hovered over all people at one time or another, in one way or another. It fell too harshly on the young. The Metts kids inherited it unjustly. Avoiding shame made them do things that caused greater pain later. She remembered the burden she herself had carried. Yet, without shame, society would be a mess. Perhaps shame was like salt. In the right measure, it made things better, while too much of it ruined food. It was one of those mysteries the people at her church tried so hard to sort out.

Chapter Thirty-One

"You know, Bonnie, she's gonna think that you're the pregnant one," Allen said. They had left Maggie's house and driven to the Metts house. They were sitting in the dark with Allen's arm around Bonnie. Usually, they would be necking, but there was no mood for that.

"Oh, your sister, you mean?"

"Yeah."

"Let her think it. What's it gonna hurt?"

"I'll tell her that one of my buddies has the problem."

"That'll work, Allen. You know we're gonna need you to take her to the doctor's place. Carter doesn't know, and I want to keep it that way. How far away is it?"

"You know as much as I do. I will ask tomorrow," Allen said. "Now, I heard what you told Maggie. If I'm not gonna get laid unless we get married, you gotta at least give me some sugar." He drew her to him, and they kissed passionately.

She broke the kiss. "You deserve more than sugar, Allen. This will only make it worse. You poor guy. Now, go home, go to bed, and dream about me. Let me know as soon as you learn something. I'm gonna tell Beth that help is on the way." As Bonnie got ready for bed, a new affection for Allen swelled. She had asked for his support with something sticky. He hadn't backed up an inch.

Allen had made the phone call, and between him, Bonnie and Beth, they came up with the money. They were able to schedule it for Saturday afternoon. That worked well. Allen was off, and the girls could both leave their jobs without much consequence. They told Aunt Polly that they had all been invited to a party, and they might come back late.

The "doctor" was not in a town like most doctors are. He was in a veterinary clinic, on a rural, but well-traveled highway. "They said we should park in the back at exactly three-thirty. There's a green door with a rippled glass window," Allen reported.

They found the spot. Allen parked, and a young man came out. He held out his hand for the money. He counted it, placed it in his pocket and disappeared, walking around the outside, apparently to the front of the building. The door opened again, and another man came out. He wore a white coat along with a surgical mask and cap, so he looked professional.

The girls didn't like it when the man asked, "Which one of you is Jane?" His voice was a little muffled through the mask, but they knew what he meant. Allen's car was a coupe, so Bonnie got out and tilted the seat forward for Beth to get out. "Only Jane can come inside. You two can go drive around. Come back in an hour."

Bonnie had the urge to push Beth back into the car. Their eyes met and Beth sensed her hesitation. Her mind was made up; she took a determined step toward the door. "It's okay, Bonnie."

"Relax, Jane," his voice was upbeat as he opened the door and ushered Beth inside. "I've done this hundreds of times. There isn't much to it." They walked down an unkempt hallway. It had the same odor as the milk house on the Hughes farm. She knew the smell was soap or disinfectant, something medicinal. She didn't find that reassuring.

"You're in a strange place, I'm a stranger to you, and what we're going to do is against the law. That's why I haven't asked for your real name, and you don't know mine. Someone I have helped in the past put you in touch with me. Things worked out well for them, or you wouldn't be here. You need to keep this to yourself so that I can help other girls who have your problem. There are a lot of them, believe me, so don't feel bad.

"You need to know that a little bleeding is normal once we're finished. I'll give you some extra pads, and you'll need to rest for a day. Most girls are a little nauseous and maybe dizzy. Most of that comes from being nervous. Once you get over that, life goes back to normal. I'm going to assume you're a smart girl and won't let this happen to you again. Sad to say, I have helped some girls more than once. They must think it's easy enough to do, so they stop being careful."

The room had a table padded with pale-colored blankets and sheets. It looked make-do. The man had Beth pull her dress up, remove her underpants and sit on the table with her legs over the edge. "Now lay back and open up for me." Those words seemed callous, even vulgar to Beth, yet he spoke so casually. She felt cheap. There were crude wooden stirrups for her feet on both sides. She realized they were crutches, what people used when they had a broken leg. Everything about the room seemed temporary and improvised. The man guided Beth's feet to the places where each heel rested. These were covered with a clean cloth that resembled socks. The man draped a sheet over Beth's knees and Beth could not see him. "You'll need to relax and hold still. It will hurt some, but it will hurt a lot if you fidget around or jerk."

The man moved with confidence, humming a little while he worked. He wiped Beth with something cold and wet. There was a strong medicinal smell, maybe alcohol. Beth had never felt so exposed and vulnerable. She tried to think about something else. She remembered Louie and how he had warned her about Frank. When she got back to work with Louie, she would listen well to everything Louie said. He was like a father to her. Better than her real father, who never tried to steer her in the right direction.

"Hold real still now. This is the tricky part," the man said. Beth felt something pushing; it stopped, started again, stopped, maybe four times, and she lost track. A mild cramping sensation came and stayed there. She felt something warm on her thigh, an intense throbbing pain. She regretted surrendering her well-being to a faceless, no-name, now probing her most delicate parts. There was a wave of intense pain, and she fainted.

When she came to her senses, the pad between her thighs seemed enormous. Someone had slid her toward the top of the table, and her legs were together. The room spun slowly, and she felt a sharp ache, like the cramps she occasionally had, nothing like the pain before she blacked out.

"Can you sit up for me?" Beth felt the doctor's arm assisting. She was eager to get out of there, so she swiveled, getting ready to stand up. She felt the pad twisting a little as she did so. When she got to her feet unsteadily, she looked around at the table and saw so much blood she almost fainted again.

"I don't feel good," Beth said.

"You'll be fine. It's gone. You bled a little more than most; otherwise, the procedure was normal." The tone of the man's voice was not friendly the way it had been. In fact, the man sounded scared.

"Your friends pulled up outside. I'll walk you to the car."

Everything was different now for Beth. Her senses, hearing and vision, took things in more slowly than before. Her thoughts were thicker, like syrup. Her feelings, good or ill, were weaker, like a heavy quilt or blanket had been drawn over them. The covering did not comfort her like it did on cold winter nights. At first, she thought it was some medicine the doctor had given her. She couldn't recall any medicine, and he had not mentioned any. The eyes of Bonnie and Allen were sharp as they looked at her, but they didn't pierce her consciousness like they had before. She was awake, just not alert. She could hear, but there was no tone or melody. She could see, but there was no beauty in the color.

Objects, though she recognized them, and could name them, had no meaning. It was like the part of her that cared had been left behind in the strange room. She had hoped to leave fear behind, and she had, as far as that went. Now, something had replaced the fear, something large, something unwelcome, something bland. The doctor's words, "It's gone," rang in her ears like a song repeating itself to the point of annoyance. She had a dull desire for the fear to return. The fear was alive, at least.

Bonnie and Allen took Beth's arms, one on each side. She was unsteady, and their arms were reassuring. She got back into the car wordlessly. She held a large paper cup and looked down, as if she needed to keep track of it in case she had to spit or vomit.

Allen held the door for Bonnie to get in, hurried around, and got into the driver's seat. He backed the car up and headed away as if they would never return and were intent on forgetting the place, which they were.

"How are you doing, sis?" Bonnie asked. Beth did not answer.

"Wait Allen, can you pull over? I want to get back there with her."

Allen complied, pulling off and back onto the road. Bonnie was now in the back seat with Beth. There was no traffic to be concerned about. The girls whispered in the back seat, and he mused as he drove carefully back toward Parker. He had not wanted to help pay for this thing, but he dared not refuse such a need, and now he saw the money as a sort of investment. This incident had drawn him closer to Bonnie, the way no kind words or gifts or flowers might have done. He felt bad for Beth. She was not acting herself and he did not know what that meant. It was impossible to imagine himself in a situation like that. He was glad to be a man.

"Where are we going to go, Allen?" Bonnie asked.

"Aren't we taking her back to your aunt's house?"

"She doesn't want to go there."

"We didn't count on that. Where else can we take her?"

Allen could hear their whispers. They weren't trying to keep anything secret. Beth didn't have any energy, and it seemed like whispering was all she could manage.

"The only other place to take her is your house, the farm," Allen said flatly.

There was more whispering. Allen thought Beth should go and see a doctor, but she had just been with one. He realized that what they'd done was ugly and shameful. Secret things were always dirty. He was sorry he'd taken part in it. "There's a general store up here; they sell some groceries, and there's a little drive-in restaurant. They have a gas station too, with restrooms. We should stop and eat. That should make Beth feel better."

Bonnie agreed. Her tone was more upbeat now. Any positive sign made Allen feel better. He got out and looked in the back at the sisters, huddled together. He looked at Bonnie, meaning to avoid Beth's eyes. "I know how you want your burger. How about Beth?"

"Get it the same as mine, ketchup and pickles."

Allen went to the window and ordered the burgers, along with extra french fries. He carried bottles of Coke to the car while he waited for the food. "She's gonna need some extra pads. Can you get them?" Bonnie asked.

"How do I know what to get?" Allen asked. He knew exactly what to get, but hated doing so, afraid he would blush, or perhaps the clerk would.

"Please, Allen. I don't want to leave her alone."

He gave in. He hated waiting for food anyhow. He had no trouble finding the distinctive blue box. Taking it to the front, he boldly set it on the counter. He could not make eye contact with the clerk, who was a girl about his age. From the corner of his eye, he could see her smirking. She knew Allen was embarrassed. The burgers were waiting for him when he returned with the sanitary napkins in a brown paper sack. He got everything into the car.

"She needs a fresh pad already," Bonnie said. None of them had begun eating, the food still in white paper sacks, the Coke bottles unopened. The front passenger seat was full of sacks. The aroma of fresh food made Allen's mouth water.

"I thought they gave her some," Allen objected.

"They did," Bonnie replied. "She needs privacy to change it. Can you pull over there to where the restrooms are? Water to wash a few things up will help a lot."

Again, Allen did what they required of him. He knew nothing about a woman's bleeding. His sister had advised him to cover his back seat with something. An old wool army blanket doubled over was the best thing he could find. He hoped no blood would seep through to his upholstery and then chastised himself for being selfish. Beth was clearly in a bad way. If not for Maggie Porter's influence on Bonnie, it might be her bearing an unwanted child. He knew they would never seek to be rid of a baby if one happened, but then, he would never force himself on Bonnie, no matter how excited and frustrated she let him get.

"Okay, Allen," Bonnie said, when the girls got back into the car. "We may as well sit here and eat before it gets cold."

When Allen and Bonnie's food was gone, Beth had still not taken a bite of her burger. Beth should be hungry, Bonnie knew. The decision about where they were going next had yet to be made.

"I guess we head for Grove City, right?" Allen asked.

"We need to get there late so that Aunt Polly and Uncle Curt will be in bed," Beth said, weakly. Bonnie and Allen were relieved to hear her speak. These were her first words, louder than a whisper since they had left the clinic.

"I hate to take you there when you're not feeling good," Bonnie said.

"I'll have all night. I can stay in my room. Sleep late. I can tell Polly I'm tuckered out and don't feel up to going to church. She'll be okay with that," Beth said. "Maybe when she gets back from church, I'll be better. Better enough, anyway. I hope I quit bleeding so much," Beth said.

"I think we should take you to a hospital, Beth," Allen said. "I know there's one in Grove City."

"No, no," Beth said. "Aunt Polly will find out."

"Better she finds out than you bleed to death."

"You don't know, Allen. We bleed a lot with our monthlies. A lot of girls stay home 'cause it's so bad," Beth argued. "It's like the doctor said. My problem is mostly nerves."

Beth sounded stronger now. Allen traded glances with Bonnie's worried face as they drove through the countryside toward Grove City.

"You call it Bonnie," Allen said. "You know about this stuff. I don't. I know we should play it safe. My great-grandpa should have taken my great-grandma to the hospital once. She was hurting bad. He thought she just had a bellyache. Turned out it was appendicitis. She begged him to take her to a hospital, and he would not do it. She died a couple days later. He never forgave himself," Allen said gravely.

"Nice try, Allen," Beth said. "I read that book too."

Allen sighed. His ploy had failed.

"Oh yeah," said Bonnie. "I remember that. 'Uncle Jimmy,' right? *The Grapes of Wrath?*"

"'Uncle Johnny,' pretty sure," Allen said. "So what if it's a story? That doesn't mean it didn't happen to someone, sometime."

"I'll be okay, Allen. You're so sweet to worry about me, though," Beth said. Allen's sincere concern contrasted with the painful words Frank had dismissed her with once he'd gotten what he'd been after. 'Thanks again, sis. I know you liked that as much as I did.' She wished Frank were a fly in Aunt Polly's house so she could watch him get smashed the way he deserved. It was funny the things that went through her head as she waited for the car to cover the distance back to Grove City. She felt a little warm; she might have a fever. She was not going to tell Bonnie or Allen, though. She picked up her now cold hamburger and ate it slowly. She had no appetite, and the meat was greasy, but

Bonnie saw her eating as a good sign. Bonnie seemed content with letting Beth go home to Aunt Polly's. They stopped another time for Beth to get a fresh pad and a third time before they got to Polly's house. She wanted to be sure it was safe to walk in, across the floor, and climb the stairs without blood running down her leg.

"Call me tomorrow around ten. Curt and Polly will be in church. Call person-to-person and ask for Bonnie Green if you're ok. I'll tell them Bonnie Green is out. If you need to talk to me, ask for me. I will say Bonnie Metts is not here. We'll hang up. I'll call you back. That way there won't be any charge on Aunt Polly's bill. If I don't hear from you, I'll be calling there, and I won't care who answers."

Allen got out and opened the door for the girls. Beth was no steadier on her feet than she had been earlier in the day. He walked her to the door. Bonnie stayed with the car in case Curt or Polly were still awake and looked out. A person on both sides of Beth would have them concerned.

Beth closed the door as quietly as possible. The stairs were only two steps past the door, and she could reach the wall to steady herself. Climbing the stairs gingerly, holding tightly to the handrail, she was grateful that the primary bedroom was on the first floor and the house had a second toilet in a closet downstairs. She could have the entire upstairs and the bathtub to herself. She was nearly to the top step when she heard a door open. A lamp came on in the living room, and Aunt Polly came and looked up the stairs at her.

"Out pretty late, huh? Have a good time, dear?"

"We had fun, Aunt Polly. I am so tired." Beth realized she had the perfect excuse for her fatigue. "My monthly started today, and I have cramps. I knew it was due and should have stayed home. I'm a dummy sometimes."

"You poor thing," Polly said. "Do you have everything you need?"

"Yes, I do. We stopped and got a little blue box on our way home." She held up the sack containing the pads. She felt a trickle down her thigh, so she spoke to Polly with a polite tone of finality, "Good night."

"Good night, dear. It will be okay if you want to sleep in. I missed church a lot before the change happened for me."

Beth breathed a sigh of gratitude. She went into the bathroom and began drawing water. She drew the water slowly, knowing that Curt and Polly might be annoyed if the splashing was loud. She took off her dress and sat on the toilet. She pushed the rug that wrapped the base of the commode to the wall in case blood dripped. She undid her napkin belt and pulled the heavy, blood-drenched napkin up from her crotch. It dripped onto the floor. She tried to fold it over but could not. The thing was too full. She laid the sickening lump onto the floor and wondered how she would dispose of it. Blood had dried onto her backside and dripped enough that the water in the toilet resembled tomato soup. She was still dizzy, and she wished she could just lie down somewhere and forget. The cramping had subsided to a dull, steady ache. She caught herself drifting into sleep, leaning forward, nearly falling off the toilet seat. She felt warm; the kind of warm she knew was probably a fever. She hoped it would be gone by morning.

It took a long time to get herself clean. She belted on two clean pads. She had never done that before. She had heard that sometimes it was necessary. She had washed every trace of bloody water down the drain. There were some bloody spots on her dress. The dress was navy blue with a rose-colored flower pattern, and what remained of the stain blended into the pattern well enough to make it nearly invisible. She took all the towels out of the linen closet until she found what she wanted, the lowest towel in the stack, older, thin, and faded. She went into the bedroom and pulled the blanket and sheets down, doubled the towel, and laid it so she could position her hips over it. She hiked her nightgown up, hoping to minimize the risk of blood stains. She expected that if she slept too well, there would be more blood, and she didn't want any blood on Aunt Polly's sheets. She reached out, turned off the lamp, and pulled the blanket up. The soft glow on the curtains from the streetlights gave enough light so she could make her way to the bathroom if she needed to. The house, the street outside, everything was as silent as a tomb. The voice of the doctor, "It's gone," played over again in her mind. The diminished light was like the hazy world between sleep and awake, where clarity is elusive. There, an idea impinged itself like an errant ray of light through the blinds, lodging like a splinter in her mind. Intending to restore her future, she had lost desire for a future. The event had drained the energy from her life. A voice, feather soft in the silence, more distinct than a thought, told her, "Not it. He or she." Mercifully, sleep came.

Chapter Thirty-Two

Beth, Beth, oh dear Jesus. Wake up, Beth," the quaking voice of Aunt Polly pierced her foggy mind. Beth felt hot, sick, and weak. She opened her eyes and instantly knew that what she had hoped to keep hidden from her aunt would be known. The knowledge didn't upset her as she thought it would. She lacked the energy to care.

"Why didn't you tell me you were sick, Beth?" Polly pleaded.

"I thought I'd feel better this morning, Aunt Polly," Beth said.

"Morning? No dear, it's past noon. You're always up sooner. I expected you to sleep in. I never thought it would be twelve hours. That's why I'm afraid you're sick."

Beth wanted to get out of bed and visit the bathroom, but she was afraid of how much blood there might be. She could not know how bad the mess might be, and too much could make her aunt panic.

"I'm going to call Dr. Morgan and see if he minds making a house call on Sunday," Polly said. "I'm afraid for you."

"Maybe that's a good idea, Aunt Polly," Beth said, as she dared to sit up. "I'll go to the bathroom while you do that."

"Do you need help getting up, dear?"

"I don't think so. I'm not dizzy anymore."

Polly retreated from the room, going to call her doctor. Beth got up quickly and examined herself. Thankfully, the blood flow had slowed during the night. Doubling her pad had been unnecessary, even with the prolonged sleep. That made sense. Her bleeding was not from her monthly, after all. She wet a washcloth and laid in on her head, the way her mother always did when one of them had some illness. She and her siblings had run the whole gauntlet of measles, chicken pox, mumps, and the other unnamed bugs that plagued them from contact with other kids at school.

She had slept way past the time she was supposed to call Bonnie. Bonnie had promised to call if she didn't hear from Beth. She was considering how to handle the problem when she heard the phone ring downstairs.

Polly hung up from calling Dr. Morgan and took a step toward the stairs. The phone rang. She turned and snatched it up.

"Hello?"

"Hi, Aunt Polly, it's Bonnie. I'm calling to check on Beth. She wasn't well when we dropped her off last night." She did not mention how she had called twice earlier. Curt and Polly would have been in church, but when Beth didn't answer, Bonnie didn't know what to think.

Polly could tell that Bonnie was more than a little concerned about her sister. "I'm glad you called. She is probably worse today. She has a nasty fever. She was still sleeping when we got home from church. I've asked my doctor to make a house call. How about you? The three of you were together. Any symptoms with you or Allen?"

"I'm okay. So's Allen. He called earlier."

"She mentioned her monthly began yesterday. Does she usually get sick when that comes?" Polly asked.

"She has a lot of cramps, more misery than me, for sure." Bonnie embellished, hoping it would be helpful. "She might get a fever sometimes. We don't have a thermometer to check. She usually puts up with it like a good trooper."

"I've got a thermometer. I think Dr. Morgan will want to use his own. No point in me getting it out. Not yet anyway. My guess is she'll be getting a shot of some kind."

"I hope she isn't so bad that he puts her in the hospital," Bonnie said. "If he does do that, please call me right away. Okay?"

"I will, dear," Aunt Polly said. "I better go upstairs now, and make sure she's ready for the doctor."

Dr. Morgan arrived twenty minutes later, carrying the black bag typical of doctors. He had been Curt and Polly's physician for forty years. He'd delivered their children. He took a few minutes to exchange pleasantries with Curt before turning to Polly. "So, where's this patient?"

Morgan was an older man, but he bounced up the stairway with surprising vigor and then paused to let Polly enter ahead of him.

"So, you're Beth Metts, Polly's niece. She tells me you hail from Parker."

Beth did not expect to see the same doctor who had told her she was pregnant a week before. She pretended not to recognize him. He returned the favor. "That's right, sir." The two of them became impromptu thespians, allied for the sake of her privacy and dignity. Her saying anything to keep her secret, him pretending not to see through her.

"You went with some friends to some kind of party yesterday?" He queried.

"That's right. We cooked outside over a fire. I don't know how well the meat was done. Could I get food poisoning from that?"

"Did you vomit?" Dr. Morgan asked, placing a thermometer under her tongue. "It's good to vomit if you've taken in bad food. Have any diarrhea?"

"I did throw up a little." She did her best to speak clearly, despite the thermometer. My bowels haven't moved at all."

"Do you have a boyfriend?" he asked, knowing the exchange with Beth might seem awkward to Polly. He'd been in a play once and knew that actors sometimes adlibbed when they forgot a line. No one had given him the script for this drama.

"No boyfriend."

He drew his head back and nodded. Their eye contact confirmed it for Beth. She clearly remembered telling the man she had a fiancé. He surely remembered her and knew she was lying.

"When did you start to feel sick?"

"On the way home, in the car."

"Your aunt said you were dizzy."

"I was, that's getting better."

The doctor removed the thermometer, read it, and went through the usual checks of ears, eyes and throat. He listened to her heart and lungs and moved the stethoscope over her stomach. "I'm going to palpate you some. Can we lower these blankets?"

Beth complied, easing the covers down no further than he needed. The doctor ran his hands across her abdomen and pressed some. When he got below her naval, her discomfort was obvious. He did a quick survey of her legs and feet.

"Do you normally have a lot of pain with your monthly?"

"Yes. Cramps, you know."

"I'm going to give you an injection, an antibiotic. And a laxative. I want you to stay in bed and eat some lunch and dinner. Drink plenty of water. Do you have any aspirin on hand, Polly?"

"I do," Polly said.

"Take two aspirins now, and two every four hours. Keep it up unless you feel completely well. I don't think you'll feel much better at all. I want you to come to the hospital around ten tomorrow morning. You need a more thorough examination and, I suspect, a procedure."

Beth looked at her aunt.

"We'll see that she gets in, Doc," Polly said.

The doctor patted Beth on the thigh, saying, "You just rest now." He gathered his things and placed them carefully into his bag.

"I'm gonna see him out, dear," Polly said. She left the room behind the doctor.

When they had descended the steps, Polly opened the door for him. "What kind of procedure, Dr. Morgan?"

"I'd rather not say, not until I get a better look. This just reminds me of a condition I've had some experience with. You know, I've been at this a long time. You develop instincts, I suppose. If it's what I think, it'll be easily done at the hospital. It can be a bit scary for a young girl, though." He smiled and made his exit.

Polly reached for the telephone. "Hello, Bonnie? You asked me to call you if Beth had to go to the hospital."

"Oh no," Bonnie said.

"Stay calm, dear. Dr. Morgan gave her a shot. He wants to examine her more thoroughly at the hospital tomorrow. He didn't say anything about her staying. He thinks he knows what the problem is, but I've never known him to give a diagnosis until he's sure."

"How is she feeling? Is she still feverish?"

"Yes, but not that high. I think Dr. Morgan would have her in the hospital today if she needed to be. What kind of meat did you three eat at the party? Beth said it didn't seem properly cooked."

"We bought her a hamburger on the way home, but she didn't have much appetite. She let it get cold. But she was feeling badly before that."

"I see," Polly said. "What did they have, ice cream and cake at this party?

"Yeah, you know, nuts, mints, punch bowl. A lot like a wedding reception. The birthday girl got teased; they said she was rehearsing for a wedding. It embarrassed her and her boyfriend."

Bonnie was terrified, and mouthed wordlessly, "Aunt Polly, please don't ask any more questions."

"So, it was a birthday party?" Polly asked.

"That's right."

"Are you coming here tomorrow? I'm sure Beth would appreciate you being there in case she has to have this procedure thing."

"I'd love to come, but Allen and Carter are my only rides, and both are working. Well, Allen's on midnights, and I can't ask him to be up all day. I can maybe come in the evening." The truth was that until she could speak directly to Beth, she wanted to avoid talking to Polly. She had not anticipated the need for their lies to match up.

"All right, dear, I'll call tomorrow after she's finished at the hospital, one way or the other," Polly said.

"I'll probably be at work. Can you call there?"

"Sure, let me take down the number." Bonnie recited the number, and Polly wrote it on the notepad.

"Thank you so much, Aunt Polly," Bonnie said. "I am so grateful to you for all the help you've given us, especially what you did for Carol and now Beth." She hoped some compliments might keep Polly from being suspicious. It was a shot in the dark, a feeble one, but she felt cornered.

"I consider it a privilege to help my nieces and nephews. My own children are so far away. I have grandchildren I haven't met. My brother's family fills a gap in my life. Thank you, Bonnie." Though it went unspoken, Polly knew that neither of them would say anything to Ward and Dorothy. She remembered when her conscience would have bothered her for keeping information like that from her brother. Not anymore. Polly knew what chaos Ward could add to a problem.

Aunt Polly didn't have a driver's license, but she had a lot of friends, and one of them drove her and Beth to the hospital. Beth didn't know what to expect. She had never been to a hospital. She now realized that she had walked past it once, when she was exploring the town, assuming it to be merely a large, well-kept house.

Once inside, the medicinal scents and white-capped nurses left no doubt this was a place of order and authority. It was harder to tell lies in a place like this. Besides that, Beth hated lying to Aunt Polly. She had never liked conspiring with her siblings or keeping secrets. No question, they had become good at it. When nobody asked questions, it was easy. There would be questions this time. Beth felt like a mouse being tormented by a cat before it killed the hapless prey.

A nurse with a clipboard full of papers took her name and pertinent information. She sat with Aunt Polly for what seemed like an hour. "There's always waiting time with doctors," Polly said quietly. "I don't know why that is."

"The nurses are nice. I like that," Beth remarked.

"They are. Kindness is part of a nurse's job, though. Doctors concentrate on medicine and operations; they have a lot to think about. Nurses try to comfort people. When you're sick, that means a lot."

The confident-sounding steps of Dr. Morgan came through the door, followed by a nurse pushing an empty wheelchair. They focused on Beth. "Good morning, young lady, Polly. We're ready to do the exam. This will be an uncomfortable experience for you, Miss Metts, but there will be two nurses present. If you have any questions, feel free to ask them. This will probably take an hour or so, Polly."

Beth tried not to quake visibly. Riding in the wheelchair felt awkward. The empty feeling she had after her experience on Saturday came back to her. They seated her on a table about the size of the one she had been on Saturday. But his one had shiny metal posts and stirrups on each side. She realized the doctor planned to look inside her. She began to weep.

The nurse took her temperature and her blood pressure. "She's 99.1, Doctor; 130 over 80."

The nurses gently positioned Beth in the same position the doctor had on Saturday, draping sheets to preserve as much of her dignity as possible, with her legs open and her feet high. She sobbed a little as the doctor went about his work, one nurse looking over his shoulder, the other seated close by, assuring Beth that everything would be alright. "You're going to feel something like a bee sting. But the pain will go away real soon," the nurse said. "It's called a local anesthetic."

Beth felt light-headed. She wished she could faint. She recalled how it was when she was little and had a splinter in her finger. Her father would sit her on his lap and take her hand in his. He would isolate the finger and mom would open a folded pack of sewing needles with a picture of a red rose on it. She would tell Beth to look at the pretty flower while her dad probed with the needle to dislodge the offending sliver of wood. Beth remembered the rose in full bloom; she fixed that image in her mind and told herself that this pain too, would end. But no matter what these medical people did with her today, she would be saddled with something for the rest of her life. There was no medicine to take away shame. No pretty flower to distract her conscience.

The draped linens gave the doctor some privacy as well. His voice got low, like he was mumbling. He obviously did not want her to hear his comments. This "procedure" was so much like what she had endured three days before. Painful as that had been, she would gladly accept more pain if she could trade away the despicable way she felt.

After some time, the doctor stood up. "I'm giving you another injection of antibiotic to be on the safe side," the doctor said in an audible voice. He left the room, and Beth was alone with the nurses.

"That wasn't as bad as I thought it might be," Beth said.

She expected some happy comeback from the nurses, more comforting words. There were none. The nurses were uncomfortably demure, both avoiding eye contact with her. They were aware of her disgrace. Her collusion with Bonnie and Allen had proven inadequate. The effort to keep things secret was for naught. Her upbeat tone was seen for the facade it was. She closed her eyes and drew into her shell like a turtle.

The nurses moved about the room. They had finished whatever tasks they had to do and were killing time, avoiding her until the doctor returned. She felt like an object, no longer a person. They brought the wheelchair back and she was seated in it wordlessly. They wheeled her to a room with a bed and explained that she would have to remain overnight, maybe two nights. The doctor came back into the room, followed by Aunt Polly, who sat in a chair beside the bed.

"You need to tell us the truth about where you were Saturday," Polly said.

Beth stared blankly at her aunt for a moment and burst into uncontrolled sobbing. The wobbly story vanished, swallowed by shame. They let her cry for a long moment. Polly stood up and moved to take Beth in her arms. Beth went stiff at first, but gradually relaxed as the emotion drained from her.

"Look at me, dear," Polly said, straightening up and handing her a tissue.

Beth slowly looked up.

"Was it Frank?" Polly asked.

Beth's sobbing began again. It became clear to both that there would be no communication with her until she regained composure. Polly held her close until she could tell that Beth was refusing her comfort. Polly knew such torment would remain until Beth faced and accepted the guilt. Confession drained the power from sin. It was the only thing that made room for grace. Dr. Morgan stepped away, and Aunt Polly followed, leaving Beth to her agony.

"Can you tell her, Polly? It might be better that way," the doctor said. "If you need me to confirm things, I can."

"I'm going to see if I can get her sister to come and be with us when I tell her. I promised to call her anyway when you finished. It was her and her boyfriend who took Beth to get it done. I had a pretty good idea they were lying to me about why she was sick."

"Who is Frank?" the doctor asked.

"Please, Dr. Morgan, do you have to know?"

"I suppose not," Morgan said. He turned slowly away and left the room.

Chapter Thirty-Three

Polly went home and made the phone call. A man's voice answered and shouted for Bonnie over the din of the busy café.

"Bonnie, it's Aunt Polly. You need to come as soon as you reasonably can. I know what happened on Saturday."

There was silence from Bonnie's end.

"Did you hear what I said, dear? Dr. Morgan has seen it before. We need to talk with your sister. She will be in the hospital, probably until tomorrow."

"Yes, I heard you," Bonnie said, now contrite and subdued. "Is Beth okay?"

"I think it is best if we keep this to ourselves, at least for the time being. I won't say anything to Curt. You shouldn't say anything to your mom and dad." Polly's tone changed, and it seemed like Aunt Polly had become an ally rather than the judge Bonnie had expected. "Who all knows about this?"

"My boyfriend Allen knows, other than that, just you and I."

"Some people at the hospital know, but they are expected to keep things like this confidential. That shouldn't be hard since Beth is from out of town. Oh, wait a minute. Does Frank know?"

"As far as I know, she didn't tell him."

"Is there any way you can come tonight? We need to keep it as quiet as possible. Carol cannot find out. That is, unless Frank or Beth want to tell her. It would be best if we could have this talk at the hospital. We can keep it from Curt this way too," Polly said.

"I think Allen was planning for us to be there tonight, just in case. He'll be picking me up. We'll head right over."

"All right, dear. I'll meet you there around six, unless you call me and say otherwise," Polly said.

When Allen arrived, Bonnie had a sack of burgers and fries for the two of them. She thanked the Tyners for being so understanding about her absence. She had not worked Saturday and had given them no details about the events in her life.

Allen took a back road on the way to Grove City. Since he'd be eating and driving at the same time, he liked the road where there was little traffic.

"I can't believe the way Aunt Polly is taking this," Bonnie said, thoughtfully. "I think she's known we were up to something from the beginning. She's not gonna tell anyone who doesn't already know. That's good for Beth. If I were her, I wouldn't want anyone to know."

"Yeah, but your folks are gonna feel like they have a right to know," Allen observed.

"They don't know anything so far. Not even Carter," Bonnie said as she fed french fries into Allen's mouth. "I kind of feel bad keeping him out of the loop."

"Isn't it asking for trouble to pretend like we don't know what Frank did?"

"Why is that asking for trouble?"

"If he doesn't know she got pregnant, he's liable to try it again. Suppose it comes out sometime in the future. Carol finds out we kept this secret from her, she'll feel betrayed, not just by Frank, but by us."

"Alright. That's all true. Maybe we wait on all that until we've had this talk with Beth and Aunt Polly. Maybe we let Frank know what my dad is likely to do if he finds out. That has been known to scare people," Bonnie said.

"All I know is that I'm not letting that son-of-a-bitch anywhere near my wife in the future," Allen said.

Bonnie was stunned. She looked at Allen. "What did you say?"

Allen realized he had blundered. "Gosh, Bonnie. I was planning a nice romantic proposal. Looks like I blew that. Me and my big mouth."

"Well, if we're going to be doing illegal stuff on the weekends and keeping secrets from our families, maybe we should get married." Bonnie was strangely thrilled, partly by Allen's intentions, but perhaps more so because the truth about Beth was out.

Bonnie and Allen arrived at the hospital with time to spare. After being cautioned about when visiting hours were over, a chattering nurse, apparently unaware of Beth's plight, led them to her room, talking all the way about the set of twins that were born that day. Beth heard a lot of her talk as they approached. She had been sitting on the edge of her bed, feeling empty. The nurse's happy voice punctuated Beth's torment. She had done away with a baby. The contrast hit her, making her head spin. The phrase, "Not it. He or she." nagged at her.

"So, how are you feeling, Beth?" Bonnie asked.

"I'm not sure. The fever is almost gone. They take my temperature about every hour. And there's not much bleeding now."

"Is the food good?" Allen asked, pointing to the tray on her bedside table. The plate looked picked over, not relished.

"It's okay," Beth responded, her features flat.

"Have they said when you get out?"

"I hope tomorrow."

"Think you'll be allowed to go back to work right away?" asked Allen.

Beth shrugged. "Dr. Morgan is supposed to talk with all of us. Maybe when Aunt Polly gets here."

Bonnie was surprised when Beth didn't ask if their other family members were aware of what had happened. They continued to struggle with small talk until Aunt Polly arrived with Dr. Morgan.

"Dr. Morgan, this is my niece Bonnie and her boyfriend Allen. They were with Beth on Saturday. They picked her up from my place and brought her back late. They had a story about them all going to some kind of party." Polly inhaled deeply, clearly not wanting to go on. "Maybe you can take it from here?"

Dr. Morgan and Polly exchanged a look. Polly dropped her eyes, knowing she had passed the uncomfortable buck to him, the excuse being that he was the professional. He drew in a deep breath and began.

"I'm not concerned with what happened before Saturday, other than saying that there are other ways to deal with the problem. Let me state the obvious in case there is some confusion about what happened," Dr. Morgan said. He continued giving what sounded like a prepared speech.

"When you discovered that you were pregnant, you learned about a person who could stop the pregnancy, or 'take care of the problem,' as they say. You told your aunt that you were going to a party and would likely come home late. You met up with someone, whose name you do not know, whose face you did not see and whose qualifications as a medical professional were unknown. You paid them a sum of money to perform what is known as an abortion. And it is an illegal procedure. That's why you didn't see the face of the person who performed it. Am I correct so far?"

Three guilty faces nodded, lips pursed in contrition.

"The person told you that bleeding was normal and that it would stop if you gave it time. That part was true. What they did not say is how susceptible you would be to infection. Neither were you warned to expect damage to your cervix and uterus. The procedure I performed this morning is known as 'Dilation and Curettage.' It is, essentially, the same procedure the person did on Saturday. If he had done it properly and in a sterile environment, you would not have had to come to me."

The doctor took another deep breath. More was coming.

"It could be that the instruments that were used were not sterile. It could be that he did not have the correct instruments or a full set of them. It could be that the person who performed the abortion lacked the proper training and experience. It could be that there was not enough light. It could be that there were no antibiotics administered. It could be a combination of all that. But the result is that your female organs will not return to the condition they were in before the abortion. This is only my opinion and you are free to consult a specialist. There is such a person in Pittsburgh; I can refer you to him if you wish."

The doctor's speech sped up, like a runner using a strong burst of energy to cross the finish line ahead of his opponent. "But the result of this badly done procedure means that there is no possibility of conception in the future."

The room was silent. Dr. Morgan moved his eyes around to each of his listeners. The only one who seemed puzzled was Beth. "What does that mean, 'conception?'" she asked. She knew what he meant, but it was too awful to take in. Her mind dodged what it could not face.

The doctor's eyes were solemn. "You will not get pregnant again. You will never be able to bear children," he said quietly.

There were a few sighs. They all needed to be stoic. Beth reached deep down and, trying to comfort the others, spoke with a convenient flippancy that they were all grateful she could muster. "I thought you would say I was going to die."

The doctor was relieved. He knew Beth's initial reaction would fade into a morbid sadness, but he would be elsewhere when that happened. He had nothing in his training or experience to mitigate that. Only the support of loved ones could help her.

"You folks can stay here as long as she needs you to. I'll be back in the morning, and I expect we can discharge her tomorrow. Any questions?"

After a long pause, Polly said, "If we have any, we know where you are. Thank you, Dr. Morgan."

The physician nodded to all and made his way to the door.

The room was silent now. Beth hung her head. Though her bed was surrounded by people she was close to, she was alone. Lonely in a way she had never been. This was different. This was permanent. She had been warned about Frank. She had wanted his attention. She had smiled at him in a way meant to draw him. She had gone with him to a private place and had let herself be fooled about what he wanted. She had become his victim. It was her fault. Shame had come with it, and she would always fear that the secret would come out. How would Carol react? She knew how people would talk about her, the awful words they would say.

She had not wanted a baby, not asked for a baby. In seeking freedom, something worse had come. The one thing about being a girl, the thing every woman anticipated in her life, had been taken, forfeited, because only a legitimate child was a real person. It was a lie, but her way of seeing it meant nothing. She had conceived in pain, aborted in pain, and would be draped forever in regret and despair. And what man wanted a girl who could not have children?

"So, what now?" Bonnie asked. Her head was swimming. There was nothing to say that seemed right.

"Now, Beth will come home to my house tomorrow, and we will go back to living." Aunt Polly said cheerfully. "There will be plenty of time to talk about this."

The door opened, and a nurse entered, carrying a tiny paper cup. "Dr. Morgan wants you to sleep well. Good sleep makes a big difference in how quickly we heal. This pill will help you with that." She handed Beth the water cup on the bedside table along with the pill. Beth swallowed. She needed to flee, and sleep was the thing for it.

They all wanted to escape the awkwardness. It seemed like a cheap thing to do, Bonnie thought, but the doctor had given them an excuse. Citing Beth's need to rest, they all said goodbye. Polly gave Beth a kiss on her forehead, and the three of them left for home.

Curt sat waiting for his wife to return from the hospital. She entered through the front door with a look Curt knew well. Polly was too soft, always had been, especially with their children. He let her have primary control over them, and by extension, their nieces. It was understood that his oversight and decisions were always the final word, "Alright now, Polly. I need to know what is going on, and I want the whole truth."

Polly took her time getting seated, ready to face him, dreading his wielding of authority. As the man of the house, he had to uphold certain standards. A decent society depended on traditional limits of behavior. They both knew it. The whole world knew it. There was a popular wave of rebellion afoot, an undercurrent you could read about on the pages of Life and Harper's. The fabric of society would not hold up if those who defied decency faced no repercussions. *On The Road*, a popular and supposedly true account of debauchery, recently published, showcased the kind of errancy that threatened to gain cultural traction if people like Curt and Polly failed to take a firm stand. Curt had stopped reading it halfway through, sensing it was poison for the mind. It was that recent exposure that hardened his heart toward the girl who had come to live under his roof and brought the degraded lifestyle of the Metts household, shoddy and unkempt, to his door.

Polly began telling him, but he cut her off. "I got the whole squalid mess already from the grapevine," Curt stated with disgust. Every wagging tongue in town knew about the pregnancy and subsequent abortion.

"You know I've never asked a thing from Ward or his kids. We never judged, scolded, or interfered. I've felt as much pity as you because of their ugly situation. I hate being in the middle of it. Maybe we asked for it; should have known better. There is nothing to be gained by going over the matter. We both know what happened. You can tell Beth, or I will, but if she's fit to be released from the hospital, she's fit enough to leave town, and that must happen," Curt said. He stood and moved to switch on the television. There would be no further talk on the matter.

Chapter Thirty-Four

THIRTY YEARS LATER......Beth wiggles the iron and presses it against another of his undershirts, straightens her stiffening back once again and stares out her second-floor window across the rooftops, trees and lawns of her neighbors. She can no longer say if these boundaries are fences to protect or a cage that restricts. She only knows that she has chosen them and has become so accustomed that the idea of being free no longer appeals. Shame put her here, wed to a man so much her senior that no expectation of motherhood was part of the bargain. The pile of laundry that has come to define Monday is finally crisp and ready for the drawers; everything tidy, all in perfect order. It is control, capturing thin and exaggerated purpose from a world where meaning is fragile, and once lost, grows more and more distant. Her absolution was purchased, little by little, with self-imposed penance. Carol had never learned the truth about Beth and Frank.

Every day, she reviewed the few weeks that had come to define her life. Like the star of a stage production, stepping into the wings only to return for the curtain call, her past was due the credit for making the show what it was. The country singer on the radio intones what she'd only heard once, long ago and could not bear. She had opted for recorded music for the months it took for the song to go the way of all popular tunes, replaced by something fresher. Since she cannot reach the dial, she endures *Manhattan, Kansas ain't no place to have a baby, when you've got no man to give it his last name.* She wonders how life might have been. She wonders how she has managed to forego suicide for thirty years. Had the alcohol made it worse or better?

The singer tells of flying west to work in a diner and provide for herself and the child. That might have worked for her, but her options for escape did not include flight. She had gone from eager, optimistic youth to an orphan of the storm, hiding in Bonnie's home, after she and Allen had hastened to a Justice of the Peace so their marriage could provide her with a place to live. She no longer mused how some people who do something stupid go to jail or pay a fine. Nothing so easy for her. The desperation was overwhelming. Trading a few years of open shame for a lifetime of secret pain proved a bum deal. She had struck that bargain with herself.

She had not known the word abortion. Who did in those days? Language like 'getting things taken care of' and 'people do this all the time' made the whole thing sound ordinary. The man was some kind of doctor, and the trappings of the place seemed clinical enough to trust, but there was no fooling the real doctor in Grove City.

She had returned the kindness of her aunt and uncle by dragging them into her shame. The knowledge that momentary transgressions could produce horrible results was just another deficit from her upbringing. She understood that now. There was no way to know what alternate life rolled past her like the ripples of the river she took her daily walk beside. Funny how much could be captured in the lines of a song. She liked poetry for the same reason. Those secret, inarticulate feelings were defined and made available. Words gave misery form and shape. Like medicine, verbal pills gave pleasant melancholy when she needed it. And hope, or something like it, gets sharper in melancholy. *I guess every form of refuge has its price* was another one. The Eagles weren't her style, but one never knows from whence insight will come and the wise drink from any clean spring.

Epilogue

The train has passed, its horn now a whisper. The night remains, having earned its place from the hard day. Just as understanding has earned its place from hard life, the sand that trapped my family did not hold us forever. The story goes on. We struggled long and broke free. Christ's harmonious song of Grace falls sweeter in the ears of the wounded. No amount of sin or shame is beyond its reach.